STAND IN PLACE

MARY CALMES

Stand In Place

Copyright ©2019 Mary Calmes

http://marycalmes.com

All rights reserved. No part of this book may be reproduced or transmitted in any form or by any means, electronic or mechanical, including photocopying, recording, or by any information storage and retrieval system without the written permission of the author, except for the use of brief quotations in a book review.

This is a work of fiction. Names, characters, places and incidents either are the products of author imagination or used fictitiously. Any resemblance to actual persons, living or dead, business establishments, events, or locales is entirely coincidental.

Cover content is for illustrative purposes only. Any person depicted on the cover is a model.

Cover art Copyright © 2019 Reese Dante

http://reesedante.com

Edited by Desi Chapman

Content/Copy Edit by Lisa Horan

Proofreading by Judy's Proofreading

Assistant Jessie Potts potts.jessie@gmail.com

❃ Created with Vellum

ACKNOWLEDGMENTS

This one is for my grandmother, Phyllis, and for my Aunt Barr, both of whom helped bring the matriarch of Kaenon's family to life. It's also for all the wonderful women who have mothered me over the years, and to others who have allowed me to mother them. Love you.

I couldn't do this without my team behind me, thank you for supporting me even when I drive you all nuts. Like really, really, nuts. And thank you to all my amazing readers; I appreciate you all so much.

STAND IN PLACE

One summer won't be enough....

Kaenon Geary was done fighting the small minds in his sleepy Texas town when he made his escape and never looked back. But now, for the first time in more than a decade, he's returned to Braxton to spend the summer with his beloved grandmother—her final summer—and no longer recognizes the home he'd left behind all those years ago.

Everything has changed.

Everything but the man he's never stopped wanting.

Brody Scott was the local football hero who became a gridiron champ, but he retired from the fast lane to forge a new life as the Chief Constable of Braxton. He longs to put down roots in the community he is now sworn to protect. Though he's not at all sure he can protect his heart from the quiet, earnest boy he once knew. The boy who has come back a man.

Starting something would be a mistake. Kaenon plans to fly away at summer's end, but his love is something Brody desperately wants to have...and to keep. Their days together are numbered. Unless some simple hometown magic can make all the right things bloom and show them the true definition of love.

ONE

The only thing on my mind was coffee as I stumbled off the plane at the Austin-Bergstrom International Airport. A quarter to six in the morning was much too early for anyone to be awake, but that was when the red-eye from Connecticut got in. Had it not been a life-or-death situation—the latter being the case—I would never have returned to Texas. The idea of seeing the town of Braxton again would have made me sick to my stomach if I were even somewhat conscious.

Thankfully, there was an open Starbucks in the terminal, and I was able to get a regular coffee with three shots of espresso that the nice barista was worried might kill me. He made me take a large cup of water to hydrate, which was kind and completely unnecessary, as caffeine and I were well acquainted. In fact, the coffee was gone before I made it to the Budget counter to pick up the rental car that my buddy Baz had ordered for me.

"How do you pronounce your first name, Mr. Geary?" the agent asked, looking at my name, Kaenon, uncertainly, as a lot of people did.

"Like Canaan from the Bible," I explained, as I'd done about a billion times in my lifetime. "It's just spelled weird."

"Oh, I love it," she said, smiling sweetly at me.

I thanked her, and she handed over one of those key-fob things and told me that the car was reserved with an open return date.

"I had no idea you could even do that," I replied lamely.

Her brows furrowed, and it looked odd on her pixie face. "Did you not make this reservation?"

I hadn't, no. "I did. I just forgot," I muttered and rushed away, not wanting to come apart at a rental car counter.

Needless to say, I had been a bit annihilated at the thought of going back to the town where I'd grown up, and Baz and his husband, Simon, who both taught at the same private college as I did, had taken things into their own hands. One had packed my duffel, the other got online with my credit card and made travel arrangements. When Baz dropped me at Bradley International Airport, he'd hugged me fiercely—which was a bit painful considering the guy was an ex-defensive lineman—and told me not to worry about coming back.

"The hell are you talking about?" I asked, squinting.

Baz's eyes rolled heavenward. "I *mean*, don't worry about anything until the summer's over. You have time before school starts back up, so do what you have to do. Simon and I will take care of your place, water your garden, and grab your mail. We may just stay in the guest room until you get back."

"Why?" That made no sense. "Your condo is amazing, and it's in that great building, and it's close to downtown, and—"

"Who cares?" he told me. "Your house is like a sanctuary. Every time you have us over, we never want to leave."

It was a really nice thing to say. "You just like my homemade tea," I teased him.

"Your tea is epic, that's true," he agreed. "Everyone in the department is addicted to it, but really, your home, your space, is the real prize, so we'll take good care of it so you don't have to give it a thought."

It was a comforting idea, having them house-sit.

"And George will love it. Let's face it, he likes me better than you anyway, so I wouldn't worry about him."

He was not wrong. My cat, a shelter rescue two years ago, actually moved whenever Baz came over. The only thing I ever got was cool disregard and occasional judgment.

Baz grinned wide. "Look how cute he is," he said, making a very uncharacteristic noise that sounded suspiciously like cooing as he flashed me a short video from Snapchat of his husband cuddling my asshole cat in my own living room. "He loves Simon."

George's eyes were closed as he rubbed the top of his head under the man's bearded chin. "Ugh," I groaned. "That cat's a filthy traitor. Not even a moment of sadness over my leaving."

Baz smacked me in the chest. "So, there. Everything's settled. You can go and not be worried about anything here. Take however long you need to be with your grandmother and then...come home."

I nodded. I didn't want to be reminded about my grandmother.

"I don't know what I'd do if it was my grandmother," he said, taking a quick gulp of air so he wouldn't get emotional.

"You're not helping," I informed him.

"I just...I know how important she is to you. I know she's your whole family, and since you don't know what you're walking into and what she's gonna need, I'm trying to tell you to take the time and spend it with her, and don't worry about anything else."

I shook my head, and not over the family part but, instead, over the rest of what my friend had alluded to. "I'm not staying there. No one wants me there. You have no clue how bad it was."

He nodded. "I'm sure, but just don't add to it by being hard on yourself, okay? Take it easy, Kae, and whenever you get back, everything will be here waiting."

"Okay."

"Except Aidan," he said cheerfully with a sinister smile. "Aidan will be in Boston, right? There's no chance of you guys getting back together."

"No. No chance. But there wasn't anyway, you know that."

"I wasn't sorry when you broke up with him."

I knew he wasn't. None of my friends were. They had all hated him. Every last one of them. The entirety of the people I knew in Connecticut all wanted the man gone. Simon, the sweetest man on the planet, offered to throw me an emancipation party.

"Lemuel wanted to push him off the balcony of his apartment," Baz reminded me.

"I know," I grumbled, because I did.

"Lemuel studied with Tibetan monks, Kae."

"I know," I groaned again.

"The man took a vow of silence for two years!"

I let my head fall back before I closed my eyes, letting the full weight of the horror that the situation was wash over me.

"He's a pacifist, for fuck's sake, and he wanted to *kill* your boyfriend. Let's let that sink in for a second, shall we?"

Jesus.

"Kill. Aidan Powell brought out murderous intent in an almost monk."

God.

"Could it have gotten any worse than that?"

"Yes." I answered what I knew was a rhetorical question.

"Yes!" Baz yelled dramatically. "For crissakes, Kae, he lectured Maya on the plight of the black man in America!"

Yes, he had.

First, Maya Grayson taught at the same exclusive private college with the rest of us, had a PhD in urban geography and gender studies, was in charge of educational leadership and policy studies at the college, was also director of the doctorate in educational leadership, and lectured all over the country on race relations and how educating everyone was the cure for all manner of stupidity. Second, she was black. When Aidan started mansplaining things to her at dinner, she did a slow pan to me, and the look of pain and horror on her face made me cringe. Her husband, James, kept opening his mouth to say something, but Maya lifted the index finger on her right hand to let him know she had the situation covered.

"Are you done?" she asked Aidan when he finally took a breath.

As she waited for his reply, patiently, like a snake coiled to strike, he finally recognized in her face that he'd overstepped, but by then it was far too late. Once he nodded, she took him point by point through his entire argument, missing nothing, destroying—logically and thoughtfully—everything he'd said. Basically, she shut him up for the rest of the evening without ever raising her voice, not once.

"I'm so sorry," I told her later, on her patio.

The fact that she forgave me for bringing my ass of a boyfriend to dinner, into her home, no less, spoke to our years of selfless friendship. "You deserve better," she said, taking my arm as we had strolled together the following day, "and I don't know why you can't see that."

The thing was, Aidan was smart and stylish—everything I wasn't. When I finally realized, after dinner that evening, that being criticized and having someone try and make you over was not, in fact, in my best interest but, instead, for Aidan's own selfish reasons, it had been time to go. When I told him it was over, I was surprised that he suddenly wanted us married and moved to Boston, like, yesterday.

"Why?" I asked, glancing around his loft for stray items that belonged to me. Not that there was anything. We had kept things separate, because that's what he wanted.

"Why do I want to marry you?" he said, like it was the most ridiculous question ever.

"Yeah," I answered softly, feeling the weight of the ending as I stood there in a place that had never felt like home.

"Are you kidding?" Aidan asked, almost leering, looking me up and down.

I got it then. It was my body he liked.

In bed, Aidan touched me constantly, marveling over the breadth of my shoulders, the hardness of my chest, my sculpted abdomen, and long, muscular legs. He praised my abilities in one place only, and that was in the sack. Aidan needed a dominant partner, and that was me. Outside the bedroom, it was apparent he thought I had little to offer, but between the sheets was a whole other story.

I huffed out a breath and was out the door seconds later. We hadn't talked since. Not that I thought we would. After basically being told sex was all I had going for me, the writing was on the wall. And I hadn't told anyone about our last encounter. I had my pride, after all. I wanted my friends to think the investment banker and a college English professor had not been a wrong fit from the start.

They were all lucky they'd never met Aidan's family. Pretentious and entitled and snobbish didn't begin to describe them.

The whole thing was on me, and I was smart enough to know why. I never liked to admit my mistakes. I liked to think all my choices were good and solid, and it was hard to suck it up and say yeah, I blew that one. Aidan moving to Boston was an easy out, and even though I was still in the headspace where I was performing the autopsy on the dead relationship—where did I go wrong?—I figured all the findings would lead to the same conclusion: we weren't compatible. When all your friends, every single one, hated the guy you were with, it was time to wonder if he was, in fact, a nozzle.

"I should write the people of Boston a note and tell them that Wallingford, Connecticut, is sorry they're getting the town jackass." Baz snickered. "Jesus."

Brought back to the present, I smiled at my fiercely loyal friend. "Just...enough. I get it."

"I need to meet whoever you pick next before you make any long-term decisions, all right?" he said, shooting me a grin complete with deep dimples. "I think that would be best for all parties involved."

"You're speaking for everyone, then?"

"Yeah. I'm speaking for everyone."

"Well, I don't think you hafta worry about it. I mean, before Aidan, who have you seen me date?"

"That's because you're oblivious when someone is hitting on you," he emphasized. "And your gaydar is nonexistent."

That was accurate. I missed lots of things that others told me were clear as day.

"I don't get how you don't notice people throwing themselves at you all day long."

I scoffed at him. Loudly.

"You're the whole package, and I wish you realized it."

He was a dear friend and had to say nice things. It was in the friend contract.

"You're beautiful inside and out."

The *out* part was what I'd heard most often from Aidan, that I had a beautiful body. I should have known something was off right then. I should have packed on the pounds and tested Aidan's interest early, but it was far too engrained in me to get up and hit the gym. I'd been an athlete. Soccer carried me all the way out of Texas to Syracuse University in New York years earlier, and even though I got hurt in my junior year—compound fractures to both the tibia and fibula of my right leg, which still hurt even years later—I ran every morning. I went to the gym three times a week, lifted weights another two, and worked on my leg, keeping it strong and myself in good shape. It wasn't something I could ever change, not that I wanted to. And besides, I was never giving up beer and cheese, so the tradeoff was exercise.

"Anyway," Baz groused at me. "Go get on the damn plane and text me when you get there so I know you're not dead."

"That's lovely."

"Eat me."

"Wouldn't Simon get upset?"

He pointed at the terminal. "Get the hell out."

I might have whined just a little.

"It'll be fine," he promised before giving me an almost-too-tight bear hug. "Go home, take care of your grandmother, get everything in order, and then come back."

That was the plan.

Now, leaving the rental car counter, I realized that, truthfully, if anyone else had called—my parents, siblings, aunts, uncles, cousins—anyone at all besides Joanna Geary, my father's mother, the woman who, along with my grandfather and her sister, my Aunt Peg, had pulled me from the fire, I wouldn't have gone. But she was the one who loved me. She was the one who moved to New York for a year when I got hurt. She was the one who stayed with me through the eleven operations I had to have just to be able to walk again as screws were drilled into bones that would never be the same.

After the surgery, waking up, groggy, my grandmother's face was the first one I saw, the first voice I heard cracking a joke about how, if I wanted to see her so badly, I could have just called. Breaking my leg in four places was just a ridiculous, childish cry for attention.

I gasped first, groaned second, and winced last. "Don't make me laugh. I'm dying."

She smirked at me. "Not today, love."

The entire time I spent recovering, she was there. My grandfather flew up every other weekend to make sure I knew he was there too. As if I ever had any doubt. Everyone who met them, Joanna and Harvey Geary, was in awe of their commitment to me, their youngest grandchild. I, of course, took it for granted. In the worst of times, I could always count on them. They'd come when I called, and now I was showing up in Braxton, Texas, because five years after the death of my grandfather, it was now my grandmother's time. It was my turn to take care of her, and not because I was going to nurse her through anything. She didn't need a lifeline or a caretaker. All she needed was her favorite grandson to bust her out of the hospital so she could die at home instead of in the care facility that everyone had planned on. I would not let her down.

TWO

I made it to the Seton Medical Center much faster than I thought I would. There was no traffic yet, the Thursday morning commute barely began, so I was parked by eight. The five minutes between the parking lot and the lobby of the hospital was not even enough time to gird myself for any accidental parent sightings. Not that running into any of my aunts was going to be any better. They had all sent me emails that I was going to be the death of their mother. I wasn't looking forward to talking to any of them.

Leaving my sunglasses on, I walked through the front door, limping a bit because I'd been folded up in an airline seat for three hours, and made my way to the front reception area. I began to head up to Jo's room but was told by security that visiting hours didn't start until ten. I was in for quite the wait.

I called the hospital, asked for my grandmother's room, and was connected moments later. The phone rang twice and was then answered in her usual cheerful tone.

"Who is this?" she asked, her voice dripping with

disdain. "Do you have any idea what time it is? Dear God in heaven, were you raised in a barn?"

I grunted.

"Oh, well, yes, you were now, weren't you?"

"You would know," I grumbled at her.

Her sinister cackle made me smile.

"Jo," I said, because unlike every other person I knew, my grandmother had insisted that all of us, her grandchildren from all four of her children, call her Joanna or Jo.

She was only fifty-five when I was born, and I was her last grandchild, so the idea that she would be called Gram, Grammy, Gramma, Grandma, or, heaven forbid, Nana, was just too horrific to contemplate. My grandfather didn't care what anyone called him as long as it wasn't Harv. He really hated Harv. But Jo was insistent. When she got old, she informed us, the endearments could begin. Not before then. As far as I knew, everyone was still waiting for her to give them permission. Now, at eighty-seven, with a body that was shutting down but with a mind that was as sharp as ever, even after her stroke two years earlier, she was finally showing her age. I had begged her to come live with me, but she insisted she was happy in the house she'd shared with my grandfather. She had lots of friends and refused to be a burden. Our weekly phone calls told me she was well, up until the last one a few days ago, and then she couldn't lie anymore.

"You know," she said softly, "there's a reason my voice has been sounding so sexy lately."

Jo had been hoarse for a while, but she had told me it was a persistent cold.

"Yeah? What?" I asked her, distracted, folding clothes at the same time.

She took a quick breath, and because I heard her do it,

heard her get ready to tell me something important, I stilled and waited, laser focused on her answer. "I've had this lump inside my cheek for a while now," she began, "and because it never hurt and it wasn't very big, I never thought too much about it," she said, taking another breath. "But then it started to bother me, and since I've been sounding like Lauren Bacall, which would have helped me get your grandfather that much quicker—"

"Jo!" I yelled.

"Don't fuss, just wait," she growled at me.

I was quiet as I sat down on my bed, holding my breath.

"It turns out that the lump was a tumor, because that's how things go sometimes, and we know that, don't we, darling?"

We did. Breast cancer had taken Peg, and that too had started out as a tiny little lump that she too thought was nothing.

My heart was in my throat. "Tell me."

"I have what's called adenoid cystic carcinoma."

Cancer.

Did I hate anything as much as that fucking disease?

"Now, usually with this kind of cancer, there is surgery followed by radiation," she explained, "but when they removed my tumor and checked a bit of the healthy tissue around it, they found that it had spread."

"Could you just—"

"Sweetheart," she cautioned me, and I could hear it in her tone, the sharp one, the shut-up-and-let-me-finish one.

"I'm sorry."

"Patience is a virtue."

"Yes, ma'am."

"Now, most cancer, as you know, spreads through your lymph nodes, but adenoid cystic carcinoma, it spreads along your nerves, which means that it could have been in my whole face or something, and I would have had droopy face," she said with a snort.

"What?"

"What?" she asked all innocent.

I was distraught, and she was screwing with me? "Jo!"

"Fine," she grumbled, sighing deeply. "Well, it turns out that I have tumors in my lungs already, and they did the brachytherapy, which is just a fancy name for radiation, and nothing is slowing it down."

"What does that mean? Tell me what that means!"

"Most people get about five years after the initial diagnosis. Others get to be happy for a bit until the cancer comes back, because, with this kind of cancer, it always does. But for me, with my age and because it's been around for a bit, Dr. Sterling says about three months, give or take."

I knew it would happen eventually. This was my grandmother, and the circle of life was that she would die before me. It was logical, and I was prepared. Or thought I was. How arrogant was I to think I could ever be ready to lose her?

"Love?"

"I...what?"

"Here's the thing," she began cheerfully, "your father wants to put me in a nursing home, and your aunts are all on his side."

"What?"

"I know? Can you imagine? Me? In a nursing home? They'd kill me in a week. It would be all over the news."

"Jo—"

"Honestly, I drive everyone nuts. I know this, you know this, so there's really only one alternative that I can come up with."

"Where are you now?"

"I'm in the hospital, and I'm supposed to be transferred to the nursing home at the end of the week."

"I'll be there tomorrow," I told her.

"Oh, don't be so dramatic," she said with a groan. "It's only Sunday. You can come Thursday and spring me. I promise not to die before you arrive."

"When I get there, I'm going to smack you," I told her.

"I'll have you arrested for elder abuse," she volleyed back smugly.

My sigh was heavy. "Okay, so I'll make a list, but first off I'll hire some movers, and with their help I can get the house packed up and—"

"No."

I was confused. "No what?"

"No, we're not packing up anything."

"But I'm going to move you to Connecticut to live with me."

"Did you listen to the part where I said I only have three months to live?"

"I—"

"Why on earth would I move out of the town I've lived in my entire life when I only have three months to live?"

"Jo—"

"I want you to stay the summer with me in Braxton."

"What? Why?"

"Because that's what I want. It's my dying wish."

"Oh my God, please don't talk about—"

"And I have another favor, but I'm not going into that over the phone."

I was back to not being able to breathe.

"I know it's a lot to ask," she said solemnly. "You haven't

set foot in this town in fourteen years, but I need to be here so you do too."

Peg—who was technically my grandaunt and not my aunt, but she, like my grandmother, had not loved the idea of having her years thrown in her face, so Aunt Peg it was—didn't want me at her funeral. To her, once she was gone, that made no sense. The same had been true for my grandfather. Jo had buried them alone, and I'd flown her to Maui both times, afterwards, because we needed the downtime to decompress. But now, finally, there was no way out of it. I had to return to Braxton because I would do anything for my grandmother.

Anything.

"Hello? Are you there?" she said, breaking into my thoughts, bringing me back to the present, to the here and now.

"Yeah, I'm here," I groused at her.

"So," she said, like she was bored out of her mind, "where are you?"

"Downstairs. Where the hell else would I be?"

After a moment of silence, I got a self-satisfied "Well, now."

"What's with that?"

"I wasn't sure that would work."

I was startled. "You weren't sure what would work?"

"The whole 'Kaenon, I'm dying' number."

But she couldn't fool me. I'd spoken to her doctor who confirmed that from the hospital she needed to go into a nursing home, and hospice would take over her care for the time she had left. There was nothing more to do. Any more radiation could kill her. There was no more surgery, no more anything. It was a waiting game now, and making her comfortable, though the doctor told me Jo wasn't in much pain. She was weak, winding down, and needed managed care. I said that I would do that.

"She needs to be in a home with trained medical professionals," Dr. Sterling insisted.

"Have you met my grandmother?" I asked her.

The soft chuckle told me she had. "Even knowing her, how she is and what she wants, I can't recommend that she go home."

"I know," I told her. "But that doesn't really matter to me."

"No. I suspect not."

"Are you still there?" Jo asked, barging into my thoughts for the second time.

"Yes, I'm still—"

"I can't believe you came."

"I'm sorry," I said, playing along. "You literally thought I'd let you die in a nursing home with strangers around you?"

"Maybe you were too busy to fly out."

"Busy?" I snapped at her.

"What? Stop with the whining. It's a lot to ask, love."

I was about to get all indignant, but she spoke before I could get another word out.

"I mean for me. All I had to do was move to Chelsea for a year while you recuperated and figured out your life; you had to come all the way home."

The guilt and sarcasm could not have been piled on any higher. She was a much better person than I was, but this was not news. She always had been. But since no one enjoyed having things like that pointed out, I griped at her instead. "Why can't I just take you home with me to Connecticut? You'd love it."

"This again?"

"Yes, this again."

"It's cold there."

"It's cold here too."

"I'll be dead before fall."

"You will not!" I yelled at her.

"I might be, and I definitely don't want to be Connecticut cold."

"Did you hear what you just said?"

"What did I say?"

"If you might be dead before fall, technically you could, in fact, come home with me and still never be Connecticut cold. You'll just get the balmy summer."

"Logic? You're throwing logic at me now?"

"Oh for fuck's sake."

"I want you in Braxton."

"Why?"

"Because I should have never let you leave."

"Dear God, woman, you have lost your ever-loving mind."

"Not at all," she countered. "You see, much like Peg, you're tied to the land. To our land. To our home. You're grounded in that space. You get power from the earth itself, and you shine like she did, just from being there."

She was mixing up me and her younger sister, for whatever reason. I cleared my throat. "Peg left Braxton all the time."

"But not for long. She always came back because she was at her strongest when she was there. The issue with you, why your light has dimmed, is because you've never been back."

"Uh-huh."

"Oh, boy, don't you dare *uh-huh* me."

I huffed out a breath of air. "Give me another reason why you want me to stay."

"Because having to see your entire family will be like doing penance from God."

I grunted.

"You know it will."

"Oh, there's no argument. And you know, really, deep down, you hate Braxton too," I reminded her petulantly. "You used to tell Papa that you wanted to live in Tuscany."

"Did I?"

"You just don't remember," I said evilly. "It's because your memory's going."

"That's low even for you, Kae," she scolded me. "Telling a senile old woman that she can't remember something," she continued, pretending to cry.

"Senile?"

"Aren't I senile now?" she asked, the fake waterworks stopping instantly.

"Hardly."

"Old, then."

"You? Old?"

She stopped the fake lamenting as well. "Good point. Old *is* pushing it."

"You better stop messing around, or they'll think you're nuts for real and get an injunction to keep you here," I warned her. "I'll have to prove you're sane before I can take you home, and good God, that could take forever. Seriously, sanity and you are only casually acquainted to begin with."

"True," she hmphed in agreement.

"Just pretend to be all there until I get upstairs, will you please."

"Can they really do that? Keep me here? I don't think they can do that."

"Stop being so—"

"I just want to die at home, not in a hospital or a horror movie nursing home."

"You're not going to die."

"I am going to die," she placated me. "But probably not today unless your driving has gotten even worse."

"I'm a great––"

"But that's not the issue here, now is it, darling? Let's stay on topic about the creepy nursing home."

I gave up. "How do you know it'll be creepy?"

"Aren't they all creepy?"

"We maybe watched too many movies like that."

She grunted, conceding that point.

"You'd like my house in Connecticut."

"Didn't we cover the cold factor?"

"And I'm reminding you that it's not cold there now."

She made a noise of disbelief.

"You would like my house."

"What if I die in your house? Wouldn't that be horrible? You'd have to move."

I groaned loudly.

"I'd be so worried about you being sad that I'd end up not being able to cross over, and then I'd start haunting you, and then your grandfather would wonder what I was doing, if I got remarried after he died and had gone to live in the hereafter with my new husband, and good gracious, Kae, it would all just be a big mess."

"I'm exhausted just listening to all that."

"Good," she said, sounding pleased with herself. "Besides, as I said, it's time you came home. You need the land and the land needs you."

"That is such horseshit."

"I don't think so."

"Jo, it hasn't been my home for years, and once you're gone, that's it. I won't ever be caught there again."

"Oh, I know, that's what I'm trying to fix."

"There's no fix for it. My home is in Connecticut."

"It's no more your home than New York was. You're a Texan in your soul."

"You have no idea what's in my soul."

"Oh, I think I know far better than you what's in there."

"I—"

"More importantly, you need to be in Braxton. It's your true home."

"Says you."

"Yes. Says I. And I know best. You'll see."

"What are you up to? And what'd you mean it's time I came home? That's not something you can fix, you know. This was all broken years ago."

"Not broken, just a bit banged up."

"A bit?" I railed at her. "You can't get me to—"

"Kaenon Joseph Geary, I'm dying. What other agenda besides final resting places could I possibly have?"

But she was cagey, my grandmother, and I didn't trust her. Love her? Yes. Think she was innocent? No, not so much.

"I'm so not letting your final resting place be Braxton, so you can just get that right out of your head," I assured her.

"I've already made all the arrangements, and besides, I want to be placed beside your grandfather."

"His ashes are in an urn in a wall. I can move him too."

"That's sacrilege!"

"Oh, it is not. That's why we did it that way, so the ashes were movable."

"I don't remember that at all."

"Seriously?"

She grunted. "All right, so maybe I remember that a little."

I couldn't help shaking my head even though she wasn't there to see me.

"We'll both be in Braxton Hills Cemetery," she said with finality.

"You'll be dead. You won't have a say. At your wake, I could dress you in pink polka dots, and you'd be totally screwed." It was easier to joke with her than to imagine her gone.

She laughed then, and it was real and good, which helped me focus. "Your grandfather hated me in pink."

"I know!" I growled at her.

"As if you have a say."

"Everything's in my name," I reminded her. "The house, the property the house sits on, and you, crazy woman. I get to decide. The only reason I haven't just packed you up is because I know that's not what you want, but I'm dead serious when I tell you that—"

"Hah!" she cackled. "That's a good one. Dead serious. Dead. You're a hoot."

I sighed long and loud.

"Get your ass up here, kid. The nurse just called down to security."

So I rode up to the fifth floor, got off in front of a door that someone had to buzz me through, and there, on the other side, was a smiling nurse in My Little Pony scrubs.

I took off my sunglasses, because that was polite even though I was temporarily blinded.

"You're her sweet little grandson?" she asked, surprised as she stared up into my face. At six foot two, I wasn't often the tallest guy in the room, but not the shortest either.

"Yes, ma'am," I answered with a smile.

And then her brows furrowed as she stepped closer to me. "You realize that she thinks you're here to check her out of this hospital."

I nodded.

"She truly believes that she's not going to the nursing home, but we have the order from Sunnydale, and they're coming for her tomorrow."

"Which is why I'm here today," I apprised her, trying to keep the smugness out of my tone, but not completely succeeding.

Her eyes widened, and her mouth fell open in surprise.

"I'm here to spring her."

"But she shouldn't—she needs to stay here and then be transferred to the nursing—"

"You and I both know that's not what she wants," I insisted even as I kept my tone soft, light.

"Yes, but she's weak and she needs—"

"She needs help, but that's what I'm here for, and I'll bet you anything that she got up and got dressed the second you left the room."

Her gasp was loud, and I shrugged and smiled, because what she didn't know about Joanna Geary was a lot.

I SHIVERED in the parking lot as I helped her into the Toyota 4Runner I'd rented at the airport, and put her small overnight bag behind the driver's seat. We had left at least twelve bouquets of flowers, a few Mylar balloons, various planters, and many stuffed animals at the nurses' station to be distributed to other patients. She refused to bring home any of the gifts people had brought her in the hospital; she didn't want to infect her house with bad juju from a place of sickness and death.

"Some people walk outta there, you know," I reminded her.

"I know," she agreed. "Us. Let's not push our luck."

Once I was pulling out of the hospital parking lot, she patted my thigh. "Thank you for getting me out of there. I could feel the white walls and the fluorescent lights starting to suck out my soul."

I shuddered a second time.

"You too?" she asked, rolling down the window.

"I hate hospitals," I said, feeling life flood back into my body, the numbness dissipating. "You know it's going to be a hundred degrees outside."

"I just want to feel the sun on my face."

"You'll be cooked by the time we get to the house."

"Drive, lackey."

I made a noise, and she smiled and closed her eyes, face tipped toward the sun.

She was pretty, my grandmother, with her short pixie cut that was gray with streaks of silver. Her skin, which had always been tan since she spent much of her life outdoors in the garden she shared with her sister under the relentless sun, was now paler, almost translucent, the wrinkles pronounced. What remained, always, was her wicked grin, the mischievous cant to her eyebrows, and her deep dimples. I loved her throaty chuckle and husky voice, now even deeper, that I'd seen many a man turn around for. A woman with a laugh that infectious you had to see for yourself. My grandfather told me that when they were younger, all the men in town used to stare at him in amazement because he'd gotten Joanna Varlett to pick him.

"I don't know how I managed that," he always told me, but from the way my grandmother always sighed when he left the house, I had a pretty good idea that the love and admiration went both ways.

I took I-35 South from the airport toward Wimberley in Hays County, because that was the town you hit before you turned north for twenty miles and came to Braxton, both of them in the Texas Hill Country. Even though Braxton was only an hour and fifteen minutes out from Austin, those miles made a night-and-day difference. Compared to a big bustling city, the sleepy little burg rolled up the sidewalks at five and there was nothing at all to do. Or so I'd thought. As I drove toward town, I was surprised at the bars and clubs that had gone up on the outskirts there right off the highway. There were easily ten more bed-and-breakfast places, but that made sense with Canyon Lake so close.

"Holy shit, will you look at this place," I said to my grandmother, who was dozing in the passenger seat.

"I know." She yawned, stretching as she sat up. "You realize that, nowadays, Peg's little metaphysical bookstore slash herb shop, or whatever it was, would be a hit."

"It was back then too, but now the whole 'organic, essential oil, crystals-and-beads' way of life is so much more widely accepted."

"Do you still remember everything she taught you?"

"What?"

"You heard me. Do you still remember everything Peg taught you?"

"Well, yeah, but your mother taught both of you," I reminded her. "She was a hedge witch, and she passed the craft to both of her daughters, you and Peg."

She nodded. "I love that you never questioned the fact that your great-grandmother was a witch."

"Yeah, but witch is relative, right? The way you and Peg

always said it, it was more in a healer kind of way than in a magical one."

"True, though I saw her do magical things with people."

"Peg used to say that sometimes magic could just be knowing when to put on a pot of tea and talk instead of letting someone walk out the door of the shop."

She sighed. "You know, sometimes I envied her."

"Peg? Why?"

"Well, I got married and raised your father and his sisters in this town. Peg's the one who made her life with the store, and healing people with her tinctures and oils and advice."

"Don't kid yourself, Jo. You took care of a lot of people too," I said, wanting her to remember that her sister wasn't the only healer in town. My grandaunt might have done it in the traditional way, by mixing up dusts, making mojo bags and spell bags, and anointing candles with the herbs she grew in the garden, but Jo had a hand in raising things as well. She had a myriad of vegetables, among them radishes, tomatoes, bell peppers in three colors, red potatoes, mushrooms, and corn. In the fall, anyone who wanted a pumpkin could traipse through the patch behind the garden, and Jo's small orchard gave needed fruit when people couldn't afford to buy their own at the grocery store. "Don't ever sell yourself short. Not in front of me."

"Yes, dear," she said fondly, patting my leg. "But you worked in that store with Peg. You watched her mix the oils. You know what was in them and what she did when she infused them with intention."

"True," I said, acknowledging that. "But a lot of that was her doing the mixing during the full moon or the waxing moon, and her intention, as you're calling it, was nothing more than her feeling as she mixed the oils."

"Don't you downplay her gift," she warned me.

I smiled at her. "I'm not. I'm just saying that Peg was such a good, open, happy person, and that touched everything she did. You believe she had the gift, and people loved her store, but I also think a lot of women wore her oils because they smelled good, and spending fifteen minutes with Peg when they came in to buy them was time well spent."

"I see what you're saying," she agreed. "But back to what she taught you. I bet you could mix those oils again, couldn't you?"

"Why?"

"And make the candles."

"You're up to something?"

"Who? Me?"

"Yes, you."

"I was just wondering."

"You never just wonder about anything."

"And my garden, I bet you remember where everything went, don't you?"

"Maybe," I agreed, grinning over at her.

I was surprised when she reached out and touched my cheek and my hair before letting her hand fall away. "Every time I see you, you get more handsome."

My snort was loud in the car. "Are they sure there's nothing wrong with your eyes?"

More of her laughter then, and it sounded so good, so strong.

Seeing my grandmother's house after so long was a surprise. It had never looked better. The tiny little A-frame that once upon a time had been a dingy gray with off-white trim was now a lovely mint green with red trim. Even the front door was a vibrant crimson. And the more I stared, the more I realized I was looking at more than a paint job. The front porch was totally redone.

"What the hell, Jo?" I said, stunned as I parked in the gravel in front. "It looks amazing. When did you have all these renovations done?"

"Everett moved back into town," she disclosed like it was a secret.

I turned to look at her. "When was this?"

"About five months ago."

"Why didn't you tell me?"

"Because it didn't affect you," she said simply.

I nodded because that was true. Whatever my brother, Everett Geary, did had squat to do with me, except that evidently his return had something to do with the changes in the house. "Okay, so Everett moved back and what?"

"Well, so, since he didn't know I put the house in your name years ago, when he moved back, he asked if I would consider giving it to him for him and Rochelle, and in exchange, he'd fix up Peg's old cottage for me."

"Let me get this straight," I said with a snort. "He wanted to move you out of your own house and into the mother-in-law cottage behind your home."

"Mmmmm-hmmmm," she murmured.

She wasn't fooling anyone. The mischievous sparkle in her eyes as well as the curl of her lip was a dead giveaway.

I snickered. "And your house?"

"Why yes, dear," she said, smiling, her eyes dancing with evil intent.

"He wanted to fix up your house for Rochelle," I deadpanned.

"Uh-huh," she replied sweetly.

"You're screwing with me."

She scoffed, shaking her head.

I turned to look at her in the passenger seat. "He thought that his wife, the ex-prom queen, head cheerleader, and Miss Bluebonnet 2005, would live in anything as small as your house?"

She waggled her eyebrows before opening her door to get out.

"Wait," I ordered to no avail as I threw off my seatbelt, scrambled from my seat, and slammed my door shut before running around to the passenger side to offer her my hand.

She smacked it away. "Get the luggage. That's what I have you for."

"That's mean, what you did," I assured her, following directions, walking around the back of the SUV to pull out my duffle before going to the side door to grab her bag as well. Once I had the car locked, I stepped in beside her, both of us still looking at the house. "You knew better and you let him fix it up, knowing the whole time that Rochelle would never go for it."

"Did I?" she asked, batting her lashes.

I scoffed. "And so what happened?"

"Well, he sank a lot of money into it, and Rochelle said *oh hell no* the second she saw it. Maeve told me he actually did it on Facebook Live because he was so sure she was going to be excited."

"You talk to Maeve now?"

"I never stopped talking to Maeve. Don't act like I did." She scolded me. "And your sister has been calling quite regularly here lately."

"That's because she wants your jewelry when you die."

"It's all divvied up already and in the safety-deposit box at the bank."

"I was kidding!"

"Well, since you're the executor of my estate, you get the fun of reading the will."

"Estate makes it sound vast," I teased her.

"I think it's vaster—is that a word?"

"I don't know. I think so."

"Well then, it's vaster than you think," she said, winking at me.

"Oh, yeah? Is it?"

"Anyway," she said, rolling her eyes at me, "back to Everett presenting the house to Rochelle on Facebook. Apparently, it was so horrible, Maeve said she had to look away. The whole thing was cringeworthy."

I loved that my grandmother knew as much as she cared to about social media, and that once I bought her an iPad, she had enjoyed using FaceTime with me every other week.

"Did everyone see it?"

"Oh yes," Jo assured me, grimacing.

"Well, I feel so terrible for Everett," I snarked, grinning just thinking about it.

"You don't give a good goddamn about your brother," she said, almost sadly.

"That is true."

"I don't know what he was thinking."

"I don't either," I said, yawning. "I'm not even married to the woman, and I could tell you there was no way on God's green earth that Rochelle Geary—"

"It's Trotter-Geary," she corrected me snidely. "She hyphenates."

"Because heaven forbid anyone forgets that she's from the richest family in town."

"That's right," she affirmed, grinning at me.

"God."

"Well, anyway, on the video she lost her mind and

informed Everett that she'd rather live in her Mercedes than in my house, and they moved over to—"

"Ridge Road where all the big houses with the wrap-around porches are," I finished for her, knowing exactly where they ended up.

"Nope."

"Really?" I was surprised. "Where else do rich people live in this town now?"

"There's a new subdivision by the golf course and the country club, and that's where they bought a house."

"By the what and the what?"

"You've been gone a long time, love," she said with a cackle. "It's all fancy now."

"Country club? In Braxton? Isn't that like an oxymoron?"

"You would think so, but there are mansions up there now too," she advised me.

"No shit."

She chuckled, and her eyes lit up as she gazed at me.

"And what about the money he sank into the house?"

"He said, when I sell it, he wants back what he put in."

"You can't sell it."

"Yes, I know."

"It belongs to me."

"Yes, dear, I'm aware."

We had put everything in my name in case, heaven forbid, something happened to her. She didn't want vultures descending on her home even before her body was cold. But I knew her, and since Everett had put money into the house, she wouldn't be okay not to give that back to him. She was far too honest for that, which was why she'd let him make the renovations in the first place—she had always planned to pay him.

"You knew you had something else he wanted," I told her, because that had to be it.

"Yes."

I thought for a moment but came up blank. "Like what?"

"I swapped him the diamond your great-aunt Georgia left me in her will, and Peg's old store downtown."

"The huge one?"

"There was only one diamond, dear."

"Yes, but she left that diamond for you," I argued. "That's not right."

"Who cares? It was old when it was given to Georgia. It has that terrible asscher cut, and it's not a quality stone by any stretch of the imagination."

I had seen the ten-carat diamond many times growing up, because it was at the bottom of Jo's jewelry box. "But it was yours."

"It was mine because Georgia gave it to me and not Peg or any of our cousins, and I know the only reason she gave it to me was because she didn't want my mother to have it when she died."

"But you gave it to your mother anyway."

"Yes, and she gave it back to me before she died."

"Georgia would have been pissed if she knew."

"She did it to be mean and spiteful—"

"Because she *was* mean and spiteful," I chimed in.

Jo snorted out a laugh. "Jesus, was she ever."

"So you thought, use the ice rink of a diamond for something good."

"Exactly."

"But Peg's store?"

"Darling, it was empty for years, even before Peg passed away. She used the cottage behind the garden after she got sick. I told you that. Don't you remember?"

"I do, but it was still hers, the property I mean."

"It was both of ours, and she put it in my name before she died."

I sighed deeply. "You know, I asked her once if she regretted not ever getting married or having kids."

"Oh?"

"Yeah."

"What did she say?"

I turned and smiled at her. "You know what she said."

Her smile was bright. "She said that her spirit was made to blend with many and not one, and that having children was never in the cards for her."

"Literally," I said, chuckling. "She said her tarot cards told her, no kids."

"That's right."

"And she never wanted any, never felt the urge."

"And yet she was maternal with all the women who ever wandered into her shop and, of course, with you."

"Yeah," I sighed, remembering. "She liked me just a bit."

"God knows why."

I snorted out a laugh as Jo leaned into me, wrapping her arm around my waist.

"I'm sorry you had to give the store and the diamond to Everett."

"Please, as though I care about diamonds anyway. The renovations cost much more than either was worth, and I'll bet you he's still trying to fix up that store."

"What's he going to do with it?"

"Rochelle wants to open a clothing boutique."

I grunted.

"More power to her."

"Why the diamond, though?"

"Well, it is big."

"It certainly is that."

"And remember the provenance."

"Oh, that's right. It's got papers that say it belonged to some colonel in the American Revolution, and he gave it to a viscount's daughter when he proposed," I said, nodding, recalling my mother explaining it to me the summer before she and the rest of my family, except my paternal grandparents and my aunt Peg, stopped talking to me altogether. "It has some auspicious history to it."

"Yes," she said, sighing, giving me her weight. "So when I suggested the swap to Everett, he jumped at the chance to get it from me."

"Stupid," I muttered, smiling at the sweet little house that had been my refuge.

"Yes, it was," she agreed. "But I bet your mother was jealous."

"She wanted it too," I said, looking down at Jo. "How come you didn't give it to Dad when he proposed to my mother?"

"He didn't ask for it. He thought your mother would want something new."

"Little did he know that big and gaudy was the ticket."

She chuckled.

"But I guess it worked out since Everett wanted it for Rochelle."

"It most certainly did."

"I would have paid him, you know. I sort of hate that you lost the diamond, no matter the reason."

"I'm not," she assured me. "I'm happy. It was a good trade, and he and I are square. I had him sign on the dotted line that I don't owe him a dime."

"Don't trust him, huh?"

"It's not that," she said, turning to me. "I just wanted to make sure that after I'm gone, he had no claim on anything."

"I would never let him take the house from me," I said, and even I could hear the chill in my voice.

She took a step back and squinted at me.

"What?"

"Why do you care?"

"Because it's your house!"

"But if you never plan to live here, whyever would it matter?"

"I just—I don't—It's your house."

"Yes, you said that."

It wasn't logical, but her house, once it wasn't hers anymore, would be mine. Plain and simple. The house, attached to the garden, with Peg's sweet rose-covered cottage in the back, would always belong to me.

"Darling?" she prodded.

"What do you want me to say?"

She stared up at my face.

After a moment, I huffed out a breath. "It's hot out here. We should go in," I said, giving her my arm.

"He works with your father now, you know," she said, changing the subject, taking hold of my forearm as I led her toward the front door.

"I don't want to talk about Everett. I want to hear more… about the…huh," I finished as we reached the porch.

"I like that blank expression on your face," she teased me as I pulled the keyring from my pocket that had my Connecticut house keys on it, as well as my car keys, and the skeleton key for her front door that everyone always commented on. "And that key doesn't work anymore. All the locks are changed. Everett made it all state of the art."

She unzipped the front pocket of her backpack purse

that I'd given her for Christmas when we were together in London, and passed me a key and a fob.

"The hell is this?"

"The thing that's not a key; you have to touch to the plate. It unlocks the deadbolt and makes sure the alarm doesn't go off, and then the key just works like regular."

"The alarm?"

"If Arlo were still alive, I'd say that the alarm wasn't necessary, because we both know that no one was coming in here with that dog around, but living alone now, I don't hate the idea of the alarm."

The dog in question, the fifth in a long line of bloodhounds, had been the sweetest, gentlest creature on the planet, unless he didn't think you should be in the house. He had treed a very nice Maytag repairman once. "Okay."

"You know the Carsons down the street there? They were robbed a couple months ago."

"Really?"

"We've had quite a few break-ins around town. There are a lot of young people addicted to that oxy and other pain pills, and so we've had a bit of a hike in burglaries."

"Oxy?"

She nodded.

"How do you know all this?"

"You think I live under a rock?"

"No, ma'am," I said, opening the screen door and then touching the small silver plate with the fob. When I heard the click of the deadbolt, I opened the new, heavy door with the key. I held it open so she could walk in first.

Inside, the house was stunning.

"Holy shit, Jo," I said, closing the door behind us and dropping the luggage.

Her smile lit her whole face. "I know, don't you love it?"

It had always been a sweet, cozy little house, but now it had a wide-open floor plan, as all the walls that used to separate the kitchen from the living room and the dining room had been torn down. The brown shag carpet and wood-paneled walls were gone. Instead, bleached hardwood floors and off-white paint with cream-colored molding and wainscoting replaced them. There was a window seat in what used to be the dining room but was now more a library, along with built-in bookcases that reached from the floor to the ceiling. Gone were the cheap blinds, and in their place were plantation shutters and curtains. One entire wall had been torn out and windows put in, which made what had once been dark now bright and flooded with light.

"Wow," I said, my voice gone, stunned at how incredible her home looked.

"Go see the kitchen," she said, sounding excited.

I crossed to the Scandinavian-style kitchen with white woodwork, subway tile, and double-tall windows. There were vintage-styled stainless-steel appliances, like the oven and refrigerator that were top of the line. The geometric black-and-white-tiled floor was stunning as was the new farmhouse sink.

I turned and looked at my grandmother. "How long did all this take?"

"He moved me out for three weeks," she said, seated now on an overstuffed wingback chair that it was clear she loved, given how she was patting the arms. "And when I came back, I was just over the moon."

"But you didn't let him know that, did you?"

She shook her head slowly.

"Well, I have to say, he did an amazing job."

"That's because he put in everything he thought Rochelle would want."

I sighed, looking around and shaking my head. "I just...love it."

Her smile was huge. "I'm so glad."

It hit me then, what had been bothering me earlier. "Hey, I know this is bad, but—"

"You look as confused as you did a bit ago."

"Could you tell me what your son does for a living?"

Her shit-eating grin came out then, along with that signature cackle she'd perfected before I was born, or so my grandfather used to tell me.

"Laugh it up, but I have no clue what he does," I confessed.

"I know," she said playfully, having fun, I could tell. "He changed jobs so often it was hard to keep track."

It was true. My father had jumped from one get-rich scheme to the next when I was growing up. "So what does he do now?"

"He owns car lots."

"No shit?"

"No shit," she mimicked me, grinning.

"How many?"

"Four or five."

"Huh."

We were quiet a moment.

"Is that a lot?" I asked her.

"I have no earthly idea," she said with a chuckle.

I thought a second. "What're they called?"

"From what Everett told me, they're named Geary Chevrolet, Geary Cadillac, Geary Buick...things like that."

"Original."

"Yes."

"Huh."

Another moment of silence.

"She has a degree in marketing, you know."

"Who?"

"Rochelle."

"Oh," I said, getting it. "So Rochelle and Everett both work for Dad."

"Yes, Everett is the general manager of one of the dealerships there in Austin, and Rochelle manages the digital marketing department."

"Where do they live now, still in Austin?"

"Yes, your parents are still there."

"I wonder why Everett and Rochelle don't live there too."

"I suspect because their house here would be two or three million in Austin, and here Rochelle can show off her diamond and her Mercedes and her horses; whereas, there she and Everett would be living in your parents' guesthouse."

"That all makes perfect sense."

"Go look at the rest of the house."

There had been three bedrooms, one for the girls, one for the boys, and one for my grandparents. Now there were only two and an extra bathroom, so whereas it used to be a half-bath for company and one bathroom for the house, now there was one in the master, one for guests, and the one still across from the kitchen. I had always wondered how they did it growing up: three girls—my aunts—and one boy—my father—plus my grandparents, in one bathroom. Just me and my grandparents in the one, when I lived with them, had been crazy.

But now, the master was stunning, open, with windows on both walls, then the enormous bathroom, walk-in closet, and skylight over the bed. The guest room, where I would be, was huge as well, and the new bathroom had no tub but, instead, a shower so big it had no doors. It had a rustic feel to it, and the traditional Mexican-tiled walls made it feel bright and airy.

Walking back out to the living room, I found Jo dozing in the chair. I moved up beside her and crouched down with my hand on her knee.

Her eyes opened slowly, and her smile was gentle as she brushed my hair back from my forehead. "What do you think?"

"I love it."

She sighed softly. Apparently that made her happy.

"Are you hungry?"

"Not yet, but I would love some coffee."

"Absolutely."

"We need to get some hanging flower baskets for the porch today."

"Okay," I said, rising to go to the kitchen, but she caught my hand. "What?"

"I'm thinking bubblegum petunias, because they'll do well even in the heat."

"But you hate pink."

"But Peg didn't."

"That's true," I said, sighing, because whether I liked it or not, there was the tug of familiarity that whispered home when I'd been walking around the house, and even looking at it from the outside.

"You know each pot of petunias gets—"

"—a gallon of water a day in the summer," I finished for her, remembering my aunt's words. "It used to take hours to do the whole yard."

She nodded, smiling. "And you bitched about it like crazy."

"I didn't see you doin' it."

"There were bees and wasps and those damn grasshoppers and—"

"We didn't have any wasps," I said, chuckling. "That's why there was basil and lemongrass and geraniums and all that damn mint."

"There was?"

I nodded. "And fennel to keep the slugs and snails away, and rosemary by the garden gate."

"You know, I used to love looking outside and seeing you two planting things and watering, her in her big sun hat and you in that stupid straw thing."

Squinting, I explained to her that Peg had brought me that hat back from her trip to Vietnam. "That was a great hat."

She nodded slowly, indulging me.

"It was."

"Well, the important thing was that, with you and Peg in the garden, I could sit on the back porch and drink iced tea and watch you work."

I grunted.

"I loved watching you two work," she sighed, grinning at me evilly.

"Yeah, Peg and I didn't so much love that." I remembered Peg and me with hoes and shovels, the two of us leaning on the handles in the sun, glowering at my grandmother as she sat on the tiny back porch, fanning herself in the shade and drinking one mint julep after another. Peg used to mutter under her breath that it must be nice to have been born a princess.

"I'm glad you love the house," Jo said, retuning me to the present.

It was a little scary how many memories were coming to visit, and I had to be careful not to let my nostalgia for my family get the better of me. I refused to get soft on Braxton. "Did I say love? I meant to say it was okay," I amended quickly.

"Okay?" She made a face.

"Did Everett pick the red?"

"I picked it. You know it's my favorite color."

I did know.

"We need to go to the store and stock the house," she informed me. "Can you cook? Because I don't like to much anymore."

I winced.

"What?"

"I'm a vegetarian now, you know."

"That's fine, I'll cook my own bacon."

I shivered.

"What? Don't want to kill Babe?"

My scowl was dark. "That's a terrible thing to say."

"Bacon tastes good."

"You're a horrible person."

"This is not news."

I took a breath. "You know I'm kidding."

"Stop being so serious, or I'll invite Everett over for dinner."

The idea of seeing any member of my family was the second worst thing I could imagine. "I'm lightening up as we speak," I assured her.

"Good, because we need to get to the store, and then you can start on that favor."

Here was the crux of the matter. On the phone five days ago, she said she needed me to do something for her, and I knew it was more than being there, more than springing her from the hospital. It had to be bigger.

"What is it?" I pressed her. "What do you want me to do? Whatever it is, I'm on it."

"Oh?" she teased me. "Anything?"

"I swear. Just please, out with it already."

"Come here," she said, getting up and walking around me.

I followed her to the kitchen and then out the back door that now led to a long deck complete with a large picnic table and other assorted high-end furniture that would have been out of place before, but looked amazing now. From there, the entire backyard, which used to be her garden, was visible, just as it was from the new larger windows over the kitchen sink.

"What?" I asked when she stood there, hands on her hips, and smiled.

"This is it."

"What's it?"

And then she did the most horrible thing imaginable and slowly lifted her arms and opened them wide, presenting the now-wretched excuse for a garden that once upon a time had been the most glorious piece of real estate in Braxton. Now, sadly, tragically, it was overrun with weeds almost as tall as me.

Back in the day, the spiral-shaped garden that sat behind a waist-high white picket fence with a rose-covered arbor, was the jewel of the neighborhood. Everyone knew Jo's little patch of heaven, home to night-blooming roses and peonies, honeysuckle and gardenia, dogwood and even hydrangeas, which thrived in the hot and humid summers. Wisteria had grown on the left side of the back fence, along with lilac and lavender and jasmine. On the right, sunflowers once stood tall. In the middle, planted in spirals, were the spices. Stepping through the arch over the back gate, where it butted up against forest, had felt like entering another world, all lush and green during the day and deep blue at night, with the songs of the crickets and the glow of the fireflies. I had spent so many nights on my back in the garden, wondering about my life and contemplating what, if any, magic was left in the world.

Now, there was dirt and a ton of weeds, and I suspected that sooner rather than later, my grandmother would have to have someone come in with a backhoe and overturn the entire piece of land so someone else could start from scratch out there. But now I knew she had other plans, plans that included me.

"Be very clear now," I said, hoping I was wrong.

"I want it back as it was," she announced like this was a movie and she was the queen of something. "So let it be done."

"I'm sorry?" I blurted, because she was clearly out of her mind. She gave me the eyebrow arch then, and it was terrifying. "No." And the evil grin on top of it. "No, no, no."

"Where's your sense of adventure?"

"You can't be serious." I almost moaned.

"The house was built to enjoy looking out at the garden, as was the cottage."

I was horrified. "That's true, but—"

"And who better than you, with the green thumb and an encyclopedic memory of where everything is supposed to go and what's supposed to be in there, to bring the garden back to life?" she asked, her gaze locked with mine.

"Are you kidding? There's probably snakes in there now!"

"I would suspect so, yes."

I turned to look at her. "Let's just hire a landscaper."

She shook her head slowly. "There won't be any love in it with some stranger."

"Yeah, but—"

"And we both know that you'll have it growing in a week. My mother had the gift, so did Peg, and so do you."

"What are you—"

"You just need to start, and the earth will finish."

"Do you know what you're talking about right now?"

"Don't play dumb," she warned me. "On this particular patch of land, you're as full of magic as the rest of the witches in our line."

"You don't believe that."

"I've always believed it."

I made a noise I wasn't proud of. "I really think a landscaper is the way to—"

"This is my dying wish," she intoned, sounding all serious and foreboding like this was a movie instead of my life.

"Oh come on, this is lame."

She howled then, and her laughter, even in the face of a Herculean labor, was an excellent sound.

THREE

Two weeks ago, my grandmother had passed out at the grocery store and was still unconscious at the local hospital when my parents drove from Austin to see her. My father had, she told me on the phone, freaked the hell out. Worried, wanting what was best for her, he had her transported by private ambulance service to Seton Medical Center. Since they lived in Austin and not in Braxton, it would be easier for them to visit her in the hospital there and then transfer her to the Sunnydale Nursing Home. Everett could put her house on the market, and they'd use the money to help pay for her care. It was all settled.

"You should have called me sooner," I stated, angry that she'd waited instead of coming to me at the beginning. "Why didn't you?"

"I didn't think they'd actually try and take my choices away from me like I was a child," she explained as I unpacked my duffel in the room that had not existed when I was growing up. "I mean, they've got some crust."

I looked at her.

After a moment, she gave me an indulgent smile. "Yes?"

"What does that even mean?"

"What?"

"That stupid, *they've got some crust*."

"You know, like bread."

"I know it's like... Ohmygod, you don't even know what your weird sayings mean," I told her for the millionth time in my life. "Like, every time I'm about to open a door for you, you yell out, 'Open the door, Richard!'"

"Yes," she said, like that made perfect sense.

"Why? What is that even about?"

"It's a song, you ingrate."

I shook my head at her. "Anyway, I know why they tried to railroad you into the nursing home. They figured since there was nobody else here to help you that you'd be stuck."

"I don't think your father had any railroading on his mind," she said, taking a seat on the end of the bed, watching what I pulled out to put into the antique armoire in the corner of the room. "He's not like that."

I opened my mouth to argue.

"But," she began before I could. "He wants me to have care that he can't give me so he thought a home was the best option."

Her defending him was going to make me sick to my stomach.

"But he didn't count on my baby coming to take care of me."

"That's because he doesn't remember I exist."

"Oh, darling, he remembers very well."

I grunted.

She shook her head before reaching into my duffle and pulling out a lightweight zippered hoodie I'd brought with me. "May I borrow this?"

"All yours," I said, watching her pull it on and wrap it around her shoulders instead of zipping it up. "You cold?"

"My body temperature is odd lately," she explained before yawning.

Before we were allowed to step foot out of the hospital, the doctor sat me down and lectured me on what was normal and what wasn't and when I should call her. Jo had lost some weight, so the chills were expected. "So Mom and Dad, they want you to continue with the radiation?"

"Yes. They think me stopping is equal to suicide."

"Oh, Jo, I'm so sorry. That's so stupid."

She gave me a dismissive wave. "It's not stupid. It's how they feel, but really, don't concern yourself with it now, darling. You're here now, so I don't have to worry."

"Do they realize that this is 2019? You can't have someone committed just because they don't want anything to do with chemo or radiation." I reached for her hand and assured her. "But, so you know, I'm not letting that happen. I have power of attorney and you have a medical directive. They've got nothing."

"I do know," she soothed me, her voice calm, soft. "And I know your father, especially, is scared, and he doesn't want to lose me—again—but yes, me not wanting any more poison in my body is not, in fact, grounds for involuntary hospitalization. Every individual over the age of eighteen gets to decide on their own quality of life."

"I'm sorry," I repeated, stopping on my third trip from the bed, where my duffle was, to the armoire, and really looking at it, noting the colors and the hardware. "Holy crap, is that Grandpa Stewart's armoire?"

"It is," she said, beaming at me. "I asked your father to get it out of storage for you."

I turned to look at her across the room. "You told him it was for me?"

"Yes."

"Me?" I said again, trying to clarify in case she was confused. "You asked my father, your son, to do something for me?"

"Yes, I did."

"Why would he do that?" And then it hit me, and I felt like an ass. She was dying, after all. Nobody got to say no to her anymore. "Oh, Jo, I'm an idiot. I—"

"It's not because of me," she said flatly, pinning me with her sharp blue gaze. "Your father did it for you."

"No. He did it for you, because you asked him."

She shook her head. "I didn't have to insist. I said, 'Kaenon will be coming home,' and it was here the following day."

"That makes no sense."

She shrugged. "Perhaps he wants to make amends."

My face scrunched up before I even thought about it. "Oh, c'mon, gimme a break."

"It's been a long time," she placated me. "He's losing his mother; maybe he'd like his son back."

I rushed across the room to stand over her. "You need to stop reminding me that you're going to die already, or I'm going to be ten kinds of useless to you."

It seemed as though we stayed like that forever, frozen, staring at each other.

"Yes, dear," she finally agreed.

"Okay," I echoed, exhaling seconds later.

"But I believe that your father, the boy I raised, wants to make amends."

I winked at her. "I wouldn't hold your breath."

. . .

Stand In Place

"You realize, to clear those weeds out of the garden, I'll need a machete," I told my grandmother three hours later as we walked through the outdoor market together. I had insisted she nap even though she said that she was fine.

"You'll probably need a scythe," she said with a cackle. "You'll look like the grim reaper out there. All the kids in the neighborhood will poop their pants."

I stopped walking and stared at her.

After a moment, when she was a few feet away, not having realized I'd stopped moving, she turned and looked at me. "What? Too much?"

"That's terrible."

In response there was more laughing.

"You know, I'll need thigh-high waders so nothing bites me," I continued, goading her once she was done giggling like a demented serial killer.

"All right," she agreed, not listening in the slightest.

"There's probably a billion spiders in there."

Nothing.

"And yellow jackets."

Not even a murmur of concern.

"And flesh-eating moths."

She was ignoring me, too busy picking broccoli and avocados, sweet corn and peaches.

"I should get one of those outfits to keep the bees off me too."

Into the basket went cherries and green grapes, cauliflower, long-stemmed mushrooms, and chickpeas.

"I want a flamethrower."

"Whatever you think's best."

"You're not even listening to me," I muttered. "And I hate vegetables."

"Yes, dear."

Definitely not. She didn't even catch my lie. Not listening one bit.

"I hate kale most of all," I grumbled.

"Uh-huh."

Really not paying a scrap of attention to me.

"Are you sure you should be walking around?" I asked, taking her arm.

She turned and looked up into my face. "You've asked me that five times now."

It was more like three. "You're exaggerating."

"I'm not feeble," she contended.

"No, but you did pass out two weeks ago, and at the hospital, they thought you were frail."

"I've never been frail a day in my life," she muttered irritably.

"Again, you passed out."

"I'm aware of that, and it's really annoying that you keep bringing it up."

"I just think we should rent you one of those motorized little carts so you can drive it around and––"

"You suggest that again and I'll invite Bill and Emma-Jean over to show you their pictures of their trip to the Grand Canyon. They just went in April."

"I don't even know them. Maybe they're lovely, and it would be like a night with David Sedaris or something."

She snickered.

"Fine."

"Just stop fussing," she snapped. "I promise you I can walk just fine, and we won't be out here that long anyway."

"I'm only worried because––"

"And," she said, her voice softening, warming as she reached up to put a hand on my cheek, "being at home with you, my angel, has helped more than I can tell you."

I scowled at her in response. "Angel? Really?"

She dropped her hand. "It was worth a shot."

"I just want you to be truthful with me."

"I am. And I had a nap for crissakes. I will tell you if I feel poorly."

"I'll make you a deal," I began, seeing the table in the shade close to the kettle corn booth and the homemade iced tea. "If you sit, I'll walk around, grab some more of your favorites, and then be back. And you call me if anything changes."

She squinted at me, weighing her options, I could tell. "Fine. But I want some white peaches, and those are on the other side by the woman who sells those creepy dolls that are supposed to be possessed by spirits."

I had to process that.

"I'm not kidding," she assured me.

"Seriously?"

"Oh yes. Don't even look at the dolls," she said with a shudder. "If your aunt was still alive, I wouldn't worry but… just don't look at them."

"Yeah, no. Don't worry."

"Make sure you walk around the whole market."

"Why?" I asked. "I'll just get the peaches and be right back so we can––"

"No." She was adamant. "I want you to look at things."

"It's produce."

"It's a lot of things."

For whatever reason, she wanted me to browse, and then it hit me. "You want me to talk to people."

"And what's wrong with that?"

"Jo, it's not like I'm moving back here. What does it matter?"

"Do what I tell you," she barked, done discussing the

topic, not sounding frail in the least before she turned and left me.

She went to sit. I kept my eyes on her, assessing her walk, and I had to say it was a stride, not a slow shamble. The moment she sat, she was joined by a couple of women. I was going to ask if she needed water, but one of the ladies passed her a bottle.

I opened my mouth to tell her I'd be back.

"Oh my goodness, is that Joanna Geary?"

I didn't look to see who it was; I didn't care. I had stopped even checking the faces of the people I'd walked by years ago. People in Wallingford, even those who only knew me in passing, would be surprised, disbelieving. Kaenon Geary was rude? Abrupt? Cold? Are you sure? He's the nicest guy, smiles a lot, he even has those crinkles in the corners of his eyes. How did you not get a wave from him or a genuine hello? Maybe he was sick, had a headache, or even the flu. I knew what they would say, because when I wasn't kind, people asked why. It wasn't like me. That wasn't who I was. And yet...back in Braxton for mere hours, I was a surly, brooding fourteen-year-old boy all over again, freshly abandoned by my parents, newly outed by my older brother, ignored by my sister, and left alone to sort through bullies and homophobia and apathy from adults who didn't give a damn what happened to me. Only my grandparents and my Aunt Peg had kept the more desperate pain away, reminded me to keep looking toward the future instead of thinking the small-town life was all there ever could be.

I found the white peaches, kept my eyes averted from the table to the left, and thanked the woman who looked pained as she placed the peaches in my basket. The market was more co-op than traditional market, as everyone had stickers on their produce and customers then paid in a central location.

"I'm moving next to the watermelon guy next week," she told me.

I gave her a smile. "Probably for the best."

"You're not even kidding."

It was funny, but the smells were the same. In summer there was always that warm scent of sun on clothes, of charcoal in backyard barbecues, and lemonade. There was also that earthiness of vegetables and freshly turned dirt. But as I walked down the long rows of tables, another aroma hit me. Somebody was smoking pot, and it struck me that Jo could use some of that to help with nausea or pain or whatever she was going through even though, as she said, she was done with the chemo and radiation because it was killing her faster than the cancer.

The closer I got to the chain-link fence, the stronger the smell got, and when I reached it and saw the three guys, at first I was excited because it would be easy to make a buy to help Jo out, but that fast, when they turned, I was disappointed. They weren't old enough for me to score pot from. They were boys, maybe seniors, at least two of them; the third looked even younger. All three resembled the incoming college freshman students I taught year after year, and so, because I was first and foremost a teacher, I went right into that mode.

"You guys are in trouble," I announced, curling my hands into the metal links of the fence and shaking my head.

"Who the hell are you?" The leader, the one the other two were flanking, greeted me with prickly defiance.

He was tall, with short black hair, his dark sepia skin with deep bronze undertones in direct contrast to the pale kid beside him with the billion freckles and the bright red hair. They were both handsome, as was the dark-tanned kid who rounded out the threesome, shorter than the others but more muscular, his hair tumbling down the back of his neck.

"New teacher at the high school," I lied, matching his glower. "And you're screwed."

"Why?" he challenged me. "It's just a hand-rolled cigarette."

I snorted and that got them all glaring at me.

"You're a teacher?" Freckle Boy on the right said, like I was full of crap. "Bullshit."

"Why? I don't look like a teacher to you?"

They all moved forward at once, leaning on the fence, making it bow toward me, checking me over, sizing me up.

"You don't look like no teacher I ever seen," Tan Kid with the crew cut told me.

That I had to smile over, because my students back home said the same thing.

My thick, loose, wheat-blond curls were too long, falling around my ears, messy, doing their own thing, and I was sporting too many different pendants on silver chains and black leather cord, and not one of them was a cross. The white tee was tight under the short-sleeve shirt, molding to my chest, but it was too hot to keep wearing my leather racing jacket, so I'd left it in the car. My jeans were old, worn, and my boots were ancient. None of it said teacher.

"Well, I promise I am," I assured the musketeers, "and since I'll have all three of you guys in class, you better hand over the weed so you can stop now, to get out of the habit before school starts."

"Man, it's June," the leader snapped at me. "We ain't sweatin' school."

"You sweatin' a constable?" I asked, seeing the cruiser turning into the parking lot behind them. "Because"—I pointed over his shoulder—"check it out."

They all did the turn and swore at the same time.

"Pass it through," I ordered, my tone sharp, brooking no protest.

A quarter of a sandwich-size Ziploc bag of weed got threaded through the links to me, and I took it and shoved it down into my pocket. The constable—there weren't cops or deputies or even a sheriff in Braxton but, instead, constables—called them over, his command bored, and I saw them pivot and head toward him, sauntering, cocky, confident, of course, because everything they had been holding was now on me.

Returning to the market, I went back to looking at more stupid vegetables, walking up and down the aisles until I was noisily joined by the three teenagers coming up beside me, jostling together, waiting for my attention.

"Yes?" I asked slowly, walking again so they had to move to stay with me.

"Give us our stuff."

I scoffed. "Not on your life."

"Man, weed ain't bad for you," the leader again argued. Since I'd gone into teacher-mode, he was responding with student-mode, trying to get me to see things his way while whining.

"Did you know that the rational part of your brain isn't fully developed until you're around twenty-five?"

"Yeah, like we've never heard that before," the redhead groaned.

I turned to look at them, arms crossed, waiting.

The leader sighed. "I'm Artie. This is Vance, and that's Mike."

I turned to Vance. "That's your first name?"

He made a noise of disgust. "Nah, it's Hoyt so yanno, I use my last name."

"All right." I couldn't very well argue with that. "Well, I'm Kaenon Geary, and from now until school starts, you can call me Kaenon. When we're in class, it's Mr. Geary."

"Yessir," they all chorused.

"You guys are lucky I didn't turn you in to the constable," I warned them. "You should be damn thankful I'm in such a good mood."

There was nodding then, and I had a second to wonder if my own prefrontal cortex was functioning. It didn't seem like it, with the decisions I was making. I had to come clean. It wasn't fair to them.

"Okay, so I don't exactly live here anymore. I'm just hanging here for the summer, and I am a teacher, well, professor, but in Wallingford, Connecticut, not in Braxton."

They just stood there, waiting, and I had a moment to think that they could have been in an ad for a soft drink or jeans or something else. They were quite the assortment for a tiny town—a Hispanic kid, a black kid, and a white kid. When I'd gone to school here, it was almost all white. I was encouraged to see some diversity.

"I won't be your teacher," I made clear.

Artie, the leader, gave me a smile then. "Okay, so then, hand it over."

"No. I'm still an adult—mostly—and you can't smoke pot."

"Aww man," Hoyt—I couldn't get that out of my mind—muttered. "I knew this was gonna happen. We took that from Hughes to sell, and now we're out the pot *and* we don't have any money to give him. We're totally fucked."

I understood. Small town, zero prospects if your folks

didn't own a B&B, do something that had you working with tourists, or own a farm. Everything else was fast food, and those filled up before school was even out. I had worked at my aunt's herbal shop, so growing up I always had a job. Not everyone had been so lucky.

"How much do you owe this Hughes guy?" I asked them.

"A hundred," Artie told me.

I had two hundred in cash on me, so I got out my wallet and gave it to him. "You go give this to him now, and don't screw around with him again."

"We won't," he agreed, and I could tell he was just a bit scared.

"Haven't you guys watched any mob movies ever? You never use your own product—first rule of selling drugs."

They all nodded like I was a sage or something.

"Pay Hughes and get out of there, and then Monday morning at around say, nine, I want all three of you guys to show up at 822 Apple Lane and help me start fixing up my grandmother's garden. It's gonna take forever, so I'll give you eight bucks an hour, and we'll start at four hours a day and see how you all do."

Instantly, the smiles were blinding.

"If you guys don't show up, or you're not there by nine, deal's off."

A lot of nodding.

"Now, get the hell away from me."

They bolted and I once again went back to looking at vegetables, wondering at my own stupidity, when I felt a hand on my back. Turning, I found Artie there, Mike and Hoyt a few feet away, waiting.

"We'll be there," he promised. "And thank you for the advance."

Okay, then. "You're welcome."

They left, and I heard my grandmother calling my name.

Worried that she was tired or getting sick, I hightailed it over to her. "What's wrong?"

"Nothing. I was just talking to these nice ladies here," she said, indicating several women who had gone to school with my sister. "And we noticed that the Chief Constable just drove up over there."

She was staring, hand shielding her eyes, looking at the man climbing out of a cruiser, as were the other three women with her. When I turned to look, I saw what had their rapt attention, and a day that was tolerable went straight to absolute hell. Not that I was surprised; that was the only way my luck worked in Braxton. At home, I had good luck, but here in Texas, I had the bad kind and no other.

"That's him," one of the women said, "that's Brody Scott just come back home from Houston. Ain't he something?"

"Was he in your class?" Jo asked me.

"No," I answered flatly.

"He and your brother, Everett, were thick as thieves in high school," one of the women simpered, glancing at me and smiling before turning back to watch the constable.

"Is that right?" Jo inquired, tipping her head, admiring the man crossing the parking lot.

"Yes, ma'am," someone answered.

"Was he that gorgeous in high school?" Jo questioned us all, me too, even if the women didn't know it.

Lots of laughter in response to that.

If we'd been alone, I would have answered her, because yes, the man had been beautiful then, and age, of course, had been kind to Brody Scott. Now, he was simply breathtaking.

He walked the same way he had when he was eighteen,

all fluid grace and swagger, absolutely certain of his place in the world. He and Everett had been friends forever, my brother the quarterback, he the guy he handed the ball off to most often. But whereas my brother had not been good enough for a football scholarship, Brody Scott most certainly had. He went off to California to be a running back at UCLA, and from there I didn't know what happened to him, losing track, my interest following no further, too caught up in my own struggles.

Since he was the same age as my brother, four years older than me, he had to be either thirty-five or thirty-six now, and most guys didn't stay in the NFL that long, so perhaps he'd had a whole career and then returned first to Houston and now to Braxton. Why he would come back once he got out was not something I could comprehend. I was just visiting, but he drank the Kool-Aid and made a commitment to the town, chose on purpose to be permanently in Braxton. Chief Constable was a four-year elected office, which meant he'd run a campaign and put his name on a ballot. The message was clear—he wanted ties to the community and all the baggage that came with that. I couldn't, for the life of me, imagine why. Not that I cared enough to ask. While it was true that Brody had never done anything to hurt me physically or otherwise in high school, neither had he been my champion. He had been popular, a big jock like my brother, and he hadn't wanted to do anything to detract from that image. And I understood, I did. He'd been young, but that didn't mean I had to stand around and make nice now, no matter how good he looked in his uniform.

"I'm gonna go buy these," I told my grandmother, taking the basket from her and turning to go find a cashier. I needed to give someone money, and anything was better than standing there waiting to say hello to a man I cared nothing about.

"Jo Geary, what are you doing out here?"

His voice behind me sounded the same, deep and rough, with a raspy edge to it that years ago had never ceased to make my stomach flutter and my pulse jump. It was unfortunate that, as far as I could tell, nothing had changed. I was careful not to run away, but it was a near thing.

Once I found the line to check out, I stood there, waiting, and then remembered that I was supposed to text Baz, and so took off my glasses and put them on top of my head as I wrote a quick message explaining that I had arrived safe, if not sound, and telling him that I would send pictures of the garden that my crazy grandmother wanted me to make green again.

The question back, *Your grandmother wants you to do what to what?,* was funny, and I was smiling as I moved up to my turn with the cashier.

"Kaenon?"

Head up, I found a woman who looked somewhat familiar.

"Jesus Christ," she said breathlessly, "look at you."

I smiled back because that was polite.

"My God, did you fill out nice."

And it was the knowing smirk and the tilt of her head and the dancing blue eyes that finally did it. "Oh shit," I gasped, surprised. "Shelly?"

Her laugh was sweet, and I realized she looked so much better than she had in high school. Hair that had once been bottle-blond was now a gorgeous rich auburn and fell in wisps around her face.

"Shelly Garber?"

"Took you long enough," she chastised me.

I grinned at her. "You look amazing."

"Yeah?" she fished, and I saw it then, uncertainty. She was holding back, excited but waiting. "You think so?"

"You're gorgeous, darlin'," I pronounced, letting the drawl I'd worked so hard to get rid of come right back out as I lifted my arms. "C'mere."

She flew around the makeshift counter to reach me, lunging, arms wrapped around my neck as she welcomed me home.

And it hit me as I held a woman in my arms who had dated my brother back in the day that being a prick the entire time I was there wasn't going to do me any favors. And I knew it wouldn't, because I'd been taught to look at things logically.

People thought literature majors just read the classics, learned to appreciate iambic pentameter, and got some history and philosophy thrown in for good measure. But first, in all areas, from reading poems to treatises on the nature of man, we were taught to look at our own experiences and gut them, to more easily extract the motivations of fictional characters. There always had to be a reason, some underlying motivation, and who cared if it wasn't what the author intended, it was something you, as the reader, excavated. So I was used to looking inward and outward at the same time, which meant that how I was acting had not escaped me.

Since I'd arrived, I'd had my head down, not being myself at all, and the reasoning was really simple.

I was angry.

I was furious at my grandmother for getting sick, and it was unreasonable and childish, but every time I tried to be a grown-up about it and think of her and what she was going through instead of how much I was going to miss her…I was back at the kitchen table and fourteen all over again.

I was mad at my parents for discarding me like a piece of trash.

I was mad at my sister for acting like I'd died.

I was mad at my brother for his callousness.

I was mad at being in a place, again, that I was never comfortable in, and more than anything, I was pissed off because I wasn't being myself even a little.

Back in Connecticut, everywhere else in fact, I lived well in my skin. Yes, I had taken a detour from my common sense when I was with Aidan, but other than that eight-month transgression, normally I was a loyal friend, an excellent teacher, a kick-ass neighbor, and a thoughtful lover. I wasn't petty or jealous or insecure or any of the things I'd been feeling in the last few hours. I could barely breathe, and if I didn't stop and just calm the hell down, I was going to have a heart attack and be zero help to Jo.

"Oh, Kaenon," Shelly squealed in my arms. "Are you still gay, or was that just a phase you were going through in high school?"

I chuckled as I gave her a final squeeze before setting her down on her feet. "Still gay. Some things you just don't grow out of."

Her smile was huge as she held on to my hand. "Well, I can't blame you. I like men quite a bit myself."

I let out a deep breath. "So, tell me everything."

And she started, catching me up on her marriage and how she was Shelly Tate now, and all about her four boys, and when she was done ringing me up and still talking, I moved around beside her and bagged vegetables as she continued speaking, ignoring the customers she was helping except to give them a total and then change.

Several people interrupted her rambling update when they said hello to me, men and women who remembered me from the soccer team or from when I worked at my aunt's store, who just wanted to smile or give me a hug or shake my hand.

It was strange and unexpected.

"You look weird alluva sudden," Shelly said, scrutinizing me.

"No, I just—no one used to talk to me except for a small group of friends."

She made a noise.

"What?"

"Honey, by the time you were a senior and an all-state—what was it?"

"Forward."

"By the time you were an all-state forward, everyone was tryin' to get your attention. My little sister wanted to be your friend so bad, but you were so private. Just you and Zuzu and Colby. No one else got the time of day."

I nodded.

"They went on off to school when you did, and ain't neither of 'em been back."

I, of course, knew where both women were.

Zuzu Wooster was now Zuzu Johnson, married with kids and living in Indianapolis. She ran a lifestyle blog with some insane amount of Twitter and Instagram followers. She tried to explain to me the importance of page views and trending whatever whenever we talked, but our conversations always ended up being about her latest adventures with motherhood or my wretched dating life. I liked those talks the best.

Colby Park lived in Paris, worked as a journalist, and juggled more men and women than I could ever hope to keep track of. She often suggested I visit. I had plans to go next year. We still talked on the phone late into my night, if not hers.

"They're good," I assured Shelly.

"Still talk to them both, do you?"

I nodded.

"Well, that makes sense. Y'all were inseparable."

And we had been.

When my phone rang, it was Jo.

"What?" I grumbled at her.

"Oh, don't sound so surly," she chastised me. "I'm hungry and tired and let's go already."

After hugging Shelly goodbye and promising to meet her for either drinks or coffee—she had me call her so she'd have my number—I left the tent and headed back to my grandmother.

"Wait."

It was only one word, but it came out as less of a request and more of a command that I had better heed.

I stopped and turned as Brody Scott stepped in front of me. "Good afternoon, Constable."

Arms crossed over his massive chest, shoulders squared, legs braced, scowling, clearly rippling with anger, the man was in his battle stance.

"Or not."

FOUR

When Brody Scott became the law in Braxton, his sense of humor was obviously the first thing to go.

"No?" I said, grimacing. "Not a good morning?"

He took a step forward and jabbed two fingers right below my collarbone, which didn't hurt but certainly wasn't comfortable. "Do you have any idea what you just did?"

I looked down at the bags of vegetables I was carrying and then back up at him. "Is there some kind of vegetable statute I'm not aware of?"

"Kaenon—"

"I know it's possible; this is Texas and all. Beef is what gets eaten around here. Am I right?"

"The boys," he snapped at me, brows furrowed, staring holes through me. "We've been watching that son of a bitch Hughes for three months, and when he finally sells to three underage boys, we think we've got him, and then you step in and screw it all up!"

I squinted at him. "Why don't you have him for giving the boys the pot to begin with?"

"Because no one saw him," he growled at me, stepping closer so I got a rush of leather and faint traces of citrus and musk. Whatever soap he was using had some hints of bergamot, which I loved, so without thinking, I inhaled a lungful of him. "I—are you listening to me?"

No, I was smelling him. "Absolutely."

More glaring. "We were going to grab the pot off the boys and then go to Hughes, match his stash with what we got from them, and seize everything."

"Why don't you just forget about the boys and bust Hughes with a lot of pot and get rid of him that way?"

"Don't you think we would if we knew where his damn stash was?"

"Oh shit," I said suddenly, because when I'd been talking to the boys, I hadn't made the connection, but standing there with Brody, lost in memories of a younger version of him, I'd been reminded of others who I hadn't given a thought to over the years. "Is the Hughes the boys were talking about Derek Hughes, Reverend Hughes's son?"

Seriously, if his glare got any darker, I might be incinerated right there. "Yes. And?"

"In high school he used to deal pills out of his dad's church."

"We checked that," he said flatly, "and the old carriage house out back."

"Yeah, but did you check the room behind the janitor's closet downstairs? That's where his father used to keep his stash."

"His stash of what? The hell are you talking about?" he barked at me, both combative and defensive at the same time.

"I'm talking about all the money he skimmed from the

Sunday offering. There were all those mason jars full of cash."

"What?"

I had to be careful so his head didn't explode. "You didn't know that?"

"When the hell was this?" He'd moved from angry to annoyed, which was better. Still not great, but moving in a deceleration of hostility was preferable.

I had to think. "I wanna say in, like, June of 2007. The church in Houston sent Reverend Larson out here to take over for Hughes after people started complaining because all the pews had to be pulled out and everybody was sitting on those folding card chairs."

"Are you kidding?" He was flabbergasted, and I couldn't blame him.

"No."

"That was their first indication that something was wrong?"

"It's a small town, man, you expect them to worry about it right off?"

"Holy shit."

"Holy," I said, chuckling. "Nice."

He was back to scowling, but it was definitely less like he wanted to punch me and more that there was something seriously wrong with me.

"You're the one making puns," I pointed out.

He shook his head. "So, let me get this straight. Reverend Hughes was skimming from the Sunday offering that was supposed to be going for the upkeep of the church?"

"What do you think that's supposed to be for?"

"No, I know. I just…that's so…." He was at a loss for words, shaking his head.

"Bad," I suggested, grinning at him. "It's real, real bad."

"It's a 'lightning bolt through your house' bad!" He was incredulous.

I chuckled, calming, finding my footing with him. "It is, but if I were you, I'd go back to the church and check behind the janitor's closet, because I'll bet you he's using his father's old hidey-hole for pot and pills and whatever else."

"And you know this because you never missed service?" he asked sarcastically.

"No," I said flatly, correcting him, because now he was pushing old, worn-out buttons. "I know this because everyone came in and complained about it to my aunt," I finished, stepping around him to get back to Jo.

He grabbed my arm, tight, holding on, making sure I couldn't take another step away from him. "What did I say?"

I looked at his hand on me until he let me go, and then my gaze met his. "I don't know if you remember, but the good reverend wasn't about to welcome the only gay kid in town into his fold, and I sure as hell wasn't listening to any hellfire and damnation shit."

His gaze held mine like he was looking for something.

"So no, I didn't go to any church services."

He nodded.

"You have a good day now, Constable."

I left him then, and I didn't look back.

"What was going on with you and Brody?" Jo asked when we were back in the SUV and headed to the house.

"Ancient history."

"What kind?" she asked, studying me. "Did he bully you in high school?"

"No."

"Then?"

"Just drop it. He's an ass."

"Oh? I thought he was very sweet."

"He was being stupid, pretending like he didn't remember what it was like for me after Everett outed me to everyone."

"I know it was hard for you."

"It was a long time ago, but I don't need any reminders."

"Yes, but—" She grimaced. "—maybe the way to fix it is to forgive him."

"What?"

"Well, I suspect that it was more Everett's crap than his, right?"

"Not stopping something is just as bad as doing it yourself."

We drove in silence, and once we were home, before I could get out, she slipped her hand over my forearm.

I turned to look at her and was surprised to find her eyes glistening with unshed tears. "Oh, Jo, for the love of God, don't get all sensitive on me."

She took a shuddering breath. "I remember how bad it got that first year, when you were a freshman and the school wouldn't help, and the law refused to interfere because they thought you were all just kids, just juveniles, and they kept asking me what I thought they were supposed to do."

Boys will be boys, they'd told her over and over.

"Things are so different now."

"Some things," I agreed. "Not all."

"I was so glad when you had that growth spurt the summer before sophomore year."

I snorted out a laugh. "You and me both."

"No one—they didn't—they—you weren't hurt once you were bigger, were you? I mean physically. No one beat you or—"

"Not once I was big enough to defend myself," I soothed her. "Absolutely not."

"But before that, when you were still a freshman, did Brody hurt you?"

"No. Never Brody."

She nodded. "Good. Because I'm gonna die soon. I could start running people over with my car now and never serve a day of time."

"Uh-huh. Been thinking a lot about this, have you?"

"Maybe a bit."

"How 'bout we get you in out of the sun?"

"Dammit, that's what I forgot to get. I need a parasol like all those old Southern ladies."

"Lemme check the attic," I told her. "And you should eat something."

"Fine. After lunch you have to start in the garden," she teased me. "Did you get those hip-waders you wanted?"

"So funny," I said, pretending to cackle. "People always say, 'That Joanna Geary is a fuckin' laugh riot.'"

She laughed until she cried.

"You're such a liar," she accused me as I was cleaning up the dishes after we ate in the beautiful sunlit kitchen. I couldn't get over what a fantastic job Everett had done with the house. He had a real gift.

"What did I lie about?" I asked her.

"You're a great cook, and those Chinese scallion pancakes were wonderful."

"Well, they're not authentic, clearly, but my friend's mom taught him and me what she calls the 'cheater way,' where you don't have to knead the dough like sixty-five thousand times."

She was beaming.

"I'm glad you liked them."

"I shouldn't be surprised you can cook. You can do all those things I can't."

"The only thing I can do that you can't is teach English."

"And score a soccer goal."

I grinned at her.

"My goodness but you turned out gorgeous." She sighed, chin on her palm as she stared at me. "I bet people tell you how handsome you are all the time."

"You're a bit biased."

She shrugged.

"Christ," I groaned, looking out the window at the backyard. "I seriously need, like, a hazmat suit or something. There could be a wolf in there."

"I'll give you snakes, even a coyote, but probably not a wolf."

I grunted.

"Let's go see," she said, smiling too big, too fake, before clapping her hands, getting up, and rushing toward the back door.

"Wait!" I ordered, but of course, she didn't listen.

Outside, I put on my sunglasses and headed toward the weeds.

"I am rethinking this," she called out to me.

I turned and found her standing there with a pair of knee-high galoshes in her hand.

"I think these used to belong to Chief Constable Coltrane," she offered cheerfully. "He probably left them over here one night when he was shacking up with Peg."

"Oh for crissakes," I whined, gagging a little, thinking about my aunt telling me how she and the good constable knocked boots all the damn time.

"Just…don't be such a prude and come take the boots."

"I bet you a rattlesnake's teeth could go right through those."

"Snakes have fangs, not teeth," she corrected me.

"Is that better?"

"Maybe not?" she teased.

"You're an ass."

She jiggled the boots for me.

After walking over, I grabbed them, flopped down on the bottom step and was sliding my foot into one of the boots when a car pulled into the driveway behind the rental. I thought it might be Everett, come to give Jo crap for leaving the hospital, or even our folks—which I wasn't ready for but was expecting—but I noted the heavy grill on the front, and grunted.

"Be nice," Jo cautioned me as Brody Scott came around the side of the house, walking along the fence line so I could see him.

"Twice in one day," Jo said sweetly, smiling in the sudden breeze. It was nice now, in the late afternoon, not nearly as hot as high noon, and it was cooler in the shade. "To what do we owe the pleasure, Chief Constable?"

"Him," he said, pointing at me, and I watched as he closed in, and tried to breathe.

It was difficult.

The man really was stunning.

With his massive shoulders, wide chest, narrow waist, and long legs, he was what came to mind when someone said law enforcement. He looked the part. But none of those delectable attributes made my mouth go dry. It was the scowl. His dark, thick brows furrowed, his deep, rich cherry-brown eyes leveled on me, and his square, chiseled jaw clenched tight. The disapproval rolling off him was made even more apparent by the crossed-arm posture, making his biceps bulge and me catch my breath when he stopped in front of me. Any man who looked like that was a churning caldron of emotions, and that kind of passion was something I wanted to see.

"What did I do?" I grumbled instead of asking if he'd like to go to bed with me. He was straight, after all, so it was probably for the best.

"You were right," he informed me.

"About?"

His face fell like he was shocked. "About Hughes, of course!"

"Oh, yeah," I said, getting up, testing the fit of the galoshes by bouncing up and down in them. "Okay."

"You were right about the stash. He was so smug about it. He even let us look around the church, because he figured we had no idea where it was."

I shrugged. "He was never very bright."

"No," he agreed, looking me up and down. It shouldn't have been hot. I was certain he hadn't meant it to be. Most likely he was concerned with my sanity, as I did have galoshes on my feet in the summer, but I felt the weight of his stare regardless.

I was back to not being able to breathe.

It was terrible, because I loved men and I had slept with my share of beautiful ones over the years, but him standing there in his boring uniform with the stupid hat...I was just a goner. It was like whatever you grew up wanting really never left you. That flavor was always the best.

"I really appreciate you giving me the tip," he said softly, then cleared his throat. "And I...I—" He squinted at me. "What the hell are you doing?"

"I'm going in," I announced dramatically.

Apparently my answer didn't clear up anything. "I'm sorry, where are you going?"

I pointed over my shoulder.

His eyebrows shot up. "Into the grass?"

Jo scoffed. Loudly.

"They're weeds, actually," I clarified for him, doing an about-face, ready to go into battle. "I think I should take a rake."

"I think you should take a gun," he said, moving up beside me. "Seriously, there could be snakes in there."

I looked over my shoulder at Jo. "You see? Even the Chief Constable thinks this could be dangerous."

"Fine," she said, exhaling as though she were bored out of her mind. "Take a shovel to ward off the beasts."

"Do we even have one?" I asked her.

"In the tool shed," she assured me. "Probably."

I glanced over at something that resembled the Shrieking Shack from the Harry Potter movies and then turned to Brody. "I don't suppose you'd like to put a few bullets in that bad boy for me, would ya?"

He was relaxing. I could tell from the flashing grin he gave me that instantaneously short-circuited my brain. I'd forgotten he had dimples and how long his lashes were and that his hair was so black that there were midnight-blue highlights in it. I took a shuddering breath. I couldn't recall having such a physical reaction to another man, ever, and it was scary and exciting, and the timing was the absolute worst, and really, of all the people who could have made me crazy, the straight, alpha-male small-town cop had to be the worst choice imaginable.

Looking down, not wanting to stare, I took a breath to gird myself for battle, but then noticed the prominent veins in his hands and forearms, and my brain went right to thinking about how strong he looked but how gentle he was being with Jo, and then everything inside was mush. I swallowed down the ache in my chest and hoped he didn't notice the shiver.

He cleared his throat. "I'd be freaked out too. Maybe you wait to go in there."

The shudder was taken for fear, which was fine with me. Better than the truth.

"Look at me."

I needed to get my breathing under control before I—

"Now," he demanded with a thread of warning that was ridiculously hot.

Fuck.

Tilting my head up, I met the man's gaze with a fake smile, noted the laugh lines in the corner of his eyes, and calmed just a little.

"I don't think just going in there is a great idea," he cautioned, reaching out to take hold of my elbow. "Maybe you should call someone, huh?"

"You know I'm dying, right?" Jo called over to him. "Did you know that? And since I'm dying and we're on a timeline here, you need to let my grandson make with the weed clearing."

He turned to her, stricken, mouth open, utterly floored.

"What?" she asked him.

"You told him you were dying," I clarified for her.

"Oh, yeah," she said, bored. "Maybe I should have left that part out."

"It's mean," I told her as he charged up to her on the deck and crouched at her feet, his hands taking gentle hold of hers.

"What're you—Jo?"

Her smile was kind as she cupped his chin in her delicate, long-fingered hand. "I have cancer that spread and that I refuse to do anything more about so...there it is."

"I don't—"

"So that's why he's gotta go in there," she explained, giving me the dismissive brush-off with her hand at the same time. "This is my dying wish."

"I'm not going in there," I informed her. "I need to go get a scythe to cut all the tall weeds, and I'll need a weed flamer to torch the rest."

"I thought you were kidding about the flamethrower," she called over to me excitedly.

"I wasn't."

"You don't happen to have one of those, do you, Chief?" she asked Brody.

He turned to look at me. "You're both nuts."

I nodded as she cackled.

"It's good that you came home, Kaenon," he said softly, those remarkable eyes of his back on me. "We all missed you."

And even though I didn't believe it, I couldn't bring myself to contradict him, because he'd included himself. He said he'd missed me, and *that* I absolutely wanted to believe.

"You were a hero today."

"No," I assured him. "I was just passing on some old information."

"That only you had," he reminded me, his voice a rumbling purr that, combined with the half smile I was getting, was making it hard to concentrate on anything but him. "And so you know, if Hughes gives us his supplier to get a deal, and we catch a bigger fish outside Braxton, I'm going to make sure you get your part of the credit."

"You can have my credit," I ground out, barely, feeling like a dorky fourteen-year-old boy all over again as I stared at him. The strength and power I had been enamored of when he was a boy was still easy to spot in the man he'd become. I could distinctly recall walking into walls, lockers, missing steps, and just tripping over my own feet because I'd been staring at Brody Scott instead of watching where I was going. He had been, and still was, the most beautiful thing I'd ever seen.

"Kaenon," he said, standing up and facing me. "I would like to talk to—" A call from the radio on his shoulder cut him off. "Excuse me," he said, walking just far enough away so he was out of earshot.

"When he gets back, invite him to dinner," Jo whispered sharply. "You can show him what a good cook you are."

I turned to her slowly.

"What?" she asked me.

"What is this, 1952?"

"I'm sorry?" She sounded affronted.

"Show him what a good cook I am?"

She made a dismissive noise, like I was ridiculous. "Cooking is still a thing men like."

"I'm a man too, you know."

"Yes, but we're not talking about you. We're talking about the gorgeous lawman."

"You do think this is 1952."

"Oh, shut up."

"And by the way, he's straight."

She made a face. "Perhaps bi, but not straight."

I loved that my eighty-seven-year-old grandmother was arguing with me about sexuality.

"Oh, he's coming back. Act natural."

I groaned under my breath. "Brody," I murmured when he got close, "could you please tell Jo that—"

"I have to go, y'all. I'm sorry," he rushed out. "Duty calls."

"Of course," Jo said, her simpering smile nearly making me gag. "You be safe, now."

He nodded, glancing at me. "How, uhm, long are you fixin' to be here, Kaenon?"

"He's staying all summer," Jo announced cheerfully. "Isn't that wonderful?"

His smile took my breath away. "It certainly is," he agreed, his voice low and husky, sounding like sex. "I'll be back, then, to make sure you don't get lost in the weeds."

"Great," I said lamely, and only when he was walking away—and Jesus, was that a nice view—did I turn and look at Jo.

"Great," she repeated, gritting her teeth, shaking her head. "Dear God, no wonder you're not married. You're terrible at this."

"He's straight," I stressed to her.

"No, I don't think so, not with that smile he gave you."

"And what the hell was with that 'not married' crack?"

"Well, you're not."

"Of course not! Why the hell would I want to be married?"

"Because even if you deny it, you're a romantic at heart, just like me."

"Well, can we go inside now, Miss Romance?"

"What about the garden?"

"I have a plan."

Her eyes narrowed. "Do you really, or are you hoping I forget about it by tomorrow, or have a stroke or something?"

"God, you say the most horrible things."

"Your grandfather said it was a gift."

"I don't think so. I don't think he ever said that."

"You don't know everything. He used to say a lot of things in bed."

I pretended to vomit, but she only cackled.

"Did I ever tell you about the time we had sex at my cousin Amy's wedding?" she asked me, excitedly, and didn't even wait for me to tell her that I'd rather have a root canal than hear the story. "Well, there we were in the last pew, me sitting in your grandfather's lap with my underwear down around my ankles when we realized that there were still more people coming into the church!"

"No...God...no," I whined, sitting down on the step below her, face in my hands.

"And well, you know, once you reach a certain point, stopping is just *not* an option, so your grandfather was doing this sort of jackrabbit move he had, and all I could really do was ride it out."

I whimpered.

"What?"

It was only the first of many stories that I was going to need brain bleach for.

FIVE

I wanted to watch Jo the first day, keep an eye on her, see what her routine was, observe as the day wore on, how easily she tired, if her memory lapsed, or if she got too weak to be allowed to do things alone, like feed herself or shower or do simple tasks around the house. What I didn't expect was for her to be taking out the trash, which she was about to do, when I got out of the bathroom.

"What are you doing?" I asked when I found her outside by the road with the heavy wheeled garbage can.

"What does it look like I'm doing? I have to roll these out to the curb," she explained. "Friday's trash pick-up."

"Well, I can do that."

She shrugged. "If you want."

"Are you tired?" I asked when I ran back from the road.

"It's seven thirty," she told me. "Are you tired?"

"No, but I'm not eighty-seven."

"We should take a walk," she suggested, her face lighting up. "I always loved doing that with your grandfather, but I'm not comfortable going alone."

"Because you're afraid of falling?"

"No, I'm afraid of stepping in dog poop that I can't see in the dark."

Both that and falling would have made sense. "I would love to walk with you."

It was a beautiful night for a stroll, and once the sun went down right after eight, with the warm breeze, the scent of lilac and sweet peas, and the long grass, I could feel myself settle in even as I tried to visualize my house and my yard at home. The problem was that, before I knew I didn't belong in Braxton, it had been somewhere I'd loved. I knew the ebb and flow of the town, and that feel for it, for the movement of things, was something etched down deep.

"It's nice, isn't it?" Jo asked as we walked.

"It's fine," I said stiffly.

She laughed at me, and when I turned to glare at her, she hugged my arm tight. "You're a terrible liar, and I love that about you."

"You make no sense," I told her as she leaned against me.

Once we got home, she had ice cream, and then she had to catch up on some episodes of *Supernatural* that she had on her DVR. I started fading before her.

"You should go to bed," she told me. "You have to be up early in the morning to get started on the gardening."

"Oh, will you give it a rest," I said, stretching out on the couch as she was comfortable in the wingback chair, with her feet up on the matching ottoman. "I will take care of the damn garden," I groused at her.

"Before I die, right?"

I didn't even dignify that with a response.

. . .

THE FOLLOWING morning my eyes opened slowly, and I found my grandmother standing over me.

"Do you not sleep anymore?" I asked her, sarcastically.

"I sleep. I just don't drool like that," she said, the disgust all over her face. "What are you, a Saint Bernard?"

"Could you go away?"

"I'm hungry. Get up and make me an omelet. I want avocado and spinach in it."

Her wish was my command.

It was nice, just talking with her over coffee before I started cooking.

"I have been told, at length and in great detail, that turning the ringer off on my phone yesterday was a poor choice," she informed me. "Everyone was terrified because you sprung me from the hospital, and I suspect that people are going to start popping by to check on me."

"We could hide in the house," I suggested hopefully.

"How does that help the garden?"

"I really don't want to see anybody."

"Well, darling, that's just too bad, isn't it?"

I met her gaze. "You never made me see family when I was in high school."

"You were a child then, and I had to protect you, as did your grandfather and Peg. It was what was supposed to happen after that idiocy that your parents put you through." Her voice as she spoke was like iron. "But you're not a child anymore. You're a grown man, and though seeing people and dealing with their ignorance may be tedious, it shouldn't hurt anymore, because you know they're fallible."

"Or, I could just ditch you while people visit."

She nodded. "That is also an option."

A couple of hours later, as I was flipping through the telephone book, Jo and I both heard a car slow down. We watched out the front window as it pulled up alongside the garden gate and parked on the small bit of dirt between the road and the house. In the older part of Braxton, where the house was, there were no sidewalks.

"Oh, look who it is," Jo said, turning to me. "It's your sister, Maeve, and her husband, William, and the kids."

"I need to go rent a tractor," I informed her.

"Since it's for the garden, I'll allow it. Go on and run away."

I didn't care that she was basically calling me a coward. I was fine with it. "Will you be okay alone?" I asked Jo.

"I won't be alone. I'm about to have company, you dumb bunny."

"I'll be back," I announced, and without another word, I got up and headed toward the back door that led out onto the deck. From there, I took the stairs and went around the side of the house as Maeve and her husband of eleven years —who I'd never met—knocked on the front door. I stopped next to the porch and waited until I heard first my grandmother greet them and then the door close behind them as she invited them all into the house.

Was it childish? Yes. Did I regret it? Not at all. And while I knew, logically, that I would have to see everyone, my whole family, at some point over the summer, my second day in town hardly seemed fair.

Bolting to the 4Runner, I pressed the button on the key fob and heard the chirp as the doors unlocked, and I slid in behind the wheel seconds later. I didn't even lift my head to see if anyone was looking out the window at me.

RED BRICK HARDWARE and Garden had been in business for as long as I could remember. The old owner, Cecil Winter, and his wife, Paula, used to trade food and services back and forth with Peg. One of her greatest qualities, in my opinion, was that unlike Jo, who never missed an opportunity for me to work on being a better person, Peg would give me a break and let me be totally antisocial every now and then. So when my brother, Everett, outed me to the school when he was a senior and I was a freshman, and all but the bravest souls—like Zuzu and Colby—turned on me, one of the many people who went so far as to try to do me bodily harm was Cecil and Paula's son, Davis. From my fourteenth birthday until I graduated from high school, I had never willingly stepped foot in Red Brick Hardware. I had only showed my face inside the establishment when I was with my grandmother, because Peg, bless her, said I could wait in the car when I'd come with her.

Now, at thirty-two, I didn't think twice about walking in. Glancing around, it took me a moment to get my bearings because the layout of the store was completely changed from what I remembered. Of course, there was no telling how long it had been this way. But once I found the rental counter, I asked the young woman there if they had different sized tractors that I could rent.

"Of course," she said agreeably, not shy about looking me up and down before her gaze met my eyes. "Tell me what you need. I'm sure I can make it happen."

I grinned wide, and her smile in response was mischievous and inviting. "Do you have the torches for burning weeds too? The long ones?"

"We do," she assured me, leaning over on the counter.

"I also need a bush hog as well as a dumpster to—"

"Kaenon?"

Turning, I found Davis Winter. I wasn't that surprised, to be honest. When we'd been friends, back in the eighth grade, he'd told me that his whole plan in life was to take over his father's store and stay in Braxton. Whenever I talked about leaving, he never understood why I would want to. What was the point of going when you knew you would be returning?

"Davis," I said, wary, waiting. "I need to rent some equipment to clear Jo's garden, but if you're not comfortable with—"

"I am," he said, taking a quick step forward before stopping himself and then thrusting his hand out toward me, "comfortable. I mean, I don't—shit. I have no issue with you, Kaenon."

Squinting, unsure, I took the offered hand anyway, and was even more confused when he exhaled sharply.

"Let me get you all set up and—tell me how long you're gonna be in town?"

It was so odd. He was acting like we were friends. "I'll be here all summer."

His face lit up as he smiled. "Oh, that's great news. I'll have to have you over to meet my kids. I know you know Angie Reed."

I used to. She'd been a cheerleader along with Shelly, who I'd caught up with the day before. "You and Angie, huh?"

He nodded, and how he was looking at me, uncertain and hopeful at the same time, was a surprise. "Yessir."

"That's quite the love affair you two have going. That's from what, sixth grade?"

"Yep. Sure is."

"That's great, Davis."

His gaze was all over me. "Man, she's gonna flip when she gets a load of you."

I shrugged. "I look the same."

"No, sir, you certainly do not."

I crossed my arms and stared at him. "Not to be rude, and I need the equipment, and arranging for it to be delivered from Austin will be a pain in the ass, but, Davis, are you sure you know who I am? Do you maybe have me confused with somebody else?" I asked to give him the out. I was having a surreal moment, but maybe he was too.

Taking gentle hold of my bicep, he led me a few feet away from the counter, near a water fountain and a door marked Manager. When he stopped and rounded on me, instantly his hands were shoved down deep in the pockets of his khakis.

"I'm sorry for how I treated you, Kae. I hoped you'd come back for the ten-year reunion, and when you didn't and—I wanted to say something to you clear back in tenth grade, but you weren't havin' it after what I'd done."

In retrospect, him blindsiding me in the back with a fastball when we were both practicing after school—me soccer, him baseball—had not been all that big a deal to me. My coach, on the other hand, had him suspended for three days. I was his star forward, even as a freshman; the man wasn't about to let me get hurt.

But when I came back for my sophomore year, anyone who had wronged me in ninth grade was basically dead to me, and I could own that. Freshman year had been a nightmare of bullying—like notes on my locker, being tripped in the cafeteria, called every filthy name in the arsenal of small-town rednecks that escalated to physical confrontations, as in being hit hard and routinely during soccer practice.

The few times I was caught walking home alone after school, when my grandfather couldn't pick me up, had been bad. Once, I was beaten so badly that I pissed blood and couldn't open my right eye. Jo had been beside herself because there were days when she couldn't leave early and neither could my grandfather. They both worked full-time, and Peg traveled often. When my soccer coach stepped in to help me, she had broken down crying. Because after that beating, my soccer coach made sure that if I wasn't being picked up, he was driving me. And when I got my license and an ancient Ford pickup the following year, he designated a space beside his car in the teacher lot so it wouldn't be vandalized.

"They have small minds, and they'll have even smaller lives, Kae," Coach Ochoa would tell me all the time. "Keep your eye on your scholarship, keep playing hard, and I'll make sure you get the hell out of here."

He never said, "Win me a championship," but I did anyway. All-state soccer champs three years running, and even though no one talked to me off the field, on it I was in charge. Captain of the team, no questions asked.

By the time I was a senior, insulated with Zuzu and Colby, going to school, taking all AP classes, playing soccer with my full-ride scholarship already signed, and working nights and weekends at Peg's store, I didn't notice anything. I stepped around people in the hallways, gave no one the time of day, and with my earbuds in and iPod cranked up way too high, I neither saw nor heard anyone.

I remembered being out with my grandfather at times and he'd pat my shoulder, and when I looked up, he'd tip his head at a few guys from my soccer team, or others from the football team, easy to spot in their letterman jackets, or cheerleaders, or random people I didn't know. I would tip my head, force a smile, and then turn my attention back to Harvey Geary. Always, on the way to the car, he'd shake his head.

"What's wrong, old man?" I teased him, putting the groceries, or whatever we were carrying, in the back first before opening his door.

He would wait until I slid in behind the wheel. "For the love of God, Kaenon, you have to talk to people and forge new roads."

I always turned to him, scowling. "I'm outta here. You get that, right?"

"Lots of folks—mostly the kids—they're sorry for what they did when Everett first ran his mouth three years ago."

I smiled at him then, and he would throw up his hands in surrender. There was no way in hell I was going to give anyone in the Podunk town the opportunity to hurt me ever again, be that physically, emotionally, or mentally. I had been more than done.

"Kae?"

My eyes met Davis's, back from my trip to the past. "I appreciate the help," I said, offering him my hand. "You should see Jo's garden. I'm gonna need a bazooka to shoot whatever comes outta there."

His smile as he grasped my hand was another surprise. He was genuinely happy to see me. "I'll get a compact tractor with a loader, and a bush hog driven over to the house for you tomorrow morning, unless you're fixin' to start today."

I chuckled as I eased my hand from his grip. "No, Saturday's good, thank you. The last thing I need is to get started and then have it get too dark for me to see."

"You forgot where you are. Ain't no dark nights in Braxton unless you're talkin' about the winter. This here's summer now. It's all moonlight and stars all around. You can always see just fine."

And I had forgotten that; he was right.

"We got us a service now where we haul weeds and dirt away, and I can deliver you fertilizer and mulch if you like."

"That'd be great."

"Well, then, let's get you all set up so you'll be ready to get started," he said, and it didn't go without my notice that when he steered me back to the counter, his hand was in the middle of my back.

Once I was done renting equipment and buying herb seeds, I drove over to The Green Thumb because I needed plants. Herbs and wildflowers I could see growing in the garden, but not all the plants that Jo was looking forward to seeing would grow to maturity in her desired timeline. I needed to help things along.

Inside the nursery, I grabbed a split-level cart and started picking the plants I needed.

"He said he can't take me," a young woman close to me told an older woman who might have been her mother, but I wasn't sure. What I was certain about was that because the older woman was watering some snapdragons, she worked at the nursery. "I mean, for God's sake, Mom, he's my advisor, but he can't take me?" she announced, her voice shrill, broken. "I got a five on the Pre-AP English exam this year. A five! He's got nobody better, but he can't take me? What the hell is that?"

"Sweetie, I'm sorry you couldn't get into the summer program you wanted, and I'm even sorrier that Mr. Hastings won't take you in his summer school class, but I've already talked to him many times, as well as left a dozen messages for the principal, and I'm not getting anywhere. Neither one of them is ever there when I've tried to see them in person."

"It's not fair!" she wailed.

"I know, I know, but I'm sure we can find you something online, and then in the fall when you start AP English, I'm sure Mr. Hastings will be more inclined to help. He just doesn't know you because you're a transfer student."

"Mom, I got a five!"

"Yes, I know, you keep saying that."

"Because it's a big deal!"

It was; she was right.

"They're all boys, Mom. Did I mention that he only has boys in his summer class?"

"You did. Yes. But, sweetheart, I promise you we'll find you a tutor; this is only your junior year. You have the entire upcoming semester to get the essays done for early admission."

She shivered hard.

It was the teacher in me. I couldn't help it. "Excuse me."

Mother and daughter both turned to look at me.

"May I ask what school the essays are for?"

"Brown," the girl said, blinking at me a moment before her eyes widened and her mouth dropped open. "Ohmygod, you're Kaenon Geary, aren't you?"

I grinned at her, because how did she know? "I am."

She rushed forward, hands closing on my left forearm. "I read your article, 'Deconstructing Cordelia,' in *The Paris Review* three months ago, and it was freakin' amazing."

She was young, a junior in high school, so all of sixteen, but she was reading *The Paris Review*, for fun. I had not been nearly so driven academically when I was her age. Though, in my defense, I had killed myself to be one of the best soccer players in the state. I'd needed a full athletic scholarship to get the hell out of Braxton. It didn't sound like this girl and I were ever in the same boat.

"You teach a summer class at Pollard College," she said,

and I was again surprised that this girl in my old hometown knew the name of the school in Connecticut where I taught Storytelling and Language in Modern Media.

"The class is taught by a whole group of people," I corrected her. "We have professors from Yale and Berkeley, from Stanford and Dartmouth and—"

"Brown," she supplied, squeezing my forearm tight, looking at me like I was the second coming. "You're good friends with Dr. Lalasa Singh."

I called my friend Lasa, because that was what her family called her, but she wasn't wrong. "I am."

"She's who I want to study with at Brown."

"Well, you can't go wrong there," I assured her. "May I ask why you're not attending the seminar, because it sounds like you wanted to?"

Heavy sigh as she finally let go of my arm. "They cancelled it."

"No," I contradicted her gently. "It was moved to Berkeley in the second week of June."

She gasped. "It was?"

I nodded and was surprised when her mother grabbed my left elbow, standing there like she'd been hit by lightning. "Ma'am?"

"We have the money to get her in. We just weren't informed that the class was still on."

"Did you enroll?" I asked the girl.

"I did, yeah."

"And you didn't get the notice that the dates were changed?"

She shook her head. "Where would that have gone?"

"To your school, because your advisor has to monitor your progress," I informed her.

"You see?" she said sadly, throwing up her hands. "This

is what happened. We moved here from Dallas, and my old teacher transferred everything to Mr. Hastings, and he doesn't care about me because I'm a girl!"

Reaching out, I took hold of her shoulder. "What's your name?"

Her breath caught and her eyes filled, but she managed to answer me in a tiny, strangled voice. "Maria De Leon."

"Here," I said, passing her the rosemary plant I wanted as I pulled my phone from the back pocket of my jeans. "Put that on the cart."

She did it quickly as I scrolled through my contacts and hit Lasa's number.

"It's fine," Lasa, one of my oldest friends, said, picking up after the fourth ring. "No groveling necessary. We will take you back into the fold. You can come teach with the rest of us. It's not a problem. I'll even let you stay at my friend's place with me."

I snorted. "That was lovely. Now can I talk?"

"Oh, come on," she whined. "I won't see you until December, in New York, if you don't come and teach the class with me."

"You know why I can't," I said softly.

"I know. I do. And how is she, by the way?"

Both my grandparents had met and fallen in love with Lasa when they came to visit me in New York for the holidays. I couldn't come to them, Braxton was out of the question, and since they refused to have me be alone, even with Lasa's large extended family there in Manhattan, they had flown out every year for two weeks. Jo and Lasa's mother, Kala, had become fast friends.

"She's okay. So far, so good."

"I'm glad. It's good you're there."

I grunted.

"Have you, uhm, seen anyone yet?"

She meant my parents or siblings. "I got close," I said, speaking of almost seeing my sister, Maeve, and her family. "But not yet. For crissakes, I just got here."

"Don't say crissakes, all right? It took me years to get all that Texas out of your voice. If you start saying *reckon* again or dropping the Gs off all your words, I will come and get both you and Jo."

"Yes, ma'am."

"No, no, that too," she said, and I heard the shudder of dread in her voice. "And fixin'. I hate that one the most."

I chuckled because she missed me, that much was clear, and the feeling was mutual.

"So what do you want, Geary?" She sighed.

"Why are you upset? I covered you with the class. I got Nate Qells from the University of Chicago, and you love him."

"I do love him, and he's cuter than you, but sadly, I love you more."

We had done our undergraduate work together at Syracuse and then gotten our master's degrees from Columbia before I stopped and she moved to England, as she'd been accepted to Oxford to get her doctorate. Along with Zuzu and Colby, she was one of my dearest friends on the planet, and just like them, both she and her husband, Bryan, had hated Aidan at first sight. Yet another sign I should have seen.

"Well, I love you back, and I need a favor."

"You ditch me and you want a favor?"

"You're going to like this," I promised.

"Fine. Hit me."

"I have a girl here, Maria De Leon, and she says that she was signed up for the class, but there might have been some kind of miscommunication because she changed schools right at the end of the term."

"De Leon?"

"Yeah."

"Hold on. Let me look."

I walked a few feet away from Maria and her mother, just in case the news was not good. Even over the phone, I could hear the keys tapping on her laptop, which meant she was hitting them harder than usual. "What's wrong?"

"Man, you're good at this."

"I know the signs after living with you for three, almost four, years, right?" After my accident in my junior year, I moved off campus and got an apartment with Lasa. By the time she left for Oxford, I knew her like the back of my hand. "Tell me why you're beating up your computer? We both know it's not to blame."

She grunted.

"Tell me," I prodded.

"So, guess who wants to talk about having a baby? Again?" she said, taking a breath, the tension clear in her voice.

"And he's willing to stay home?"

"He says he is."

I shrugged even though she couldn't see me. "It's up to you. But I also think that the surrogate idea should be back on the table."

"Bryan says if I don't carry the baby and then he's the one home with the child that I won't have any ties to motherhood at all."

"Oh, that's crap."

"My mother agrees with him."

"Your mother, bless her heart, thinks that your sister

should take her husband back because it was only three women, not five, that he fucked in Vegas."

"Oh God," she groaned.

"Just talk to Bryan."

"I will. And don't say *bless her heart* ever again."

"You're ridiculous."

"It's Texas. I hate you being there."

"Join the club."

"Oh, oh," she said, her voice lifting. "Yes. I—who is Todd Hastings?"

"I think that's Maria's new AP English teacher here in Braxton."

"Well, I have an email from him saying that he won't mentor her for the summer, or monitor her progress, as he's only teaching the first four weeks, so he asked that I drop her from the class."

"You're kidding?"

"Nope."

"What an asshole."

"Well, that's what I thought when I first saw this, but I also thought he had to have communicated this to Maria and that she was all right with it."

"Well, she's not."

"Yes, but she still needs someone to mentor her who I can check in with after she leaves. They have to submit four articles to *Thread* now, not just two. We changed it last year because we didn't think it was rigorous enough, remember?"

Thread was an open-access online academic journal that accepted junior and senior work of students preparing to go to college. It was prestigious and considered a springboard to scholastic scholarships in the field of humanities.

Crap. "Will you let me do it?"

"What?"

"You heard me."

"How will you do that when you leave at the end of the summer?"

"I'll Skype with her."

"Along with your usual teaching load? You insane, man?"

"Just—you know you want to let me. This girl got the shaft big-time."

"Well, of course I'll let you," she assured me. "But I need her money for the class first thing Monday morning, you understand?"

"I do."

"And God help you if you're not in New York for New Year's. I want to dress up and go dancing, you understand?"

"Kiss Bryan for me," I told her.

"Wait."

"What?"

"I'm going to email the principal there about this Hastings guy, because as we both know, he doesn't need to be in summer school to mentor her, and I suspect he knows that too."

"She thinks it's because she's a girl. She said he has an AP class just for the boys that's going on now, for the first summer school session."

"All righty, then," she huffed out. "I'll be doing this immediately."

"Remember not to use any curse words this time."

"That was just the one time!" she said defensively.

"Will you send Maria out all the new info?"

"As we speak."

"Bye."

"Love you."

"I know," I teased her, hanging up.

Walking back over to Maria, I smiled at her.

She shrieked and leaped at me, throwing her arms tight around my neck and squeezing the life out of me.

"By the way," her mother said, openly weeping beside me, rubbing my arm, "my name is Isadora De Leon, and my husband, Ramon, and I, we've owned The Green Thumb since 2010, so really, whatever plants you need, you let us know."

I smiled at her even though her daughter was throttling me. "And I appreciate that, but that could be construed as academic bribery. I will, however, accept any coupons and free delivery."

"Yes," she said, nodding fast. "Absolutely, a hundred percent yes."

"It's a lot of money for her to go for two weeks," I said to her mother.

"Money we have. Teachers on her side have been harder to come by."

I nodded.

"Some of them don't think a Hispanic girl with a passion for English literature should be taken seriously."

I took hold of her hand. "She's got me now."

And Mrs. De Leon tackled me then as well.

SIX

Back at Jo's, I noticed that there were now two more cars in the driveway in addition to the one beside the fence.

Parking the 4Runner across the street, not wanting to block anyone in, I jogged to the front of the house. I came up the stairs and opened the screen door, and the front door was thrown wide at the same time.

"No, I don't think he—Kaenon."

It had taken Everett Geary, my older brother, my parents' firstborn, a moment to notice me, because he was in the middle of a conversation with someone. But now he stood there, staring, not moving, caught halfway in and out of the house.

"Hey," was all I could think of to say as I stepped sideways, holding open the screen door so he could walk by me and leave.

"Hey," he echoed, holding on to the door now but making no move to do anything.

I cleared my throat. "Are you coming in or going out?"

His eyes were all over me, from head to toe. "Where were you?"

In every possible scenario I had imagined over the years, the first encounter I would have with my brother, after eighteen years, would not have started like this. Civil, anticlimactic, and utterly ordinary had never entered my mind.

"Oh, well," I began as though I were addressing anyone on the planet but him. "Originally I was going to do something really stupid and attack the garden by hand, but my brain kicked in, so I have a tractor coming tomorrow, and—"

"You'll need a bush hog," he blurted out, cutting me off, and I saw him wince like perhaps he hadn't meant to do that.

"Yeah," I agreed with a nod, not firing back that, of course, I was aware. It surprised me that I curtailed my own attack mode. "Davis Winter, he has that covered. He's bringing it by in the morning first thing."

I hadn't seen my father, Robert Geary, in years, but in my mind, Everett looked just like him. Or more likely now, at thirty-five—his birthday wasn't until late June—he most resembled what I could recall about our father. For whatever reason, both Everett and Maeve had pulled more of the Geary side and had the same dark brown hair and blue eyes that my grandfather, Harvey Geary, had. But I had pulled from my mother's side, from the Cabot line, and so there was dirty-blond hair and golden tan coloring and hazel eyes for me. I had always looked just like my mother, like Tessa Cabot, who married my father the second he returned to Braxton after college.

"So, we thought—" He cleared his throat, trying to smile at me. "—Maeve and I, I mean, that we would come over and check on Jo."

"Okay."

"Everyone's worried about her," he said, waiting, like I should have a comment.

"Which is nice," I offered, unsure what else to say.

We stood there, silently, neither of us moving, almost like we were standing on each end of a teeter-totter and if either of us shifted even an inch, the other would go flying.

"Maeve and Will and her kids, they drove out from Austin, but Rochelle and I, we live back here now. I don't know if Jo told you."

I nodded. "She did."

"Oh, good, well, so like I said, we just—we thought we'd come by and visit and then have an early dinner, if that would be okay."

I could feel the anger roll up my spine, the tension lifting my shoulders and making my mouth dry. It was easy to understand why, because just looking at Everett reminded me of being fourteen again and back at the dinner table on that Sunday night a week before I started ninth grade.

I had come out to my family. It was time. I couldn't keep it a secret and didn't want to. If my mother said to me even one more time, "Oh, Kae, that girl's smiling at you. Why don't you go say hello," I was going to go stark raving mad.

I was still being dragged to church then, Braxton Baptist, and every Sunday after service, there was the luncheon, and my mother had me sit with one girl after another and another. Everett had confided to me in a whisper, with his arm wrapped around my neck, clutching me tight, that a lot of church girls were wild, so I should just go along with it. He'd had lots of so-called good girls in the back seat of his Trans Am.

The whole thing made me sick to my stomach. And it wasn't the girls. I liked girls. Two of my best friends, whom I'd met over the summer, were girls. It was just the burden of expectation of something I could never want. The lying was just not me.

That night, Sunday night, after dinner, I asked everyone to wait a second before we cleared. I had something to say.

All eyes were on me, and I could remember my mother in her pale blue sweater set with her pearls and her flowered blueberry print headband. My sister was in a peach sundress, and she was looking at me like she was bored out of her mind. My father was squinting, trying to be patient but wanting to go watch football, and Everett had his right index finger out and was making circles in the air for me to get on with it already.

"I'm gay," I told them without fanfare, because that was how Jo had suggested. I had, of course, told her first. I had sat her down on her then tiny back steps, taken her hands in mine, and said that I had to tell her something about myself.

"What's that, angel?" she asked gently.

It had taken another twenty minutes to get the words out. "I like, I mean, I don't want to kiss any—wait, no. I feel like when I look at girls that that's not what I'm supposed— you see the thing is that—"

"You like boys?"

I turned, stood, and threw up in her knockout roses. Once I was done, she took me inside and stayed with me while I washed out my mouth, brushed my teeth with one of the spare toothbrushes she kept on hand for company, and then took me to the kitchen and made me a cup of chamomile tea.

She asked me all the questions, like how long had I known I liked boys, was I certain, did I think I wanted to tell everyone right now or just sort of play it by ear?

"Do you think I should keep it a secret?"

"I think if you do, that's okay, but if you don't, then that's okay too."

"It would be easier to keep it a secret."

"It might," she reasoned, putting her hand on my cheek, "but keepin' things inside has a way of tearin' you all up as well."

I took a breath. "Well, I don't want to tell anyone else, but I want my family to know," I told her, shrugging. "I think that's important."

She smiled and nodded, and because she accepted it, no change, still her, still me, still us, when I told my grandfather, I did it without vomiting.

"I don't reckon I know any homosexuals," Harvey Geary told me, smiling, giving me a pat on the back. "So you'll have to be patient with me if I put my foot in my mouth."

"Yessir," I said, tearing up, smiling back.

Peg knew without me telling her. "It's boys for you, isn't it, darling?"

I nodded, watching her as she poured the beeswax into the glass tubes, making sure the wicks of the candles were straight, and then sprinkled the tops with her homemade herb mixture.

"Me too," she said, grinning. "You see? It's another wonderful thing we have in common. We both like hot men."

I should have been smarter.

My mother was the president of the Ladies Auxiliary, she was the choral director at our church, and she was in charge of the food drive every Christmas. She had standing in the community and in the church. It made sense that she took a breath, screamed, and then backhanded me as hard as she could across the face.

Everett laughed; he thought I was screwing around.

"I'm serious," I barely got out, holding my face. My mother had drawn blood with her ring.

"Fuck you, no brother of mine is a faggot!" he roared, shoving to his feet so fast that his chair fell over before he was around the table, punching me first in the stomach and then in the face harder than I thought he ever would.

He didn't break my nose, but there was enough blood to make me think he had.

My father tore us apart, sent Everett to his room and then shoved me back against the wall and held me there, one hand on my chest, the other pointing at me, jabbing me in the collarbone as he ordered me to take it back.

"How can I take back something I am?" I asked him, sounding nasally as my nose was filled with blood.

My mother brought my father his belt and told him to beat the devil out of me. He told her to call Pastor Edwards instead.

Maeve wouldn't look at me as she walked out of the kitchen, and she hadn't laid eyes on me since.

My mother told me I was unclean, that I would burn in hell with murderers and child molesters and baby killers.

I started to shake.

By the time Pastor Edwards and Reverend Hughes showed up, I was terrified and close to hyperventilating. When they started to set up like they were going to have service right there, I asked my father to please call Jo.

"Your grandmother knows about this?"

"Yes."

He looked at Pastor Edwards, who had brought what looked like a riding crop with him and put it on the table. "I think you should have all your family here," he told my father and then looked at me. "Take your shirt off Kaenon."

"No," I gasped, trembling as I took a step back from him.

"Reverend," he said softly, directing his counterpart to me. "Robert," he said to my father. "I need you both to take hold of the boy."

It was fight or flight, and I ran. Having already earned my spot on the junior varsity soccer team, I feinted left, spun, and then bolted for the back door. I would have made it out of there if another of the elders had not been coming in as I was trying to get out.

"Oh no, Kaenon," he told me as he grabbed me in a full nelson, bent me forward, and walked me back to the kitchen table.

Bending me over, he held me down as my father and Reverend Hughes took hold of my arms, and then once he moved, he yanked up my dress shirt—we'd been at church that morning, after all—and I had a moment to feel the air on my bare skin before I braced for the hit.

"So help me God, if you strike my grandson with that crop, it will be the last thing you ever do on this earth."

I didn't need to see him. I knew my grandfather's voice when I heard it, always strong and powerful. Normally, though, there was also a warm, gentle drawl that made everyone smile. At the moment, however, that piece was completely missing. I had no idea he could sound so cold and hard.

"Harvey," Pastor Edwards said, "for this reason God gave them up to dishonorable passions. For their women exchanged natural relations for—"

"Do not quote Romans at me," my grandfather warned him, crossing the room. "And if you don't want this walking stick up your ass, I suggest you all get your damn hands off him."

They let me go, and immediately my grandfather's arm was around me. He pulled me close to him and kissed my forehead before he patted me on the back. He then took a deep breath and turned to my father.

"I think, for now, that Kaenon should come stay with your mother and me until we can all see our way clear to a resolution."

"He wants to be a sodomite, Harvey," my mother cried out, beside herself, overwrought and broken. "If a man lies with a male as with a woman, both of them have—"

"I don't want Leviticus preached at me neither," he told my mother, scowling at her. "Before anything else, Tessa, this is your child."

She shook her head violently. "Not anymore. Never again."

I would have broken right there. This was my mother, after all, who had been my whole world, who read to me when I was little, who ran with me in her arms six blocks when I was hit by a car on my bicycle when I was five, and who made sure I had the best cupcakes to take to school for every holiday. She was my shelter, and now she was throwing me away.

"There is an excellent conversion therapy facility in Allen," Pastor Edwards told my parents. "That's just three hours or so away, and you can visit him and—"

"No," my grandfather growled, holding me tighter. "I forbid it."

"He's not your son," my father yelled at him. "He's mine, and I will not allow him to become a depraved and—"

"We're here," Jo announced, rushing through the front door with Peg right behind her. "How did the announce—what's going on?"

"Your son wants to send your grandson to conversion therapy," my grandfather roared out, smacking his heavy walking stick on the floor. It was more a staff than a stick, one that Gandalf the Grey could have easily carried.

"What is that?"

"It's where they try and make him not homosexual," my grandfather answered her.

She looked at him, then at my father and the minister, and then back at him. "That's ridiculous. He's gay; he was born gay. What's to change?"

"Ask them, Jo, honey, not me."

She turned back to them, shifting her stance to face them. "I don't understand."

"Kaenon needs to go to conversion therapy so we can save his soul," Pastor Edwards informed my grandmother.

"Over my dead body," Jo thundered, and her voice, because she'd taught high school history for her entire adult life, easily filled the room.

"Joanna," Pastor Edwards began, "we don't want—"

"Hello, Pastor," Peg said, leaning around my grandmother, her smile sly. "How are you? And how is your lovely wife?"

He opened his mouth and closed it.

She turned her head to look at Reverend Hughes. "How are the renovations on the church coming, Reverend?"

"They're—well," he said with a gulp.

How Peg had known he was stealing money from his congregation before anyone else, I had no idea, but he certainly was in no position to test her.

The elder who had grabbed me earlier decided at that moment to get out of my house as fast as humanly possible. Apparently Peg scared the crap out of him, for whatever reason. And my father and mother watched in absolute shock as the two ministers grabbed all the items they'd brought with them—oil, a cross, the terrifying riding crop—and left.

Peg almost purred before she turned to my parents. "How about we grab some garbage bags, throw all Kaenon's things into them, and just get him out of your hair for a bit? Doesn't that sound just fine?"

My mother rounded on Peg. "Thou shalt not suffer a witch—"

"A literal reading of the Bible, Tessa," Peg said, squinting at her. "Really?"

"I—"

"If we're going to do that, then you can't talk in church anymore. That's in Corinthians, and Everett will have to give up football—the skin of a pig and all—so that means no scholarship, of course, and even though you love crab, Leviticus says that's a big no-no too."

"It's not the same, Peg. Homosexuality is a sin against God!"

The look my mother gave me when she said it, the hatred and pain, the betrayal I saw on her face because I had done this to her, had broken me in a way that took years to mend. The fact that both she and my father could turn on me in the blink of an eye, over two words, *I'm gay*, would be replayed in my mind a thousand times. I had parents before I spoke the words, and afterward, did not. The fact that it had never once occurred to me that they could stop loving me was an innocence that I lost that day.

"Do you know what else is a sin against God?" Peg asked my mother, taking my hand in hers and squeezing it tight. "Eating bacon."

My mother ran from the room then, and we all heard the door slam down the hall.

"We can't pick and choose what we like and don't from

the Good Book, now, can we?" Peg intoned, hand on my cheek for a moment.

"Go comfort your wife," Jo told my father, her son. "I'm going to pack up my grandson. We'll talk before school starts."

He looked at her, then my grandfather, then his aunt, but not at me. He never even glanced at me. He left the room and didn't look back.

Stunned, numb, shaking, bruised and bloodied, I stood there like a zombie until Jo put her warm hands on my face, kissed my forehead, and took me into her arms. She had never hugged me so tight.

"It's going to be okay, sweetheart, because we're all going to love the hell out of you."

And they had. Promise kept.

My grandfather had always been proud of me and told me often and never missed an opportunity to give me a hug.

My Aunt Peg rained all her secrets down on me, showed me everything she knew, and I filled journals that I had in my bookcase at home. We laughed often, and she was forever putting a new amulet around my neck, giving me another stone to carry in my pocket or tucking a dried herb or flower between the pages of my school books.

My grandmother, though, was my anchor, the bedrock of my life. I had always needed her, and when school started and Everett outed me in the cafeteria on the first day of my ninth-grade year—he stood up on a table and basically announced that his little brother was a pervert—I had needed all three of them to breathe. The fact that I had Zuzu and Colby as well, had been a blessing I never saw coming. I had a sudden urge to call them both.

"Kaenon?"

This was the problem with visiting where you grew up.

It was easy to get caught up in a time loop and forget where the hell you were. I had to keep in mind that the bad parts were over, and I was living in the promise of better days. "Yeah, dinner's fine with me as long as Jo's up to it."

"Good," he said, exhaling fast like he was nervous. "We were thinking that, for the Fourth of July, Rochelle and I would have everyone over to our place. We could have a big four-day weekend, and everyone could enjoy the pool and the tennis courts and the stables."

"I'm sure you'll all have fun," I said, because I was running out of pleasantries.

"All of us," he clarified, lifting his hand like he was going to reach for me and then taking hold of the doorframe instead. "We all want to spend time with Jo."

"Of course," I agreed, moving forward. "Could I get in there, please? I need to let Jo know I'm back, and I need to make a couple calls."

"Oh, yeah, sure," he rushed out, stepping aside so I could walk by and not touch him, making my way toward the kitchen. "Kaenon."

I stopped and turned to face him and his jolt of something—not fear, surprise maybe—was readily apparent in his wide eyes and parted lips.

What did I look like in that moment? Did he see hatred? Fury? Or was it worse? Did I look bored because there was nothing anymore? Indifference and apathy would be harder to bear, for me, if our roles were reversed.

Seeing him made me remember, in sharp, vivid detail, one of the worst moments of my life as well as his vicious betrayal at school that had followed. It was impossible to hide the anger that I'd felt then, and still carried around now, and the mask that I'd been trying to keep in place had slipped enough that he saw everything I was feeling, I was certain, for a single moment. But the fractured, vulnerable boy I'd been was gone. I wasn't broken anymore. And yes, he'd done great harm and inflicted damage that had taken me years to heal, but I had, without him.

The new frustration I was feeling came from being back in town, sharing the same space with him. It conjured up dark thoughts and bad memories that I didn't want to relive. If he thought we were going to talk, he had another thing coming. I had no intention of ever telling him how I'd felt when I was fourteen, fifteen, sixteen and so on. It wouldn't accomplish anything, and I'd stopped caring about him a lifetime ago. Ancient history, no matter how cathartic it might be, was just that—an unchangeable past. I owed him nothing and that was all he was going to get. I had no more emotional coin left to give him.

"Are you all right?" he asked warily, gazing at me like I was a dog baring its teeth while wagging its tail at the same time.

"Fine," I answered stiffly, trying to shake off the lingering bitterness that I could taste in the back of my throat.

"Well, so," he said with a cough, "since you're going to be here the Fourth of July, we would love it if you came by too."

It was hard not to grimace or scowl, and I tried not to, but I wasn't sure how successful I was. After high school, I'd promised myself that I would never walk around being stoic again. I would be the guy people could read. Ever since college, my face showed more than I wanted it to a lot of time. "I don't know, Everett. I don't want to make anyone uncomfortable, and Mom and Dad and everyone else—I think they would be if I was there."

"Well, maybe I don't care."

"But you do, though," I couldn't help but assure him, snidely, before leaving him in the living room.

Finding Jo alone in the kitchen, I leaned in and kissed her cheek.

"Oh, well, I like that," she said seriously, giving me a smile. "I see you're back."

"And I've got lots of news, but first I need to go make a couple quick calls."

"Go, go," she ordered me.

Walking down the short hall, I went into my room, and closed the door before dropping down onto the huge bed. I had no idea why a California king was necessary for a guest room, but I wasn't about to ask.

I called Colby first, because it was just after two in the afternoon where I was, as I had slept in, which meant it was after nine at night in Paris. I had a clock on my phone with all time zones of everyone I loved.

She answered on the second ring. "I'm interviewing an actual Italian race car driver who is hot like the surface of the sun," she informed me, her voice cool, all business. "The hell do you want, Geary?"

But that was the point in a nutshell, right there. In the midst of doing her job and maybe even getting laid, she'd seen my number and answered the phone. It was how we were with each other. We cared and it more than showed. "I just want you to know that I appreciate you always being such a good, loyal friend, and I love you."

Silence.

I smiled because I could visualize her scowling on the other end.

"Why the hell would you need to call me for that?" she asked irritably.

"I was feeling sentimental," I told her.

"Oh God, you know why, don't you? It's because you're stuck in that armpit of a town all summer long," she assured me, all the contempt and snobbery she felt toward Braxton thick in her tone. "You need backup."

"I'm fine."

"I can come."

She could not. "I'm good, I promise."

"Yeah?"

"Yeah."

"All right, then. Throat punch your brother for me."

I snickered.

"You should really work on Jo. Remind her how much she loved Paris the last time she was here. I'll get tickets for you guys the second you say the word."

"Thank you."

She made a disgusted noise. "Ugh, Braxton. You know, sometimes I wake up in a cold sweat because I've had a nightmare that I still live there."

I could be in my old hometown now, only because I had Jo and years of memories before I came out to my family, but Zuzu and Colby had both moved there in the ninth grade. Colby came to Braxton because her parents got divorced and her mother got a great job with the forest service. Zuzu's family relocated to the Texas Hill Country town in order to open a bed-and-breakfast. A year after she graduated from Braxton High, her parents sold it to a land developer. Both Zuzu's and Colby's families had left Braxton years ago.

"Anyway," I mollified her, "enjoy the race car driver. I love you."

"Righbackatcha," she said softly, so I knew she meant it, and then hung up.

Zuzu was next, and she picked up on the third ring. She didn't say anything in greeting, there was only whimpering.

"Wait, let me guess," I said, trying not to laugh. "You're at your sister-in-law's house, and it turned out to be another meeting of the garden club."

More whimpering.

"You're at one of those parties where you have to buy cooking utensils."

Whining was added to the whimpering.

"It's not another themed birthday party, like when you were a cloud and Ben was a giant umbrella, is it?" I asked, dissolving into laughter, needing the emotional release for my own sanity, but also, the video—that I still had on my phone—was enough to make anyone lose their shit. Her son was clearly disgruntled, horrified as only a five-year-old could be over being dressed up as a rainbow-colored parasol, and the only adjective that accurately described Zuzu in her get-up was constipated. She'd looked like a giant constipated rain cloud.

"Are you done?"

I fell back on the bed and laughed until, eventually, I was smiling through the tears I wiped from my eyes.

"I'm in hell, and you're laughing?"

"Oh honey, I'm so sorry," I lied.

"You are not!" she accused me.

And then it hit me. "You're at that scary place with the mechanical animals and the clowns for some kid's birthday party, aren't you?"

"Yes! And you know Ben got strep the last time we were here!"

"Some kid peed in the ball pit too, remember? Ella got covered in it."

"God fuckin' dammit."

"Be careful, you don't want it turning into a Five Nights at Freddy's situation."

"Why did I even have children?" she asked, and I was

back to laughing for a moment before she said, "Ma'am, I'm on the phone with one of my best friends, and I can assure you that *he* knows I was being facetious. So you can shove your fake outrage right up your ass."

She was killing me, and I had an image of us back in high school, walking the halls together, the three of us along with my soccer coach, practically the only diversity the school had to offer, with me being gay, Zuzu black, and Colby Korean.

"It's good that you're calling so I'm distracted from manslaughter," she informed me.

"I just want to tell you I love you and to thank you for always having my back."

"Aww, baby, I love you too, but—" She paused dramatically. "—are you day drinking?"

"Z!"

"What? It's a question."

"Of course not."

"Rolling?"

"I'm not stoned either!"

"No judgment either way," she assured me, cackling.

"You know, I was thinking about you guys and high school and everything that happened and how supportive you both always were, and I got a little sentimental, so I thought I would reach out and it would be sweet—"

Her laughter got louder and interrupted my train of thought.

"The two of you are insensitive pieces of crap," I growled at her.

It sounded like she could barely breathe on the other end.

"Goodbye," I announced petulantly.

"No, no, wait," she barely got out. "I love you, and you can just go ahead and take that for granted, all right?"

"Yeah," I said gruffly, the surge of emotion making it hard to speak.

"Listen," she said with a deep sigh, "all of us—me and you, Colby, my folks, her mother, Jo—we stand in place in one another's lives. We're permanent fixtures, we never leave, and we remain steadfast, always."

Yes, we did.

"It's sweet that you wanted to call and tell us you love us, but, baby, really, we know."

I knew that. I was the same.

"Did it ever occur to you that maybe you're a little overly sensitive because you're stuck there in the butt crack of hell?"

It had, actually.

"Braxton'll do that to you. It's soul-sucking."

"It's been all right so far, surprisingly enough, except on the sibling front. But you'll never believe what Davis Winter said to me."

"Oh, do tell."

And so I did.

SEVEN

After I finally got off the phone with Zuzu, I went in search of Jo. I found her on the back deck sitting at the round glass table, shaded with an umbrella. Both that and the picnic table were new. I was fairly certain Everett had purchased them when still under the impression he and Rochelle would be moving in.

After moving one of the chairs over beside her, I flopped down gracelessly and yawned.

"Well, lovely of you to finally join me," she said grumpily.

I grinned at her, bumping her with my shoulder.

She *hmphed* at me but smiled as she sat there, cooling herself with an embroidered lace fan that had been Peg's.

"Leave it to you not to have a sun hat," I teased her, reaching out to touch the brim of the straw fedora she had on.

"Why in the world would I ever have a sun hat?" she sounded horrified.

My whole life, I had never known Jo not to be dressed

for the exact occasion. At the moment, her sleeveless black top, khaki pants, and gladiator-style sandals looked sleek and stylish. The black band on the fedora and the chunky gold necklace she was wearing were both nice accents.

"Do you want something to drink?" I asked her.

"Only if I can have booze in it," she said, sounding dejected.

"Why can't you?"

"I can?" she asked, sitting up straight, looking wary.

"Why not? What's it going to do, kill you?"

Her deep, throaty laughter was my reward for teasing her.

"I'll get the stuff to make bourbon slushes tomorrow, but for now, I could make margaritas if we have mix."

Her gasp made me realize what I'd said.

"Shit."

She reached out and took my sunglasses off so she could see my eyes. "God help you if you've forgotten my homemade margarita recipe."

"I got lazy while I was gone," I confessed to her.

"Well, you're here now, so get to it," she ordered me. "We bought an entire orchard of lemons and limes yesterday, and there's lots of sugar in there."

"Do you have tequila and triple sec?"

"Do I have tequila and triple sec," she repeated, scowling at me. "Just because I haven't been *able* to drink doesn't mean the *desire* wasn't there."

"So that's a yes on the booze."

"We're a go for launch," she said happily, giving me the mischievous smile I loved before turning her attention to the collection of people returning from either a short walk or a long stroll. I had no way of knowing. They were making their way around the edge of the overgrown garden, having passed Peg's cottage. Once upon a time, it had been covered in climbing roses, and though I couldn't make that happen overnight, I would try and return the rest of Jo's sacred space to her in at least some of its former glory.

"Hey, y'all, does anyone want a margarita? Kaenon's going to make up a batch."

When she called over the question, only then did I check the faces of the people traipsing through the backyard. There was Maeve, her husband, Will—I was assuming, but it seemed a good bet—Rochelle, with an eyesore of a diamond ring on her finger, Everett, and lastly, the man whose smile made my stomach flip over, twice, just seeing him walking with the others.

"What's he doing here?" I asked, my mouth dry, the hitch in my breathing audible, and a flush of heat running down my spine.

"I can get rid of him," Jo offered evilly, batting her eyelashes at me. "If you like."

"That would be rude," I assured her.

"And you're never rude," she said snidely, pretending to elbow me in the side.

"I'll just let him know we don't expect him to stay."

"Oh, yes, absolutely. You do that."

I shot her a look, but she just smiled at me like she'd been lobotomized.

It was stupid to be so excited that he was there, especially considering we weren't really even friends.

When he broke from the others and jogged to the stairs, I got up and rushed over to intercept him. "I'm sure you're way too busy to stay and have margaritas with us," I said, the words coming out as more an accusation than me letting him off the hook.

His answering chuckle as he climbed the few stairs to

me was low and seductive. I became aware, the closer he got, of how hot and sticky the air around me was, even with the slow breeze. "It sounds like you want me to be too busy," he said, putting his hand on the railing beside me. "Is that it?"

He wasn't smiling, and he seemed much too serious, almost sad. It was like he was expecting me to tell him to go.

"Nope," I said, smiling as he leaned close into my space, near enough that I could smell the citrus scent from the day before along with pine and firewood and salt that I knew was the sweat on his skin. "You're missing the question."

"Tell me," he insisted, and I watched him inhale, his jaw clenching for a moment.

"What I'm asking is, do you have time to just hang out here?"

"I do," he answered, his lazy grin making those russet eyes of his glint with a sliver of heat. "I switched some things around today."

"Why?" I pressed, pushing as I normally didn't do. It was funny, but I didn't want to guess what he was thinking. I wanted to know.

"So I could come see you."

I didn't play games; it wasn't me, never had been. "That's a nice thing to say."

"I'm a nice guy," he said flatly, not being flirty or playful, but serious. "I am. You'll see. You just need to start fresh with me."

"A do-over from when I was a kid?"

"We were both kids, as you recall."

I took a breath. "Can you come talk to me in the kitchen?"

"Whatever you want," he replied gruffly, the gravelly rumble of his voice hurtling me back to a time when my clothes felt too tight, my collars choked me, and my pants strangled my cock. It had happened whenever I laid eyes on Brody Scott. Whether it was the cocky swagger in the hallways at school, the powerful burst of speed on the football field, or the fluid stride when he ran at night, always, without fail, just a glimpse of him flushed me with want. I squirmed in my own skin, never comfortable, always wondering what it would be like if Brody ever put his hands on me.

Heading inside, I felt him at my back, close. When I opened the door, he was right there, closing it behind us so when I rounded on him, he was only inches away.

Taking a small step back, I lifted my head to meet his gaze. "You ignored me."

He nodded. "Yes."

I took a breath. "Some people would say that not sticking up for me was the same as bullying me. That allowing something to happen and being complacent is just as bad."

"Those people would be right."

I watched as he swallowed hard, wet his lips like he was nervous, and put a hand down on the kitchen counter, bracing himself.

"And I'm sorry, so sorry that I didn't stick up for you or stop the bullying or do any of the million things I thought of doing with you."

"You mean, on my behalf," I offered, amazed at my entire lack of anger toward him.

The truth was that yes, he should have stepped up, but how many seventeen-year-old boys did or could? And Brody's whole life was about being the big man on campus, and football, and getting out of Braxton. Because he was right. We were both kids, not just me.

"I *mean* doing with you," he growled, brows furrowing. "Don't correct what I'm trying to tell you, all right?"

Other memories came then, of him and my brother. Everett would try to goad Brody into calling me names, had egged him on, and then, when Brody wouldn't, had turned around and accused his friend of being a fag for not going along. When Brody would flip him off, Everett always recanted, apologized, and scrambled after him, wanting to smooth things over, never having meant anything in the first place.

I would hear my brother pleading with him as they walked away. Those encounters were bad because of Everett. It didn't so much hurt when I was slammed into walls or lockers; it was more the surprise factor, the jump-scare of it all that bothered me. But when it was over, if Brody was anywhere around, or close, he was the one I resented, because he never lived up to my fantasy. The Brody in my dreams would have stood up for me, fought for me, and after he vanquished my brother for his slurs, or whatever Neanderthal was giving me a real beatdown at the moment, then there would be the big movie moment where he announced to the entire school that I was the one for him.

"I was a coward, and you have every right to hate me."

I loved romantic comedies almost as much as Marvel movies, but neither was real life. In my small hometown, Brody Scott had done the best he could. He didn't actively hurt me; he ignored me and left me alone. That was as good as it got and could not be said for everyone I'd known then. He hadn't charged in on a white horse, but neither had he ever thrown a punch, tripped me in the hall, or "accidentally" dumped a tray of food on me in the cafeteria.

"I don't hate you," I told him honestly, glancing away from him.

"You don't?" he asked, softly, which drew my attention right back.

"No," I said, releasing a deep breath, and with it whatever lingering hurt or disappointment I'd been carrying around. I'd cast him unfairly as the villain, but I could amend that now and shrug off another layer of the betrayal I'd been carrying around for so long.

Now I could put Brody on the list of people I was cautiously optimistic about, like Davis Winter and Shelly Tate. He hadn't helped me when I was younger, no, but neither had he hurt me. Him not being actively against me, as my entire family had been, save for my grandparents and Peg, was a huge distinction.

"Does not hating me mean that you'd be open to that do-over I mentioned earlier?" he asked, leaning in, mouth close to my ear, his warm breath laying a molten trail of heat down the side of my neck.

"It does," I said, feeling good, almost drunk with his closeness, knowing that under just one layer of polyester blend and a cotton t-shirt was miles of sleek, warm skin. I could strip him in seconds and have my hands and my mouth all over him. No one could worship him better.

It hit me then, like a freight train, because I'd been going along and not thinking about it one bit.

The man was one hundred percent flirting with me.

Holy. Crap.

Brody Scott was putting the moves on me, and it was amazing, and I wasn't about to question it, because who in their right mind did that when their wildest, sexiest, deep-in-your-heart dreams finally came true?

"You look about ten pounds lighter," he said with a grin.

"Yes," I agreed, pleased with him for owning what happened, for not making excuses, and for being sorry. I'd been angrier at him than someone like Davis, because Brody had meant more to me. I'd felt the hurt more sharply because he was my fantasy. But unlike my parents, who deserved every little drop of betrayal I still felt, Brody I could have a do-over with and have a clean, fresh start.

"So now," he said, the mock-serious tone making me smile, "can I have a margarita?"

"Yes, you can," I said, stepping away to move around the kitchen.

"And will you invite me to dinner?"

I looked back over my shoulder at him. "Would you like to stay for dinner, Constable?"

The laugh lines in the corner of his eyes crinkled as he smiled at me. "Nothing I'd like to do more."

"Do me a favor and go tell Jo that I'm making with the alcohol already."

"Yessir," he agreed and started for the door.

"It's nice of you to take time off to come over and talk to me and hang out," I said, because it was, and I needed him to know that it meant a lot. "Thank you."

Hand on the doorknob, he turned to look at me. "You're welcome, but so you know, I wasn't gonna let it go. I was going to keep showing up here until you forgave me. Day and night, I would've worn you down. I had a whole plan ready to go."

"Is that right?"

"Yessir," he said thickly, his voice all gravel and smoke.

It was a mistake to play with fire, but I couldn't...help it. "Aww crap, so now I blew my chance to see you every day?"

"Oh no," he assured me, eyes narrowing, shaking his head. "I'll be around, don't you worry none about that."

Keeping things simple for the summer should have been

my only goal. What the hell was I thinking? "Go already," I pleaded with him, needing a second to cool down.

The wicked grin I got before he opened the door and left made it very difficult to breathe let alone think.

"Margaritas!" I heard Jo yell from the patio, which was good, because it reminded me what the hell I was supposed to be doing.

Christ.

I was just getting my bearings when the door opened and Everett walked in.

"Hey," he said stiffly, trying to smile. "Jo suggested I come in and see if you needed help with anything."

"Uh, no, thanks, though," I said, getting down the glass pitchers from the new open shelves. "You did a really nice job in here."

"Oh, yeah, thanks. I thought so too," he croaked out, gesturing at the built-in hutch with glass doors by what had become a small nook where the house phone sat on a shelf. "You saw that, of course."

"It's just like she always wanted," I admitted, because it had been thoughtful. "Did you add that after you knew she was going to stay here instead of you and Rochelle moving in?"

"No," he said, crossing his arms. "I just always thought it was a good idea."

Jo's mother had left her a beautiful set of bone china that she never had anywhere to display. It had been a persistent lament when I was young. Many a time my grandfather and I had gone somewhere specifically to buy her a hutch, only to have her point out flaws in each one. Peg had even found one made of gorgeous teak and intricately carved that my grandmother said belonged at the store and not in her home. But apparently she had liked the hutch that Everett built enough to fill it, for the first time, with her mother's pride and joy.

"Well, she clearly loves it."

He nodded, uncrossing his arms and raking his fingers through his hair. "The shelves below were a nice touch too, don't you think?"

Why the hell did he need any approval from me? "They are. She's got all her cookbooks in there, her address book, and how it turns into a shelf for the phone, it's quite modern."

"Except for the house phone, of course," he commented with a shrug.

"Yeah, but she's had a house phone for years. Not going to change that overnight."

"No."

It was grueling, making small talk, and I was so relieved when Brody came back in that I said his name a little too loudly.

"Are you all right?" he asked, glancing at Everett and then back to me.

"Yeah, no, we're fine. I just—how are you?"

"Fine," he answered slowly, squinting at me before giving his attention to Everett again. "Why are you still here?"

Everett gestured at me. "I was talking to Kae."

"Yeah, well, that's great and all, but you're supposed to be at the store."

"Right now?"

"This was your idea," Brody told him. "You suggested dinner, so you better go get some meat to throw on the damn grill."

"I—"

"Besides meat, we're also gonna need corn on the cob, mushrooms, bell peppers, zucchini, and either some new potatoes or, if you can't find those, then red," Brody told him as he charged toward the front door. The man was used to issuing orders, that was obvious.

"Why?" Everett called over to him.

Brody wheeled around and scowled at my brother. "Because Kaenon's a vegetarian, and Jo said she is now too." He looked at me, and damn if his gaze didn't soften, warm. "Except for bacon, I understand."

"That's right," I agreed, smiling at him. "She's not giving up that."

"Someone should come with me and—"

"And don't forget skewers," Brody told him. "And cauliflower florets. Those do really well on the grill as well."

"How do you know this?" Everett asked him.

"Malin's a vegan," he answered before glancing back at me. "That's my niece. My sister, Shannon's, kid. She won't even eat eggs. It all has to be plant-based."

I nodded. "I'll get there eventually, just not quite yet."

"More power to you. I have no idea what I would do without a steak once in a while."

"Well, thanks for thinking of all the veggies. That'll be good."

"That grill is new out there too. Jo just bought it, but it looks like they forgot to get her a new propane tank, so I'm gonna run and get that, and I'll be right back."

I nodded, smiling at him, taking him all in, noticing his clothes as I hadn't before.

The white fitted t-shirt he wore was lightweight and hugged his powerful shoulders, wide sculpted chest, chiseled biceps, and carved abdomen. The short sleeves showed off the roping veins in his forearms, and I admired the huge silver watch he wore. I was also a fan of the tanned skin of his throat and chest where the V-neck dipped low. On the whole, he looked good enough to eat. Even the cargo shorts were hot, showing off his long, heavily muscled legs. The white Converse shoes made me smile.

"What's funny?" he asked in that tone of his that was a bit rough, almost a growl, all slithering heat and hunger.

"Not funny. I just have those same sneakers," I explained, taking a breath and turning my back to him to glance around the kitchen, not sure where the pots were.

"They're comfortable, right?"

"They certainly are," I said, guessing and being rewarded, pulling out a large saucepan. "You know I like you in civilian attire, but I get why you don't dress like that on duty. You're not too scary at the moment."

"Oh no?"

I was going to answer, trade banter with him, flirt hard, but I realized Everett was still standing there. Brody must have noticed the same thing, because we both turned to look at him at the same time. He was watching us but not moving.

"What the hell are you doing? Go already," Brody directed him. "We'll be drinking when you get back."

"I could use some help."

"Take Will. He doesn't strike me as a drinker anyway."

Everett went out the back to the deck, and Brody pivoted and headed out the front. Alone for a moment, I thought about going to my room and changing out of the olive-green pocket t-shirt and the pair of beige shorts I had on into something nicer, tighter, but then I realized I was being ridiculous. I was off-balance because of him, and added to that was the whole having both my siblings in the same house with me for the first time in eighteen years. I really needed to start drinking.

I found a new bottle of Patrón Reposado that I opened and took a quick shot of, because why the hell not? The bottle of triple sec was hidden way in the back of the liquor shelf, but it was there, thankfully. Once I had the sugar and water in the pan, making the simple syrup I needed, I took a breath. Everything was going well, I was whisking, nothing was burning, and then the front door opened and Brody came back into the house.

"That was fast."

"I think you're forgetting that you're home, in a small town, and not back in the city."

"True."

"Besides, I called ahead, and they just brought it out to me."

"You don't pay for things, Constable?"

"Again, small town. We call that a running tab in these here parts."

I snorted as he came up behind me.

"You want me to juice the lemons and limes for you?"

"No, I—you should go get the grill going and take some drink orders."

"So, I'm the help?" He chuckled, bumping against my shoulder as he washed his hands in the sink. "When did that happen?"

"You just seem awfully comfortable in Jo's house."

He shrugged, gave me a smirk, and bit his bottom lip for a second. He had all my attention focused right there on his mouth. "Yeah, well. When I moved back to Braxton, I think she was worried I was going to starve, so she fed me quite a bit."

"Which is interesting, because she acted like she just

realized you'd returned home when she saw you yesterday," I informed him.

"Did she?"

I grunted, knowing what my grandmother was up to. She was matchmaking, and I was going to have to call her on it. "Yes."

"That's funny. I wonder why she'd do that?"

I ignored the question. "So how long have you been back?" I asked, lifting the saucepan from the heat and pouring it into a large glass measuring cup.

"Just about six months now."

Moving around the kitchen, getting a chopping board from the drawer near the refrigerator, the ancient juicer from another, and pulling a knife from the block on the counter, I glanced over at him as he leaned against the sink, looking utterly relaxed. "May I ask why?"

"Why what?"

"Why Braxton?" I said, like it was obvious. "You got out, you got away from here. Why on earth would you ever come back?"

He levered off the counter and scowled at me. "This is my home. You don't stay away from your home."

I nodded. "Okay."

"No, don't be so dismissive. It's really douchey."

I stilled in midmotion, about to cut into a lime. "I'm sorry?"

"Just because you hate Braxton doesn't mean we all do."

"Well, I have every right to hate Braxton," I said snidely, shooting him a look that I hoped conveyed the level of ass that he was being at the moment. All thoughts of how ruggedly handsome he was and how sexy his voice sounded evaporated instantly.

"Oh yeah? And why's that?"

"You know why," I snapped, slamming the knife down hard on the chopping board before I turned to face him.

"Look, I get you having issues with a few people, but to blame the whole—"

"People in this town thought I was a fucking pariah!"

"So you're saying you were what, some kind of outcast?"

"That's exactly what I was," I assured him flatly. "Once my brother outed me, everything changed, and you probably don't remember that because being a senior all-state running back in a state where that made you a god, I'm not sure how much filtered through your happy bubble."

"You think I had it so good?"

"You were *it* at our school," I reminded him, returning to the task of cutting the limes. "There was nothing and no one bigger than you, more important than you. Even Everett being the quarterback came in second to Brody Scott, hero of the gridiron."

"I had no idea you were this full of shit," he said, sounding disappointed, the judgment thick in his voice. "You think you had it worse than the kids that were on welfare? What about the ones who didn't play a sport like you, or have their own cars like you did? What about the kids who couldn't find jobs because they weren't the right color?"

I shook my head.

"Well?"

Turning, I tried to stare holes through him. "No, I get it, I do. Who cares about being jumped behind the school and having the shit beat out of you by guys who played football with you and Everett? What about the time I got held down in the locker room by Dean Waylon and the rest of his boys?" I snarled at him, because it was ages ago, but the humiliation and fear were still fresh. "They were gonna fuck me with a broom handle, but lucky for me I got loose just enough to pull the fire alarm."

His brows knit together, and he was squinting at me hard. "Dean Waylon and who?"

I shook my head. "No, no, come on, that's ancient history, right? Nothing to be upset about, nothing to carry around. And besides, that was the ninth grade, man. When I came back in my sophomore year, I was bigger, and there were guys on the soccer team who wanted to go to state, and so they didn't let other people hurt me anymore."

"You—"

"Not that they were my friends, mind you," I said, wanting to make that clear. "None of those guys wanted to be buddies with a faggot."

"Kaenon—"

"But they certainly weren't going to let me get beat to shit when I was that valuable to the team," I finished, my voice cold and flat, feeling faded all of a sudden, and wrung out. "I lived my high school years in fear that someone was going to hurt me if I wasn't always on my guard, if I wasn't hyper-vigilant."

He was quiet, studying me with his dark mahogany eyes.

I still remembered going away to college and being on the soccer team at Syracuse and attending my first team meeting, where I came out to them all. I wanted everyone to be aware of my sexuality so I could see their hatred out in the open, unlike how it had been in high school. If they were going to hurt me, I wanted to know. I wanted to meet it head-on. I never wanted to be blindsided again.

Even now, thinking about the faces of the coaches and players on my freshman team giving me various looks of disbelief could make me smile at the memory.

They didn't care.

No one cared who I slept with. The only important part was that I could play. And because I could, because I was an asset, teammates became friends for the first time in my life. It had been hard when I got hurt to remain close. For them to look at me and see that my dream was over, that I would never go pro, was far too difficult for most. Only a few were strong enough, and the number dwindled even more of those who stayed in touch after graduation. But even now, I had a handful of friends who lived all over the world because they had played fútbol in places like Barcelona and Liverpool and Paris before retiring and never returning to the United States. The fact that I had an open invitation to their homes, as they did to mine, was still a great source of comfort. I had good friends, so I was doing something right even if no one in my hometown, besides my grandmother, knew it.

"Look," he said gruffly, taking a breath. "You hate this town. I get it. But I don't, all right? I came back here because I wanted to help Braxton grow. I wanted to be close to my family and make a life and home here."

I nodded, returning to my lime cutting.

"There are things I didn't count on, but everything is a work in progress."

There was nothing to say, so I kept quiet.

"So, can we just leave it at that?"

"Absolutely," I agreed.

"Could you just—"

"You should really get the grill going, don't you think?"

"That's it? I'm dismissed?"

"It's not going to start itself."

His growl was loud and frustrated as he slammed out the back door, leaving me alone in the kitchen.

For a brief moment, I'd lost my mind over Brody Scott

because I'd forgotten that he returned to Braxton by choice, and I came back only because of Jo. He was a man fond of sleepy Texas Hill Country towns. I was not. Brody wasn't about to dig up his roots, and I wasn't going to put any down. I was there for Jo, and it was good to be reminded.

EIGHT

Once I had the pitchers of margaritas made, I carried them out on the deck and put them down near Jo. She took hold of one of the handles and slid it closer. After a moment of admiring the liquid, she looked up at me.

"Can I have a straw?"

"No, you can't have a straw," I scolded her, smiling.

"Then go get the damn glasses," she snapped at me. "Jesus Christ, the ice age didn't take this long."

I was chuckling as I returned to the house and came right back out with four glasses rimmed in salt. Since there was more than one pitcher on the table, Jo went ahead and poured for herself instead of offering the first to her guests. When she realized, after a moment, that Rochelle was waiting, she told her to pour from the other and not wait on her.

"Oh," she said, surprised, glancing up at me. "I wasn't sure if we should start one and finish it before—"

"We don't care about that," I assured her. "We'll drain them all eventually."

"I thought maybe you were confused because it took so

long for him to make margaritas that you forgot if you wanted one," Jo grumbled, shooting me a disapproving look. "It was like waiting for winter to roll back around."

"And people say you're grouchy," I said cheerfully, giving her a big fake smile.

"Oh, thank you for this," Rochelle murmured before she stood up. "This was so nice of you, and you even salted the glasses."

I grinned at her. "We try and provide the whole experience here, ma'am."

"Well, so far the service is excellent."

"The service is slow," Jo chimed in grumpily, half done with her first drink.

"So you know," I told Rochelle, "the mix is from scratch, so you may not love it because there's things in there that Jo and I—and Peg, of course—love but not everyone does."

"I'm sure it's fantastic," Rochelle offered, her smile not quite working, unsure of me. "It's so good to see you, Kaenon. You look amazing."

She looked different than she had in high school. Gone was the big teased, and frosted-tipped brown hair, and in its place was a silky chestnut bob that framed her face with long wispy bangs. Her makeup was light, and her jewelry, other than the rock on her finger, was elegant and tasteful. I was betting she fit in well with the country club set.

"Thank you," I said sincerely, giving her a smile. "You look great too."

"I look the same except for my hair, and I'm not wearing acid wash anymore."

"Which is a good thing," I teased her.

She gestured at me. "But you—I had no idea you were going to turn out so pretty."

"Aww, you're gonna make me blush."

"Was your hair always that curly?"

"It was," Jo assured her before slipping her hand into mine. "Pour me another drink."

"Oh, now we're friends again?"

"I want a kiss too," she said tapping her cheek. "Now."

"So demanding," I said, chuckling. I kissed her before pouring her another drink. "Take it easy, all right?"

"The first one always goes down fast," she told me. "I promise to nurse the second."

"Okay," I said as Rochelle retook her seat, and I passed her the pitcher.

"Sit and tell me all about the garden," Jo demanded.

Taking a seat next to her, I explained about the tractor that I was going to be using, and then what plants were being delivered, not enough to bore her but enough so she'd get the general idea. I was going to make it as beautiful as I could.

"Oh, you know I forgot to tell you that I have a ton of Peg's old books along with what was left from the shop, all the crystals and beads and whatever else, stored up in the attic."

"Really?"

She nodded.

"When did you get all that?"

"I guess it was all still at the store, and when Everett cleaned it out so Rochelle could take over the space, he just had it brought over here."

"I'll go up after dinner; I'd love to see what's there."

"I'm curious to know myself."

"You know," Rochelle said, leaning in, smiling at us. "If there are any old malas or bracelets left over that Peg had made, if you all don't want them, I'd love to sell them in the boutique. She made such beautiful things."

"Yes, she did," I agreed, smiling back, "but I doubt there's any finished pieces left. When she died, so many people came by to get anything she'd had her hands on."

"Do you still have any?"

"I have—" I had to think. "—three, I think. No, four, because when Papa died, I got his as well."

Jo smiled and nodded. "Your grandfather's mala was gorgeous, but she made you the prettiest one out of all that red beryl."

Rochelle gasped. "Are you serious? Red beryl is—I wanted a ring, but the cost was just—and you have a mala made of that? How?"

"Peg knew"—I glanced at Jo—"interesting people?"

"How do you mean?" Rochelle asked me.

"What's the best way to put it?" I said, still looking at Jo.

"That a few of the people she did business with would scare the bejesus out of the rest of us." Jo was cracking herself up, and it was fun to watch. "There were some nefarious characters, and if she asked them for something, she usually got it."

"And why is that?" Rochelle asked, leaning forward, sipping her margarita. She was interested, enjoying talking to Jo, I could tell.

"Peg was special," Jo told her, smiling, and I saw Rochelle sit up straighter, like a flower reaching for the sun, soaking up Jo's attention. "She was just the most charming woman, and I know I'm biased, of course, because she was my little sister and I adored her, but really, she spread warmth wherever she went."

"So these scary people she did business with, they loved her too?"

"Well, my stars, yes," Jo said, chuckling, reaching out to

pat Rochelle's hand. "People would drop by from the most exotic locales just to say hello."

"How did she meet them to begin with?"

"Oh, well, she would go on mineral trips to find different crystals and rocks and learn about traditional medicine and study with healers all over the world."

"I had no idea."

"Remember that time that exiled king who lived on a cruise ship flew her to Bora Bora just so she could read his tarot cards on his birthday?" I asked, laughing.

"Oh, I do." She grinned at me. "And that Russian oligarch who said he'd kill her if she left him, so of course she did, and he sent her all those amethysts by courier."

"I'd never seen a guy handcuffed to a briefcase in real life before that."

It took a second to realize no one else was talking. When I turned to Rochelle, she appeared stunned.

"What?"

"The two of you are painting a whole new picture of Peg."

"She was fearless," I told her.

"You should have seen her passport with all her stamps," Jo said excitedly. "And all she ever took was her big carpet bag, and she'd come home with so many treasures."

"And then the boxes would arrive," I reminded Jo. "And Papa and I would have to unpack them all."

"Oh, it was fun." No one was missing the sarcasm or her eye roll.

"Yeah, because you never had to do it," I groused at her. "Don't mix the fire agate and the carnelian," I snapped, doing my best Peg impression. "That's alexandrite, boy, not amethyst. Do you even know what kind of fossil that is? Or, how in the world are you confusing dried mullein with dittany of Crete?"

Jo snorted, and it was adorable.

"If you don't know the difference between polychrome jasper and septarian, why are you even in this shop?"

"She liked things a certain way," Jo offered, giving me the side-eye.

"That's putting it kindly," I said with a grunt. "She was ridiculous when she got home because, until everything was put in its place, I didn't get any sleep."

"Which is why she only went in the summer, so you were always free to help," she said smugly, her quiet burp making her giggle.

"Are you drunk?" I teased her.

"On one and a half margaritas?" she scoffed, reaching over to tuck my hair behind my ear. "Not hardly. Think about how many times I drank you under the table."

"Yeah, but that was when I was sixteen."

Rochelle gasped, her eyes huge.

"He's kidding," Jo stressed, swatting me on the arm. "Stop that. Rochelle will think I was a crappy guardian."

"No," Rochelle corrected her. "I know you were amazing."

"Oh," Jo said, looking pleased before she elbowed me in the arm. "Amazing, she says."

"Don't let it go to your head."

"Yes, dear," she said with a sigh. "Now, since we're drinking, I'd like to be eating too."

"Guacamole?"

"That sounds amazing, but will it take as long to make as the margaritas?"

"Don't be snide," I warned her, getting up.

"Is that a yes on it being made in this century?" she called after me.

"I refuse to dignify that with a response," I volleyed back.

What my grandmother didn't know was that I already had everything prepped from the night before, all except the avocados, which took no time at all to cut up and mash.

I was in and out quickly, delivering the guacamole on a tray along with a pitcher of water containing slices of cucumber, lemon, and lime.

"Oh, now see, that was much better," she praised me as she took a sip of her drink, sighed deeply, and leaned back in her chair. "I think I'll keep coming to this restaurant."

We all heard the car drive up and park. I took that opportunity to bolt back into the house and got to work cleaning up the kitchen to get ready for the imminent arrival of groceries. Someone was already in the house, though, and I heard the floors creak behind me.

"Kaenon."

Taking a quick breath, because there was no mistaking the voice, I turned and faced my sister. I was surprised by how much she'd changed in the years since I'd last seen her. The long, dark brown hair of my memories was now short, in a style that flattered her features, and dyed ash-blond with lighter highlights. She had always been small, almost fragile, with delicate features that she inherited from our mother. My sister—Jo was told and had therefore told me—had been homecoming queen and captain of the cheerleading squad as well as editor of the school newspaper in both her junior and senior years. She had gone to Emory College in Georgia and gotten a degree in human resources. Having moved back to Austin rather than Braxton, the last I'd heard was that she went to work for Dell. I also knew she was married and had children. Staring at her now, though, I realized I knew very little about her life.

"Rochelle is right," she said, smiling. "You look fantastic."

"So do you," I replied, stepping away from her and going to the sink. "It was nice of you to take a trip out here before the weekend."

"It was no problem," she conceded, voice faltering, catching for a second before she coughed softly. "It's not every day that your brother who you haven't seen in a hundred years comes home."

"Well, Jo needed me," I said, rinsing the measuring cups and spoons I'd used.

"Yes," she agreed, trailing me to the sink. She picked up a dish towel to dry what I was placing on the rack. "And we all know you're her favorite."

I shrugged.

"Both her and Papa," she conceded. "You were it."

"I lived with them; it was bound to change the dynamic."

"And Peg."

"I didn't live with Peg; she was in the cottage."

She gestured out the window over the sink. "Yeah, but it's what, fifty feet from the back door? I think we can safely say that you were in her orbit as well."

My Aunt Peg was the aunt every kid wanted. She had a wicked sense of humor, loved fiercely, and always, without fail, had the most interesting stories you ever heard.

Peg didn't just have a sapphire ring. She had a sapphire ring given to her by a pirate off the coast of Borneo. In private, she would dance naked under the light of the full moon, mix up oils that people would drive hours to buy, and had women and men waiting every night by her back door to beg her for a love spell or a banishing spell, a spell for fertility or a spell for luck and money. Price was no object, but after hours it was surprising how many times payment became of no importance, only the conversation mattering.

She had me carry different stones in my pockets that I learned all the names and properties of, had me wear bead bracelets before they were in fashion, and there was nothing I ever had disease-wise that she couldn't take care of with some sort of herbal tincture. And while she was all about children being immunized, she had an oil for whatever else ailed me, everything from hay fever to cuts and scrapes.

My grandmother was a classic movie-star beauty, but Peg was a force of nature. I always told people she smelled green. Everything about her was like fresh-cut grass and sunshine and warm summer rain. She wore her thick brown-black hair long, falling in waves to her waist, and favored long skirts that dragged in the dirt and gypsy-style blouses that fluttered in the breeze. In the winter, she was always in her hooded black coat that trailed behind her like a cape, and her knitwear, which was coveted by all, she only ever created in shades of blue.

"I used to see you and Peg at the store when I walked by, before we moved to Austin," Maeve said as she dried the mini chopping board I'd used, as well as the garlic press.

"You should have visited her."

She shook her head. "No. Not after you left."

I didn't pounce on her wording because what purpose would it serve? If I got immediately defensive and corrected her with, "You mean when I was thrown out at fourteen?" What would that do for me? It was water so far under the bridge it wasn't worth mentioning, except that I could feel it. Same as I had with Everett earlier. The tightening way down deep in my gut that told me the wound was still there, still bleeding, even after all this time.

Having it matter, having *her* matter, was inconvenient. Residual anything was more than I owed either of my siblings.

"Jo and Papa and Peg, they sort of closed ranks around you."

They had, it was true, and she damn well knew why. "Yeah, but you had a set of grandparents," I reminded her. "You had Mom's folks, the Cabots."

"They live in Jacksonville now. They love Florida."

I didn't care. Both of them, my grandfather and grandmother, had told me that I would be better off dead than being a homosexual. They had applauded my parents for throwing me out, and from what Everett had told me—he used to love to drop bombs on me at school when he saw me in the hall—had destroyed every picture of me they were ever given.

I recalled walking home in the rain, crying, and when I reached Peg's store, I blew by her to go sit in the back. She always found me beside her kiln because it was warm, and I was freezing. Without a word, she'd pass me a tumbled piece of kambaba jasper and tell me to carry it for a few days.

"Why?" I asked her.

"Because you need a little healing right now," she murmured, enfolding me in her arms and hugging me tight, nuzzling her face in my wet hair.

I shivered, then, but not with cold.

"Let's have some peppermint tea," she suggested softly, and I felt her fingers tracing over the nape of my neck, and they were slick with oil.

"What are you writing on me now?" I sighed, smiling at her. She was forever drawing sigils and symbols on my arms or back or shoulders, and though at times she used henna, oil was more constant. I always smelled strange, woodsy and warm.

"Hush," she whispered.

"Is that marjoram?"

"Good nose," she complimented me before I got another hug.

"Kaenon."

I had been lost in thought for a moment, and so I smiled at my sister. "Sorry. Memory lane and all that."

She nodded. "I'm sure it's strange for you, being back in Braxton."

It was beyond that.

"Everyone wants to talk to you about Jo."

"Yeah, I bet."

"Dad, all our aunts, me, Everett, all our cousins—we all know you're it, her golden child, but she needs to listen to reason as well."

I was saved from telling her that it was Joanna Geary's life and no one else's by the opening of the front door. In came Everett and Will, Maeve's husband, and two kids, a girl and a boy, and Brody, who had gone from priming the grill in the backyard to the front where he had helped carry in groceries. With just a quick glance, I could tell that Everett had bought far too much food, unless, of course, there were more people visiting. I really hoped that was not the case.

"How many people do you have coming?" I asked him.

"Just us," he answered, filling the counter with plastic bags. "What are you trying to say? You think I got too much stuff? Do you think we need a bigger boat?"

I grinned at the reference to a favorite movie from our childhood, from another lifetime, but my smile died as quickly as it had surfaced, buried beneath a rolling tide of regret over what I'd lost and why I'd lost it, under the lingering residue of a hurt I'd had a difficult time shedding. There would come a day when I forgave Everett for what he'd done to me, I was sure of that. But right now, in this moment, was not the time. I didn't trust him or the feelings of nostalgia that were being dredged up over fond memories of better days.

His answering smile evaporated along with my own.

"I think maybe you went a little overboard here."

He nodded and looked me in the eye rather than flinching from my sudden change in mood. "I don't care, Kae. How often do I get to feed you?"

And it hit me then, the realization that he was making an effort with me, here in Jo's house. Of course he was. Our grandmother was dying.

"This is true," I affirmed, getting into the bags. "You should go have a margarita with your wife. I made guacamole too."

But he didn't move, instead just standing there, staring at me.

After a moment of his fixed regard, I turned to face him. "You're creeping me out."

"I'm sure I am, but...I haven't seen you since high school."

This was not new information. "Yes, I'm aware. You were seventeen the last time I saw you," I confirmed.

"That can't be right," he said hesitantly, like he wasn't at all sure.

"It is," Maeve chimed in. "Dad moved us to Austin the summer after you left for Texas A&M. I haven't seen Kaenon since I was fifteen."

My parents, of course, hadn't informed me that they were moving. Jo was the one who sat me down and explained what happened, because she didn't want me to drive by the house and see a For Sale sign in the yard or be surprised to find a new family there. She also told me that my parents, Robert and Tessa Geary, had signed over custody of me to my grandparents on their way out of town. I'd had my brother's last year of high school with him before he graduated, and one year of school with my sister before she transferred. It had been odd at first, not to catch a glimpse of either of them in the halls.

"Look at you, my little tax write-off," Jo teased me, pinching my cheek.

She was being playful, trying to make light of a catastrophic situation, but still, when I burst into tears, abandoned for the second time, she had held me until the sobs became hiccups. After that, I washed my face, and we went out for ice cream.

Brody cleared his throat, and the three of us turned to him.

"Maeve, Will's never met Kaenon."

But my sister was overwrought, because she waved her hand like she just couldn't deal at the moment before she rushed from the room. Will looked at me, opened his mouth to say something, but then stopped and darted after his wife. That left Everett, Brody, my niece and nephew, and me in the room.

Just seeing the two kids put me into teacher mode.

"Hi," I greeted them, hand out, moving forward, approaching first the girl, who was older. "I'm Kaenon."

She took my hand, smiling, and I noted my sister's face stamped there. "I'm Bebe—well, Belinda, but let's not go there, all right?"

I grinned at her. "Absolutely."

"And this is my brother, Kurt."

Releasing her hand, I was ready when Kurt reached for

me. "Good to meet you," I told him, because it was. He was a mini-version of Will, as far as I could tell, though his hair was lighter and his eyes darker.

"You too," he said, staring at me.

"How old are you guys?"

"I'm ten," Bebe told me, "and he's eight."

I took a breath. "Well, I could really use some help in here, if you guys are up for it."

They were both ready to be put to work.

"Will you take care of the steaks?" I asked Brody.

"I was just hanging around to say goodbye to Everett. I'm thinking I should go."

"Oh, okay," I said, flashing him a smile. "I'm sure you're busy."

His brows furrowed like they had earlier, but instead of leaving, he moved in close to me and put his hand on my shoulder. "I want to stay," he said hoarsely, "but I don't want to fight with you, because that's not helping anything."

I nodded quickly. "We could call a truce about Braxton for one night."

He searched my face for whatever it was he needed.

"I could use grill help."

"Okay, then," he said, releasing a deep breath, sliding his hand to the side of my neck. "Truce it is."

I bumped him gently and then turned to the kids. "Who can peel a kiwi?"

"Oh, me," Bebe said excitedly. "I'm super good at it."

"Can you chop without cutting off your fingers?"

She scowled at me. "Hello. Ten," she said and held up her fingers to show me that it wasn't just her age. All ten digits were there as well.

Brody scoffed, grinning at me, and I smiled at my niece. She was a smartass. We were going to get along great.

I got Kurt busy washing the zucchini and carrots, and had Bebe slicing strawberries, bananas, and kiwis to make fruit salad skewers. Once Kurt was done with that, I had him use the melon baller on the cantaloupe and watermelon.

I prepared the veggie skewers as Everett and Brody went outside to put the steaks on and have some margaritas. The kids and I had a whole production line going by the time Maeve came back into the kitchen, holding her husband's hand.

"You guys helping Kae?" she asked her kids.

"We're almost done, and then we're gonna go outside with Kaenon," Bebe said excitedly.

"Did you know that he's gonna make all the weeds into a garden?" Kurt asked her.

"I did know that," she said, sniffling. "I heard him telling your great-grandmother about that earlier."

"I'm Will," her husband stated, smiling, leaning forward to offer me his hand. "We didn't get to meet earlier."

I wiped my hand on the dish towel hanging over my shoulder and then shook. "It's my pleasure. You have great kids."

"Thank you, I would agree."

"Go sit, relax, but grab the third pitcher from the frig, if you would."

"Absolutely," he replied cheerfully, glancing at Maeve and back to me. "This is such a treat, Kaenon. Thank you for cooking."

"I think I'm doing more delegating than anything else," I said, chuckling.

His smile got wider. "It's great to finally meet you."

"Same here," I agreed and realized I meant it. My sister and I had been done years ago, but her husband and her kids were a clean slate for me.

Maeve took the pitcher of margaritas out, and Will kindly took the veggie skewers and delivered them to Brody, who was manning the grill with Everett.

As promised, I walked the kids out to the garden gate and showed them the dandelions, which they thought were just weeds, and explained how every part of the plant was useful and edible.

"You would eat that?" Bebe asked me, horrified.

"I would, but I'd rather have a Pop-Tart," I teased her.

She laughed and took the daisies from her brother that he kept bringing her.

As I pointed out chickweed and shepherd's purse, which she thought, like dandelions, were just weeds, and told her what they did, I saw her eyes light up with interest.

"How do you know all this stuff?" she asked, watching me as I took the flowers from her and started to make a chain.

"My aunt taught me," I said, smiling, glad that I had slipped on my sneakers before we went outside, as the ground was rocky. Once I had the garden put back in order, which I was certain I would soon, I could go barefoot again in the soft dirt and grass.

"Is that going to be a lei?" She sounded excited, watching me.

"Have you been to Hawai'i?"

Quick nod.

"Well, this is actually a daisy chain. Have you ever made one?"

"No. Can I see?"

I showed her how to make a slit in the stem right under the flower and to push the stem of another through that.

"Kurt, we need more flowers," she called over to her brother.

"I'm on it," he said eagerly, and I could tell that he was excited to do something she asked. He was at the age where tormenting his sister and pleasing her was a moment-to-moment choice.

Once the daisy chain became a daisy crown, I set it on her head, and Kurt and I stepped back to admire her.

"You look pretty," he admitted to her.

"Thank you, Kurt," she told him, blushing. I was guessing that praise from her younger brother did not come her way often. "And thank you, Kaenon. I can't believe you just made this for me."

"In my aunt's store, we used to braid flowers into hair for weddings and stuff."

"You did too, or just your aunt?"

"Me too."

She nodded. "Can you teach me?"

"Next time you visit, if there's flowers in the garden, I totally will."

She launched herself at me then, wrapping her arms around my waist.

"Oh, you're a good hugger. I could tell you would be," I said, patting her back.

Everett called us over when the food was ready, but instead of eating off skewers, I carried everything but the meat inside and separated out the grilled new potatoes, the garlic and butter mushrooms, the zucchini, red bell peppers, and the red onions. I unwrapped the ears of corn from the tin foil and then brushed them all with butter before carrying the platter back out to the table.

"Oh, the corn is amazing," Jo said from beside me, eating it with her fork as I'd cut the kernels off the cob for her. She'd never enjoyed "gnawing" at her food. It was simply undignified. I myself loved eating it that way. "Did you put olive oil on it before you wrapped it in the foil?"

"Of course," I said, shooting her a look. "You're the one who taught me to do it."

"Well, I didn't teach you how to make the roasted carrot fries. Normally carrots make me gag."

"Jo," Maeve cautioned her, glancing at her kids. "I need them to have healthy relationships with veggies."

She laughed at her granddaughter. "They seem to be eating just fine."

Maeve noticed both her kids shoveling down the zucchini and mushrooms and bell peppers. They weren't hoovering down the onions, but that was fine because Everett was. "Of course they eat for you," she said, looking at me like it was my fault.

Kurt told everyone about his pains using the melon baller, and Jo assured him that it was the best fruit salad she'd ever had. He seemed quite pleased with himself.

After dinner, Brody had to go check on some paperwork at the station. I walked him out to his car.

"Thank you for cooking," I said as he opened the door of his cruiser.

"You're welcome," he rumbled, smiling at me. "I usually drive through here on my way home, so if you're still up, maybe I could stop by and we can talk some more."

I squinted at him.

"What?"

"Should we talk anymore? Is that a good idea?"

He shrugged those impossibly broad shoulders of his. "Maybe not, but let's do it anyway."

"Okay," I said, sniffing the air because something smelled like sweat socks and armpits, and it certainly wasn't Brody. He smelled clean, and I knew he did because I'd inhaled him all through dinner. "What is that?" He made a face, and when he did, I got it. "That's the car?"

"God," he groaned, opening the door wide and stepping back. "My car, the chief's car, is a Tahoe, but it's in the shop, so I've had to use one of the cruisers, and the garage keeps them in great shape mechanically and cosmetically, but the interior...horrible."

"Okay, hold on," I said and darted back into the house.

Jo kept certain dried herbs in her kitchen at all times, the same way I did in my own home, and one of them was dried lavender in an enormous stoneware jar. There were small burlap bags in one of her drawers as well, the same ones I used, because I shipped them to her. Filling a couple, I added a bay leaf to each as well. Back outside on the porch, I smiled at him as I walked toward the car.

"Whatever you're gonna do, you should wait and I'll bring my car by tomorrow when I get off, and you can magic it up."

I scowled at him before I wheeled around, heading back for the door.

"No, no, no—wait," he choked out, laughing behind me, and since I was turned away from him, I allowed myself to smile. Yeah...definitely not straight, that one. "I don't mean I don't believe, or that anything you give me isn't appreciated," he said adamantly, coming up behind me and wrapping his arms around me in a viselike grip.

I couldn't move, but that was hardly the problem.

He was plastered to my back, the rock-hard chest like a wall of muscle, his arms coiled tight, and his groin shoved up against my ass. There was electricity that popped between us, crackled, like a live circuit that flowed from him, through me and back, making me jolt in his grip, pushing back into him.

The groan that came out of him was deep and low and very sexy before he clunked his forehead down on my shoulder.

It was surrender. He gave up, gave in, and my smile, had I been able to see it, would have been utterly wicked and smug.

"I really think us fighting is a bad idea," I stated softly. "It's the last thing I want to do with you."

"Me too," he confessed, his tone deep and dark. "I want us to not fuckin' argue, but it's like a minefield of shit from the past."

It was. I couldn't change the past, but I could be honest with myself about it. Brody was never guilty of anything but being a teenager who was so caught up in living his own life that he wasn't aware of everything that was going on in mine. I couldn't fault him for being human. "So, maybe we just go forward," I suggested, trying to focus but having trouble because the man was wrapped around me and turning every thought carnal. I could feel my desire twisting, clawing at my chest, wanting out, to be acted upon, no holding back. It was a primal, pulse-racing, blood-pounding need.

"You're still judging me," he said, rubbing his chin over my shoulder, "and I'm doing the same to you."

"Yes," I rasped, taking a breath instead of whimpering, which was damn impressive considering how razor-thin my control was. My emotions had been all over the place in a few short hours, and he wasn't helping. Not that I wanted him to go away or leave me alone or do anything other than just stay near me and try and build a bridge that we could meet on halfway.

"I know you were hurt, and I would give anything to fix that."

I had no doubt. "And I know you love this town and you see the good and the bad and want to help grow the good."

"I like this," he said, and I heard the happiness infuse his voice. "Compromise is good, because if it's not already clear, I want to see you. I want to be here."

"Why?"

"You know why."

I'd missed it before. I missed the reason he was hanging around. I thought he was trying to make amends for whatever he thought he'd done, or hadn't done, in the past, and then, of course, we'd argued about Braxton, and maybe he felt bad all over again, and that was the reason he stayed. Or maybe he was just hungry and a steak sounded good. I had flipped through many reasons for his continued presence, but not once had I allowed *Brody Scott wants me* to be one of the possibilities.

"You want to fuck me?"

"Fucking sounds fast," he said hoarsely. "I want you in my bed."

"Okay, then," I whispered, turning my head so I was speaking into his hair, wanting nothing more than to rub my face in it and inhale deeply. I didn't, though, not wanting to push it, to break whatever spell I had over him at the moment. "I would love to talk to you later tonight on your way home. We can start there."

He clutched tighter, and I would have crowed, but it was in poor taste. I did, however, wriggle in his grip and lift up on my toes, just enough so that my crease dragged over his groin.

His pained moan, almost too low to hear, sent a flush of prickling heat over my skin. Already I was out of my depth, swimming in the deep end. How had we come this far in so little time? Normally I was in control. Even with Aidan, when it was over, that was my choice, my say. I steered everything, made all the decisions, but with Brody...the power didn't only flow one way. Suddenly, inexorably, I was there, at a crossroads that I had never seen coming. Because if I did anything with the man at all, I knew, at the end of the summer when I drove away, I would leave my heart behind in Braxton. I had to decide, even though I'd already invited him back, if I wanted to reconsider.

I could say I was kidding, that it was a mistake or that his nearness had shorted out my brain, but I was confident, mind clear, logic returned.

"Kaenon," he husked, lifting his head at the same time.

The second my gaze met his, I knew my decision was already made. Whatever he wanted he could have. For as long as I was there, I was his. It was simple in a way it had never been before. I overcomplicated everything, rationalized and reasoned everything to death, but now, with this man, it was easy. Because yes, when I left, it would hurt, I would ache, but that wasn't now. Why on earth would I screw up the here and now worrying about the future? It was the same with Jo. I needed to live in the moment, not six months from now, not a year from now, but in the present, with her, just as I needed to with Brody.

"I love that you can't seem to let me go," I murmured, smiling at him, leaning closer so he could reach me.

His mouth was not even a hairsbreadth from mine. Normally I would take the kiss I wanted, but instead I whispered his name. He drew closer, dipped his head down, as though unsure, and I could hear my heart pounding in my ears before he lifted and kissed me.

I had thought he would be rough and take-charge, that I would be manhandled and pushed around. The opposite was true. He moved slowly, seductively, and when he broke the kiss only to turn me in his arms, I wrapped mine around his neck so he couldn't get away.

"This will hurt," he said under his breath, and I knew what he meant.

"Yes, it will," I agreed, drawing him back into the shadows, taking his mouth, kissing him languidly, expertly, until he went boneless in my arms and opened for my tongue.

I had wanted to taste him since I was fourteen, and while most things didn't live up to the hype, kissing Brody Scott certainly did.

Bumping me back into the wall, he pressed up against me, hard, and moaned when I reached down between us and groped his thickening cock. The feel of him, the weight and length in my hand, made me whimper into his mouth, the thought of riding him making me squirm.

Coming up for air, he pressed his forehead to mine, breathing my air as he panted out humid words. "When you were fourteen, I wanted to take you driving in my car, but it felt so wrong because you were just a baby, and—"

"You were only seventeen," I reminded him. "We were both young, so—"

"I was older," he insisted, and I could hear the frustration edging his voice. "It would have been like taking advantage, but the thought of you, in my lap, naked, with your beautiful long legs wrapped around my waist...I—"

I kissed him so he'd know it wasn't just his fantasy, so he could feel how much I wanted him now, because then, the past, that was over. Whatever guilt he had, whatever blame I'd assigned to him, all of that was when we were both kids. That wasn't us anymore. We were men now and could start again.

I didn't just kiss him, I kissed him breathless, mauling his mouth, sucking on his tongue, my hands all over him, in his hair, digging into his shoulders, yanking on his shirt so I could touch bare skin.

Lifting his head, breaking the kiss, he gasped for air even as he clutched me tight, making sure I couldn't move.

"I'm sorry I was carrying around anything but lust toward you." My smirk that came along with that statement assured him I thought so much more of him than that. "The anger I feel toward my family, at Everett, has nothing to do with you."

Taking a step back, letting me go, he dragged his fingers roughly through his hair. "I should've done more. I—"

"It's okay," I soothed him, my voice a fierce whisper. "Let it go, Chief Constable."

His grin even as his eyes filled, the surge of emotion—I knew because it had happened to me many times in my life—was almost too much to bear. Closure, forgiveness, balance, all those things were gifts, but it took a heavy toll on the heart.

Moving forward, I kissed him softly, my lips barely grazing his, needing him to know things were solid and good between us.

"No, don't stop."

I kissed him again, deeper, taking his face in my hands, and his hand was there, on the small of my back, pressing me forward, closer, before his other cupped the back of my neck.

I'd kissed so many men in my life and not one could light me up, head to toe, like Brody Scott. *Brody fucking Scott.* How was this even happening with the guy I'd spent nearly two decades crushing on? I wanted him almost desperately and was now, suddenly, far too close to pulling him around the side of the house and dropping to my knees.

Pushing free, I stood there panting, staring at him. "I thought you had to go."

"I thought you had something to put in my car."

"Shit," I grumbled, because I'd dropped the bags on the porch.

Darting around him, I snatched them up and walked back out to his car. I opened the front door and bent and tucked one of the bags under the seat and then did the same on the passenger side. He was there behind me when I closed the door.

"That should help, and I have some spray I'll mix up so you can do the others over the next few days."

"Thanks," he said before he leaned in and kissed me, there in the driveway, for anyone to see, bumping me back against the car.

I couldn't help it—I wrapped my arms around his neck and returned the kiss, pushing against him. When his hands went to my ass, I moaned into his mouth.

"Okay," he rasped, pulling away, letting me go and taking a step back. "I'll be by later, so you need to be out here, on the porch, waiting, because I'm going to either take you for that drive I've been dreaming about since I was seventeen, or I wanna be invited to your bedroom."

"Is that right?"

"I'll beg," he said flatly. "You want me to beg?"

I smiled at him. "No begging necessary."

"Then quit saying things like 'is that right?' Fuck yeah, that's right. I can barely think right now," he snapped, reaching for me, wrapping his arms around my waist. "I just want you."

I put my arms around his neck and leaned close, kissing the corner of his mouth. "I want you just as bad."

"Then do what I say and look for me in about an hour or

so," he grumbled, kissing my throat, taking a tender bite. "And get everybody else out of the goddamn house already."

"Just tell them to hit the road?" I asked playfully.

"Hell yes," he said, hooking his hand around the back of my neck and drawing me forward, crushing his lips down over mine.

The hunger, the throbbing, pulsing want hit me hard, had me reeling, and I put my hands on his chest to keep my balance as his tongue swept inside my mouth, tasting all of me.

He was never going to leave, because I wasn't going to let him. I was ready to take him to bed now.

His lips curved against mine, and when he eased back, the smile I'd felt was there on his face. "I think you should just go ahead and get in the car."

My laughter made him smile.

NINE

After Brody drove away, I went back inside, and Jo was in the kitchen rolling a joint.

"You have weed already?" I asked, walking over to her.

"What do you mean *already*?"

"Is that medical marijuana?"

"Of course," she informed me with a grin. "I have a supplier in Austin."

"Well, crap, I wish I'd known that yesterday when I was trying to score you some, but I ended up throwing it away because it was from that guy Hughes."

"That one was always a bad egg," she assured me, licking the end of the paper and smoothing out the joint.

I snorted out a laugh. "Kind of big, isn't it?"

"It's a doobie," she teased me, waggling her eyebrows.

"God."

She cleared her throat as I started rinsing the dishes.

"What?"

"Don't what me," she said, holding the joint but not

lighting it. "I want to know about you and Brody Scott. I saw you kiss him."

I was quiet, opening the dishwasher, loading it with the items that didn't need to be hand-washed. All the small things, like measuring cups and corn holders, had to be done individually and put on the rack to air dry.

"Hello," she sang out, her smile wide before she sighed like a lovesick schoolgirl. "I want to know what your plans are."

"I'm going to sleep with him," I confessed to her. "That's the whole plan." She was quiet, and when I noticed after a bit that she hadn't said anything more, I turned and looked at her. Her eyes were narrowed, and she was studying me. "I can tell you have an opinion."

She shrugged. "It's not my place."

"That's never stopped you before," I said, chuckling.

"Yes, but this...this is different."

"How so?"

She thought a moment. "You've carried a torch for Brody for a long time."

"I—what? I have not carried...it's not that...I wouldn't say—"

"Oh dear God," she groaned loudly. "You're ridiculous."

"I have not carried a—"

"Oh yes, you have," she countered, her voice rising as she pinned me with her deep blue gaze. "He's been a lifelong fantasy, and on your first day back, you helped him close a case."

"I don't see what—"

"Not only does he think you're amazing, considering how he went on and on about you at dinner—and I was going to throw up if he didn't quit, I swear to God—"

"You can stop that any time you want."

"Well, as I said, you've been pining, and now you're his hero."

"Pining?" I said snidely.

"Well, perhaps not pining," she agreed, taking a moment, thinking about it. "Hoping is what I meant to say. You'd always *hoped* he was a possibility from the moment you laid eyes on him in high school. And now, here you are."

"In what realm of the imagination could I have guessed that Brody Scott was in Braxton?"

"I'm sure I mentioned it."

"And I'm just as sure you didn't."

"That doesn't sound like me. I'm sure I would have dropped it into casual conversation to torture you."

"Jo—"

"I would have, because you have the hots for him bigtime."

"No one says *has the hots for* anymore."

"Well, I'm old, so I can say whatever I damn well please."

"Fine."

"And you are his hero, and he could barely stop looking at you at dinner long enough to carry on a damn conversation with anybody else!"

I squinted at her.

"Don't be obtuse, Kaenon. It's not a good look on you."

"You're reading too much into this."

"He came all the way over here just to talk to you, and even though you fought about something, he still stuck around and then stayed for dinner. And now what, you're just going to sleep with him and that's all? Just muck around with his heart?"

"Muck around?"

"Kaenon—"

"Give me a break. His heart. Are you serious?" I said irritably, because what was with the guilt trip? "How on earth could his heart be involved?"

"The same as yours is."

I made a strangled noise of disgust. "It's just sex, Jo. It's just fucking. It's nothing more than that. This isn't one of your goddamn romance novels."

"Down on romance now, are we? Since when?"

"God," I snapped at her. "Don't make a big deal out of it."

"You're getting awfully upset," she said calmly, putting the rolled joint on top of the microwave. "Why do you think that is?"

"Because you're trying to make this into more than it is," I retorted, hearing the bite in my words.

"Or you're trying to make it less."

I shook my head and returned my attention to the dishes.

"I'm not saying don't sleep with him. I certainly wouldn't put off an opportunity to do so were I fifty years younger, but don't be surprised when you find yourself swimming in much deeper water than you ever intended to."

I glanced over at her. "Nothing will keep me in Braxton."

"And yet," she said sweetly, tilting her head and meeting my gaze, "your heart was in your eyes every time you looked at him."

"You're being overly sentimental."

"And you're being an idiot," she assured me. "We'll just see who's right."

"Why don't you go smoke that," I said, indicating the joint with a jerk of my head.

She grimaced. "I don't want to do it around the kids."

"You and Peg smoked pot around me my whole life," I reminded her.

"Only at night to sleep, and you were older, and well…

you were mine by that time. I don't want Bebe and Kurt to get the idea that they should smoke anything."

"That's probably for the best," I conceded, grinning at her. "Don't want them to pick up your shitty habits."

"What time is it? Shouldn't they be going home soon?"

"It's summer," I apprised her, "and it's only a little after eight, and tomorrow's Saturday, so they're probably not in any hurry."

"That's true," she agreed.

"They all like you for some reason."

"Well, that's just crazy," she said, chuckling.

The others came in then, carrying the dishes, having cleared the table.

"Excuse me, but, Kaenon, did you promise the kids stones or something?" Maeve asked as she set one of the platters down on the counter.

"Oh, I was going to go up to the attic and see what was up there from Peg's shop."

"I'm going to make some tea," Jo announced, smiling at me, putting the joint in the pocket of the cardigan she'd put on. "I'm mad about that one you sent last month."

"You liked it?"

"Oh my, yes," she said, walking over to the cabinet above her Keurig that I had sent a year ago and pulling down a latched glass jar. "It's just like that one Peg used to make before she did a reading."

"It's close, but I think I'm missing something in it."

She shook her head. "I don't think so. I think you're just remembering all that horrid patchouli that got in everything."

I snickered. "Come on, you love that smell."

"I hate that smell!" she declared, her voice rising. "That's the reason I didn't take up that other habit we were just talking about years earlier, because all the people who did wore patchouli."

She was adorable getting all pissed off.

"Don't smile at me like I'm cute."

"Yes, ma'am."

"Come smell this, Maeve," she ordered my sister.

Maeve hurried over to my grandmother, pleased to be asked, and Rochelle followed as well, because just from listening to her at dinner, I realized she liked to be included, and both of them inhaled the contents of the jar.

"Oh, Kaenon, what is in that?" Rochelle asked, smiling at me.

"I remember the smell of that tea," Maeve said softly, her eyes on me. "And it has, let me think, chamomile, dried orange peel, spearmint, and eucalyptus, right?"

"Very good," I told her and watched, surprised, as she blushed with my praise. "There's skullcap in it too, which, as you know, is just another kind of mint, and thyme, oat straw, dandelion root, hibiscus, and lemongrass."

"Like lemon balm?" Maeve pressed me.

"No. Lemon balm is a shrub; lemongrass—"

"Is an actual grass," she said, smiling. "Got it."

"Lemon balm is minty too."

"That's right," she said quietly. "I remember Peg telling me that before she stopped talking to me."

I took a breath, considering what to say. "I'm sorry about that."

"Hey," Jo said suddenly, putting the tea down on the counter before she turned to the kids. "Why don't you two come up to the attic with me and your daddy and your aunt Rochelle, and we'll just look through the chests that are on the floor and see what we find?"

"And we'll bring whatever we find back down to Kaenon," Bebe said excitedly.

"I think that's a wonderful idea," Will agreed, reaching out to squeeze my shoulder. "Though I feel bad letting you clean up."

"No, I'll help him," Everett said huskily, clearing his throat, glancing away but still talking. "Don't worry."

"Up we go," Rochelle chirped, and then looked back at me. "Would you mind putting a pot of that tea on?"

"Absolutely not," I told her. "Do you take lemon or cream?"

"I like honey," she said softly, nodding, her eyes filling, and she wiped at them and plastered on a big smile for the kids. "Let's go."

They bolted out of the room.

It took me a second to understand why Rochelle was getting so emotional, but it had more to do with Everett than her. He wanted to fix things with me. I wasn't stupid, I saw him trying to talk to me, to engage, and she saw it too. Watching us, seeing me and him together, was gutting her.

"I'll lead," Jo announced.

"Let me walk behind you," Will implored her, taking gentle hold of her arm. "I know you're not crazy about me, but—"

"No." Jo clipped the word out and at the same time, reached up and put a hand on his cheek. "That's not true. You're a dear man, William Sanford. I've just never gotten the chance to get to know you since I'm always gone for the holidays and for big chunks of the summer. My boy needed me because I was all he had. Do you understand?"

He was choked up. It was there on his scrunched-up face, in the way he couldn't speak and in the way he nodded.

"I'd love to have you help me in the attic," she said, patting his cheek before she turned and left the kitchen.

Will glanced at Maeve and then me before he followed her out.

Alone with my brother and sister, I felt like a tightrope walker with no net. I had no idea how to be with them anymore; they were both strangers to me. It was so odd to realize that, though we were siblings, I had no connection to them at all. Instead of fixating on it, I concentrated on the task at hand. Filling the electric kettle with water, I scooped tea into the infuser and asked Maeve if she wanted to rinse and load the dishwasher or hand-wash the things that couldn't go in.

"I don't care as long as we talk."

"You can scrub pans, then. I'll load the dishwasher," I told her. "Everett, you get to dry and put away," I said, directing, not commenting on her desire to have a conversation with me.

"I don't care either," he said softly.

We worked quietly for a few minutes.

"I'm not stupid, you know," Everett said out of nowhere.

I glanced at Maeve, who appeared as confused as I was, and then turned and looked at him. "Who said you were stupid?"

"I knew Rochelle would never live in this house. I fixed it up for Jo."

"Then what was with the Facebook Live thing where you presented Rochelle with the house?" Maeve asked him.

"So Jo wouldn't know, and I figured if everyone got to laugh at me in the process—if that was what I had to do to fix it up for her, then it was a small price to pay."

"That's really selfless of you," I acknowledged, even

though there were issues with his story. "You should tell her."

He balled up the dish towel in his fist and slammed his hand down on the corner. "You don't believe me."

"What does it matter what I believe?"

"Because it does!" he admitted miserably. "You think because I took the diamond and Peg's store that those two things in any way paid for the money I put into this house."

"Let me guess," I offered as I stacked plates in the dishwasher. "You did that for Jo too. "

"You know I did! You know how much pride she has. She would have never kept the house if she thought we weren't completely square."

"Well, she would have had to suck it up since the house is in my name, but yes, you're right. She would have tried to give you money if—"

"What do you mean the house is in your name?"

"Oh for God's sake, Ev," Maeve snapped at him. "Of course everything of hers is in his name," she said, waving a hand at me. "He's her favorite. He always has been."

"No," I contradicted her, my voice harsher than I meant, but really, how could it be any other way? "She has a lot of grandchildren, and I don't mean just us. Aunt Rose, Aunt Linda, and Aunt Debbie all have kids, and we've got a sea of cousins, but I got to be hers. She got to have a motherhood do-over with me once Mom and Dad threw me out."

"Why wasn't the store in your name?" Everett wanted to know.

"Why does it matter?" Maeve said shrilly, her eyes having filled again.

"Because he was Peg's favorite too, so how did I get the store?"

"Peg just worked in the store, the cottage was what she made sure was in my name."

"Oh, so the land too, then?" Everett clarified. "The house, the cottage, the garden, the plot that goes down into the canyon, all of it is yours?"

"It is," I apprised him.

"Did Jo tell you that I wanted the land because I'm in talks with a developer about a resort here in Braxton?"

"She did not."

"It's like me and five of our cousins."

I started stacking the bowls in the dishwasher. "I'm sure there's a lot of land between here and Wimberley that will work. Everyone wants to see Blue Hole, so I'm sure a resort will be a great investment."

"That's not the point, Kae. We wanted it to be Geary land."

I took a breath. "But it's never been Geary land."

"Fine, Varlett land. You know what I mean."

"It's been in our family since Samantha Varlett came west with her mother in 1835, even before Texas was an actual state."

"I know how long our—"

"Both of those women were midwives, you know."

"Kaenon, I—"

"I'm just saying that the land comes from Jo and Peg's side of the family, not Papa's. Jo's father gave them the house when they got married and then had the cottage built for Peg."

"Yes, I know. What is your point?"

"Did you know that sweet grass doesn't grow naturally this far inland? It's not normal for it to be in hill country."

He threw up his hands in exasperation. "What does—"

"But before Jo married Papa, when she and Peg were

hiking with him, she found this random growth of sweet grass, and she told Jo right then and there that she needed to marry that guy Harvey because he was going to bring her all kinds of blessings."

"I don't—"

"Sweet grass grows wild on the Varlett land, Everett," I explained to him. "And no one ever knew until Jo found it, walking for the first time with the guy she wanted to marry."

"Please, for the love of God, tell me what this has to do with anything."

"It's a good story is all, and the sweet grass should be protected."

"Kaenon, just—"

"But there are also the fossils to consider."

"I'm sorry?"

"At the base of the canyon, there's a permanent dig there."

"What are you even talking about?"

"Jo gave the University of Kansas paleontology department permission to excavate through 2035 or something. I'd have to check the paperwork, but it's in my file cabinet at home."

His mouth fell open.

"You have to check before you leap, or put all your eggs in one basket, or whatever metaphor you'd like to attach."

He appeared shocked. Poor bastard.

"That's why it's hard to believe you when you say you fixed the house up for Jo," Maeve said, her tone sharp and accusing. "Because you don't think. You never think. You just blurt or do something and then you wonder why everything is so screwed up."

"I feel that we're not talking about my busted land deal anymore," he said snidely.

"No, we're not," she intoned and now, suddenly, her voice was icy.

"That's bullshit," he hissed at her. "You were just as guilty as I was for how you treated Kae. You and I were—"

"No," I said with absolute conviction. "Maeve stopped seeing me. To her, I was dead."

"Kaenon," she rasped. "I—"

"It's ancient history," I conceded. "In my day-to-day life, I don't ever think of you. The whole sibling thing doesn't exist anymore."

Her eyebrows scrunched up as she stared at me, and I saw the tears swamp her eyes and overflow.

"I'm not trying to hurt your feelings, Maeve, but come on, you don't think about me either. Why would you?"

She took a heaving breath. "You have no idea how—"

"It doesn't matter," I reiterated. "However you feel has nothing to do with me. But you, Everett," I said, my attention back on him. "You didn't just forget me or ignore me or tell yourself you didn't have a brother anymore—"

"Kaenon!" Maeve shouted at me, and the pain in her voice was like broken glass, scattered everywhere, jagged and sharp.

I wasn't about to stop and acknowledge her. I needed this all out in the open so everyone was clear about where we were at the moment. "What you did, Everett, was a hundred times worse than Maeve pretending I was dead."

Snatching a dish towel from the handle on the oven door, she covered her face with it before she took a shuddering breath.

"I know I fucked up, Kaenon," he declared loudly, his voice as fractured and pained as my sister's had been moments before. "I outed you in front of the whole school and—"

"You took away my choices, Everett," I explained, trying like hell to keep the betrayal out of my voice. I was going to hit him with both barrels, just blow him apart, but as I stood there, staring at him, I realized that it wasn't necessary. Me being angry, holding on to resentment, none of it was helping anything. "It wasn't my story anymore, it was yours."

It was so quiet.

"Fuck," I growled, turning off the water and walking out of the kitchen, straight out the back door and onto the deck.

I stood under a million stars, everywhere I looked bathed in shades of blue, listening to the crickets sing as the warm summer breeze slinked around me. I could smell the wildflowers and the approaching rain, and wondered about holding on to things and letting go.

There was righteous anger to consider, because it was my right to remain so, to never let Everett or Maeve forget what they did and the choices they made. And what did it matter anyway, because I wasn't in their lives and they weren't in mine. If I remained unbending, unyielding... unforgiving, what did it hurt? I was out nothing if I lived my life behind the walls I'd built. Neither one of them meant anything to me.

Except, if that was true, then why did it still twinge? The hurt was done years ago, but now and then, it was like a ghost limb; it was gone, but there was still the occasional ache.

"Hey."

Turning my head, I found Brody on the back stairs, leaning on the railing, staring at me. "There's no way I've been out here that long," I said, taking a breath.

"No."

He was beautiful to look at, my old, and now new, favorite focus.

"I came back."

"Why?"

"Well, it occurred to me that leaving you here with just Jo as backup was not the best idea ever," he said gruffly, climbing the stairs and crossing the patio to reach me, his hand immediately settling on the nape of my neck. "I think I should stay and be your buffer until everyone goes home."

"I'm not weak," I assured him even as I twisted my fingers in his shirt, holding on, not about to let go.

"I never said you were."

I couldn't count on him. It was ridiculous.

Releasing him, I turned to head back to the house, but he caught me fast, arms wrapping around my waist as he stepped in behind me, his chest pressed to my back.

"I know you can handle yourself, Kae. You had to be so strong for so long, but maybe, just for now, you could lean on me a little."

"Why would I do that?" I husked, my voice thready, stuck in a place where I was feeling too much with not enough time and space to sort through anything.

"Because you can and because you want to," he said under his breath, resting his stubbled cheek against mine.

"I don't want to," I lied, leaning my head back on his shoulder, giving him some of my weight, drinking in the closeness, the hardness of his body, the strength there.

"The fuck you don't."

"I don't want to get used to wanting you or..." And I didn't finish because the word, the thing worse than want—need—was not something to be uttered.

"So stubborn," he said, and the low chuckle made me bristle, ready to defend myself, but he turned me in his arms and hugged me.

A kiss I would have known what to do with. Heat, lust,

fucking, that was easily put into a category I could process. But hugging? He was crushing me against him, pressing me to his heart, his face buried in my shoulder as he held tight.

"You can't tear me down and then leave me all alone," I warned him, speaking into his skin, into the side of his neck, opening my mouth to taste him.

He wobbled like his knees went weak for a moment, and when he spoke, it was a rumbling growl. "You're not fuckin' listening, so really try and concentrate this time."

My desire kicked in then. I wanted to be under him.

"Are you listening?"

"Yes," I breathed into his ear.

"I've wanted you since before I even knew what that meant, and when I saw you yesterday, my first thought was holy shit, lookit me getting a chance to make things right."

"And the second?"

"The second was that you turned out even prettier than I figured you would."

"Man," I groused at him playfully, lifting his head so I could see his face, his gorgeous dark eyes, "I am sick of people saying I'm pretty. How about hot or handsome or—"

He took my mouth in a mauling kiss that I sank into. I wrapped my arms around his neck and tasted him, sucking on his tongue, pressing, grinding against him until he broke away and shoved me back.

I had a moment of concern, like maybe he was having second thoughts about me, but the tremble that ran through him, accompanied by his panting, told me everything I needed to know, and something even more surprising.

Taking a step forward, his eyes fluttered shut for a moment as I reached for his hip and held him still as I edged in close.

"We're not alone, and if you keep kissing me like that, I'm gonna—"

"What?" I teased him, grinning as I drew his full bottom lip between my teeth and nibbled before tracing the bite with the tip of my tongue.

He peeled himself away and went to the edge of the deck, into the shadows, to the side close to the house, his hands on the railing, gripping tight. Moving up behind him, I slid my hands up under his shirt, over his warm, sleek skin, and watched as he dropped his head, giving me unspoken permission.

"Where do you normally do your fucking, Chief Constable? Do you drive to Austin for a day or just a night? Do you go home with different guys, or just screw in bathroom stalls?"

"It's not like that," he answered solemnly, but his breath caught when I slowly ran my hand down over his ass and squeezed.

"I think it's exactly like that."

"People in this town know I'm bi," he told me even as his rock-hard muscles clenched under my wandering hands. "I didn't hide anything."

"But they don't see you with anyone," I countered, stepping behind him, pressing my groin to his ass, sliding my thickening cock, straining beneath two layers of fabric, along his crease. "They don't see you shiver in anticipation."

He straightened up and spun around to face me. "The hell do you think you know?"

Stepping into him, I put my hands on his hips and then kissed a line along his jaw. "I thought I wanted to be under you, but I decided that I'm going to be on top."

"I do the fucking," he informed me with a growl.

"Because you've had to, because you don't trust anyone,"

I murmured, slipping my hand around his hip and then down, under the waistband of his shorts and briefs to the top of his crease. "But you can trust me."

Instinctively, he arched his back and lifted his ass making it easier for my hand to slide lower, my middle finger dipping between his cheeks. The shudder that went through him, the heat and electricity rolling off him, brought a groan out of my chest.

"Kaenon," he ground out, pushing back, trying to get my finger inside.

"You better stay here while I get rid of my family, you understand?"

He nodded, voice gone as he swallowed hard.

"As soon as they're gone, you're mine."

"I don't let—"

"I know you don't," I said, easing my hand free and opening my mouth to suck and lave two fingers, watching his eyes as they stayed riveted on my every action.

"You can't just—"

"Stop me, then," I whispered as I eased my fingers from my mouth, letting the saliva drip off them, unbuttoning his shorts with my left hand and sliding the zipper down just a fraction.

He took hold of my wrist, and I opened my hand, pressing my palm to his already hardened cock, my other slipping down the back of his shorts again, under the waistband of his briefs, and this time dipping lower, spreading his cheeks and then pressing inside.

Bucking forward, I gripped his cock as I pushed in deep and took his mouth in a brutal kiss, all teeth and tongue.

"Kaenon," he rasped when I let him breathe, his hands gripping my shoulders as he pushed back onto my finger, gasping as I added the second, and then forward into my grip on his cock. "This is—we have to…stop."

It was insane, but the idea of having this man addicted to me, of what I could do to him, make him feel, was so much more than just hot. I had to have him, and not just for this one time. I wanted him over and over, and it was hopeless and stupid to even start, but he'd come back just for me, to be with me, because, when he drove away, he couldn't get me out of his mind.

People could say it was infatuation or lust, minimize it, try and make it nothing, but I felt familiarity and heat and something deeper, a grounding in my core that was entirely unexpected and so welcome all at the same time. It was impossible, but I wanted to keep him.

Dropping to my knees, dragging his shorts and briefs to his thighs with a sharp tug, I lifted my eyes to his as I swallowed his cock, wet with pearly drops of precum, to the root.

One hand fisted in my hair, the other grabbed hold of the railing as I worked my lips over his length, my hand there for a moment just to get my fingers slick again.

"I'm not…like this," he muttered, his breathing rough as he fucked my mouth.

When I pushed two fingers into his ass, sliding them back and forth, scissoring and stroking, his strangled, guttural cry was my reward.

"I can't—Kae, you gotta stop or I'm gonna come all over—"

Making the suction stronger, I took hold of his balls as I thrust my fingers to the spot I knew well. I'd been lavishly praised for my blow jobs by every man I'd ever given one to, and this one I wanted to be perfect.

He came hard and I swallowed fast, sucking the whole

time, laving and licking, gripping his ass with both hands, grounding him through his splintering orgasm.

When he finally went limp between my lips, I slid free and rose to my feet, easing his underwear and shorts up with me.

Instantly, he took my face in his hands and kissed me thoroughly, tasting himself on my tongue, on my lips, sucking on them before easing back to meet my gaze. Even in the faint moonlight, I could see the blown pupils and his lashes glistening with tears.

"Did you know," I murmured, "five minutes with someone who really knows you has been known to change a life?"

"I believe it," he said hoarsely, before he reached for me again. "You're like a bolt of lightning, you are."

"Is that a good thing?"

"Yeah. It's a very good thing," he said before he kissed me.

TEN

When I stepped back inside the kitchen, Everett charged across the room toward me, but stopped when he saw Brody behind me.

"You came back?"

"I wanted to see Kaenon," he rumbled out, hand on the back of my neck, squeezing for a moment, unable, it seemed, not to touch me.

Everett nodded before his eyes met mine.

"As you know, I'm going to start on the garden tomorrow," I announced to my brother. "If you want to come by at some point and help out...that would be all right."

He jerked like I'd touched him with a livewire. "It would? Are you sure?"

"Yeah," I assured him, wanting to lean sideways into Brody but standing still, crossing my arms instead. "I think Jo would really appreciate it."

"But would...would you want that?" he asked hesitantly, his breath catching.

If I wasn't honest, he'd know, so I thought about it a

moment before I answered. "I'm not sure, but I'm willing to see."

Turning his head away, when he spoke again, the words were muffled. "That's better than I—I'll be here."

"Kaenon."

My sister was leaning on the counter close to the sink, and I noted that everything was clean, nothing left for me. She and Everett had taken care of the kitchen.

"Thank you for doing all this. That wasn't my intention."

"No, I know," she said. "I just thought that—"

"Maybe you could bring the kids back," I suggested to her. "If you want."

She took a step toward me. "There's things going on tomorrow at home, activities the kids are —"

"Oh, then never—"

"But Sunday," she rushed out. "We could come back on Sunday, and I could make you guys my lasagna."

I squinted at her. "Is your lasagna any good?"

She smiled at me even as her eyes filled. "It's amazing. My roommate in college was Italian, and her grandmother taught me."

I nodded. "Okay. I'll make Peg's chicken with lemon and garlic, and we'll have Italian night on Sunday."

Maeve gasped. "You know how to make that?"

I made a face.

She put her hand over her heart. "I—that was my favorite, but I could never remember what went in it, and Dad, he had no idea."

"Do you roast the chicken?"

She nodded. "I do."

"The garlic has to be sliced like razor thin so it blackens and you lose it in the lemon juice," I told her.

"That might be what's messing me up."

"I'll show you."

The noise that came out of her, like a broken squeak toy, I just couldn't ignore the sound. Strangers on the street would have had me checking to make sure they were okay, but my sister I was going to let quietly fall apart across the kitchen from me?

It was a weird thing, wanting to hold on to my hate. Or, technically, not even hate. Because, as so many people had said over the years, hate was the opposite of love and required the same amount of focus and passion. On a day-to-day basis, she didn't occupy my thoughts. But at the moment, I wanted to cloak myself in my indifference, and I was having trouble.

I blamed Brody.

The new connection I felt to him was palpable. When I turned to look at him, he smiled softly, slowly, his hand sliding down to the small of my back.

"You're making me different."

"There's only one thing about you I hope to change," he said throatily, giving me a wan smile as he threaded his fingers through his thick hair.

I wasn't stupid. I knew what that was.

"I won't stay," I told him as I started across the floor toward Maeve.

"We'll see," he said almost smugly, but I didn't want to fight, so I went to my sister instead, stopping a couple feet away.

"There's a lot of pride in knowing you took the moral high ground that comes with holding a grudge, especially one that is righteous and just."

Maeve's watery gaze stayed riveted on my face even as her tears overflowed and ran down her cheeks and dripped off her jaw.

"Does it make me weak if I forgive you?"

She shook her head, trembling as she held herself still, not daring to take a step toward me even though I could tell she wanted to.

"Tell me," I whispered.

Deep breath in before the words came out like a dam breaking. "I'm sorry," she said, sobbing, heaving for air. "I'm so sorry. I have been for years! And you're wrong, Kae, because I think about you all the time."

I stayed quiet because, if I spoke, I'd argue with her and accuse and remain cold and unyielding, and that wasn't helping either of us.

"I know exactly what I should have done, starting with sticking up for you that day, and if I could do it again, I would change everything. There's not one thing I would keep the same."

"My whole life changed that night," I said solemnly.

"I know!" she yelled, crying at the same time. "Or, I don't know, can't truly know how you felt, but I understand, now, how much I hurt you. My life changed too, and I've been ashamed of myself ever since, because I was selfish enough to be mad at you for taking yourself away from me. I loved you so much, and then I not only lost you, but I lost Jo and Papa and Peg. Oh my God, Kaenon, I lost Peg! I lost all the history and knowledge and just…everything that had to do with being a woman and a Varlett. And it was my fault. It was *all* my fault."

I knew what she wasn't saying. All the things I'd been taught, the things I knew and the treasures that had become mine, alone, because I was the only one there to learn Peg's craft.

"I want my daughter to have what I didn't," she said, brushing away the tears from her cheeks. "And my son."

She was beautiful with her glistening eyes and apple-shaped face staring up at me with hope and trepidation and fear all wrapped up together.

"And I'm terrified of what you're going to say, because I want this more than I can truly express, but, Kaenon...could you please just forgive me for being an idiot?"

I'd been fourteen. She'd been fifteen. And the question was, would fourteen-year-old me have forgiven her?

The answer was that fourteen-year-old me would have leaped at the chance to have his sister back. How could my choice now be any different?

I gestured for her, and she sprang at me like she was shot out of a canon. She hit me so hard I grunted as her arms locked around my neck and her legs around my waist.

The sobbing was instant. She could barely catch her breath as she clutched at me, hard. It took me a second, feeling her come apart in my arms, to dip my head and hug her tight.

"Forgive me," she wailed, and I heard it, her heartbreak and frustration over having no control of the situation to fix anything.

I had taken the power I gave her when we were little. Growing up, she'd been my world. She was closer to my age, my partner in crime. She led, I followed. But once she abandoned me, I had shut her off from me. Forever. There was no going back, no do-over, no second chance.

"I've written you so many letters, and I put them in envelopes, and then put them in a box," she rasped between sniffling. "I was just so terrified of you turning me away, and it was gutless, and I should have just thrown myself up against whatever wall you put up, but I just...I have my kids and my life too and—Oh, Kae, honey, I'm so sorry."

She broke down again, washed away in a flood of tears, and I exhaled.

I breathed out all the pain, the betrayal, all of it, and squeezed her so tight that she squeaked. When her head lifted, I smiled at her through my own tears and hers. She was tentative at first, biting her bottom lip, and then, slowly, her own smile grew bigger and brighter, and that did warm, soft things to my heart, because the sister-sized hole she'd left in me was now plugged back up. She was there, and I felt her and saw her sweet little face once more.

"You suck," I told her.

She nodded, her voice abandoning her.

"But I do too, because I'm a grown-up now," I said as I set her on her feet.

Lifting up, she wiped away my tears and held my face in her hands. "I love you so much, and when I saw you with my kids, I thought my heart was going to explode."

I wiped her eyes, gently, and put my hands on her shoulders.

"You were so kind to them, and you could've taken out your anger at me on them, but you just went right into teacher mode. And yes, I know exactly where you work and what you do—"

"Maeve—"

"You acted like an uncle, and when I told you that the kids said you were going to find them some stones, it almost broke my heart because it was all so normal, and yet, I knew it wasn't. The kids could have you, and so could Will, but not me. Never me."

I grabbed and hugged her again, and she melted against me, soaking me in.

"Just the fact that you were willing to see them, to be yourself with them...who does that? Who doesn't hold a grudge against the family of the person you hate?" she said into my chest, her arms wrapped around me, holding on for dear life.

"Hate is a strong word. Hate takes a lot of energy."

"Yes. I just want you to love me again."

"For fuck's sake, Maeve—I never stopped loving you."

She lost it all over again, and I sent her to the bathroom to wash her face. I went to the sink, took a breath, splashed water in my eyes and then scrubbed my face with paper towels.

"You should blow your nose," Brody suggested, and I saw him wipe under both his eyes as well. His voice, a smoky bourbon rumble, soothed every little part of me.

"On a paper towel?" I asked indignantly. "What are we, barbarians?"

He chuckled as I blew my nose, loudly, and then he hooked a hand around the back of my neck and eased me into his arms. It felt way too much like coming home, like shelter and sanctuary and safety, and I should have pulled free and not leaned in and given him my weight, but there was just no way.

"So, what? Everyone but me gets forgiven?"

I lifted my head up off Brody's solid shoulder so I could see Everett.

"I know what I did."

Stepping free of Brody, I faced Everett as he stalked across the kitchen to stand in front of me.

"Maeve did what she did passively."

"Yes," I agreed, my voice husky from crying, hoarse and nasally.

"I did what I did actively," he explained. "I did things to you purposely."

I nodded.

Carefully, slowly, he reached out and took hold of my shoulder. "I want to see you over the summer. I want to try. I want to see what I can do, if anything, to fix this."

I couldn't get over how much he looked like my father. It was uncanny, really, and that wasn't helping anything between us.

"And I want to see Jo too."

"Of course," I sighed. "I mean, yes, I think I love her more than the rest of you do, but I'm also smart enough to know that that's my own ego talking. There's no way I know the depth or your heart, or Maeve's, or any of our cousins'."

"True," he agreed. "But"—he squeezed my shoulder —"will you try and keep an open mind where I'm concerned?"

"I'll try," I told him as the room imploded with everyone returning at once: the kids, Jo, Will, and Rochelle from the attic, and Maeve from the bathroom.

"Honey," Will said sharply, rushing over to her. "Are you okay? Have you been crying?"

"Yes," she told him, slipping into his arms even as she looked over at me. "But the good kind of tears, the happy ones."

The kids pushed around Everett and shoved stones into my hands.

"Where the hell is my tea?" Jo groused from the other side of the room.

MAEVE WAS WRUNG OUT, and so she promised that she and the kids would be back Sunday morning right after church. Kurt was happy with his small slab of rough fire agate after I explained to him that it was for protection and that he should put it on his nightstand when he got home, and Bebe was in love with her labradorite palm stone shot through with beautiful flashes of teal and blue. They both made me promise to find them more stones so we could talk about them when they came back.

Will hugged me really tight and really long, and I understood. I'd been good to his kids, and his wife and I were on the road to reconciliation. All in all, a pretty good visit.

I had just started to make tea when the house phone rang and, interestingly enough, it was for Brody. Evidently he'd left his phone in the car by mistake, and they needed him down at the station. It was funny that they knew where he was, but then, the town was only so big.

"I never leave my phone anywhere," he grumbled as he strode toward the front door. "I'm always—you're screwing with my brain, Kaenon Geary!"

"Why am I in trouble?" I asked Jo as she fired up her joint, waved at the smoke, and then reached for a nonexistent cup.

"Oh, that's right," she said sarcastically. "I don't have tea yet."

I rolled my eyes at her, and she cackled as I got back to work.

Fifteen minutes later, I had the teapot on the table along with honey, lemon, and milk. When I put the sugar down, Rochelle picked up the clear, hinged jar and looked at the bottom.

"What are you doing?" Everett asked as he rifled through what looked like one of Peg's old jewelry boxes. It was one of the ones she used to have on display in the shop. There were six drawers in all, but instead of it being filled with necklaces and bracelets and rings, it was filled with various-sized stones.

"Is this sugar?" Rochelle asked me.

"It is," I said with a yawn before smiling at her. "It's got lavender in it too, that's what you're seeing mixed in there. I used the rose one for the margaritas earlier."

"And you just mix sugar with whatever you want?"

"Yeah. It's just organic herbal-infused sugar. It won't hurt you."

"No, I didn't think it would, I just—did Peg use sugar in her spells?"

"It's not a spell, per se," Jo told her, taking another hit from her ridiculously oversized joint. "Peg used to say that people could be sweetened up is all, and if you added things to the sugar, it gave it even more properties and chances to do good."

"Well, I don't know about that," Rochelle said, putting the jar down and smiling at me. "But it's lovely to look at."

I nodded, taking the joint Jo passed me.

Everett and Rochelle both took a hit as well, before pouring themselves some tea.

"What is this?" Everett asked, holding up a small, round tumbled stone.

"That's a carnelian," Rochelle informed him.

He looked at me and I nodded.

"Oh, you rat, you didn't believe me," she said, laughing, swatting his arm.

His grin was wide, and suddenly he looked more like my grandfather than my father, and that warmed me up inside.

"It's the dimples," Jo sighed, reaching out to touch Everett's face. "He has your grandfather's dimples."

He leaned into her hand for a moment and then held up another stone.

"That's turquoise," she answered, and I nodded when he glanced at me.

"How 'bout if she's wrong, I'll tell her," I said, chuckling as she swatted him again.

"Fine," he teased, his grin full of mischief.

They were good together, and watching Jo as she in turn watched the two of them, her chin propped on her hand as she sighed, was nice. She looked quite content.

I was surprised that Rochelle knew her stones.

Rhodonite, aquamarine, blue lace agate, jade, amazonite, red jasper, blue apatite, citrine, kambaba jasper, rose quartz, and everything the stones did. She didn't get hung up until carnelian and fire quartz.

"How do you know?" she asked me, leaning in close to look at the stone in my hand.

"Peg would catch me on this all the time, and she would say, 'You should be able to tell from the vibration of the stone,' but that requires a level I'm not at."

"He was when he was in the shop every day," Jo told Rochelle. "He could sort them by touch. It was amazing."

Rochelle turned to me, and I shook my head. "She's screwing with you."

"Everett, hit Kae," Jo directed him with a mischievous cackle.

"No, ma'am," he told her, "I'm trying to get him to like me."

She grinned at him. "I wouldn't worry."

Ignoring her, I pointed out the red hematite striations in the stone. "You have to remember that carnelian is that darker, deeper red, even when it's more transparent. And yes, some people sell carnelian with agate in it so the colors get wild, but you can still tell it apart from fire agate or fire quartz, if you really look."

"What's the vibrational difference?"

So I talked to Rochelle as Jo and Everett chatted, and

every now and then, Everett would pull something out of the box that I would really have to look at.

"That's dravite," I informed him, passing the stone back. "It's brown tourmaline and—what is that?"

Jo waggled her eyebrows at me as I looked at what could only be described as a cigarette ring holder. "This way I don't get stains on my fingers."

"Yes, but who gave this to you?"

"Me," Rochelle chimed in. "It's a replica of the one Sabrina's aunt Zelda uses on *The Chilling Adventures of Sabrina*. It's on Netflix."

I squinted at her. "You wanted to be a witch when you were little, didn't you?"

"Still," she assured me.

"Okay," I said, grinning at her as she leaned into my side. "And you, old woman, you feel fancy with that, do you?"

Jo nodded. "And I don't burn my fingers either. It's a lot easier to use than the roach clip I got along with my last order. That wasn't glamorous at all."

I couldn't stop laughing.

BRODY CALLED my cell as I was lying in bed hours later, dozing, about ready to pass out, emotionally drained from the day I'd had.

"I'm guessing I'm not getting laid," I teased him.

"Oh, that's happening, just not tonight."

"Are you okay?"

"Yeah, I'm fine; it's just that one of my deputy constables told Hughes that you were the one who gave us the tip about where his stash was, and he used his one phone call to call his supplier and put out a hit on you."

"And yet, you don't sound concerned for my safety."

"Kae, he called his supplier from the station."

I snorted out a laugh.

"From the station, Kae," he repeated. "Holy fuckin' shit."

I had to put my pillow over my face so I wouldn't laugh too hard and wake up Jo. Once I had myself under control, I got back on the phone.

"And so..." I drawled, still giggling since I was just a bit high.

"And so, I called Austin PD, they traced the call and picked up some other small-time middleman fucker, but it doesn't even matter because Hughes is dead meat. They put out a hit on him, so I'm handing him over to Austin PD so they can sit on him and the guy he implicated."

"Oh, that ought to be a blast."

"Don't get me wrong, I'm thrilled to have Hughes out of this town, and I don't need the official kudos. It's enough that he's gone."

"But?"

"But it sucks because I have to stay here until the detectives from Austin show up to take him into custody."

That made sense. "Well, I'm sorry you're stuck there, but it's probably for the best. I'd be crappy in bed. I'd just want to snuggle and sleep."

"Huh."

"See? I told you. It would be a—"

"It sounds great," he sighed.

And the way he said it, longingly, gave me the impetus to ask. "Are you working tomorrow?"

"No. Why?"

"Maybe you'd like to pack a bag and come help me in the garden and stay all day and sleep in my bed tomorrow night."

"Oh fuck yes, please. Whatever I have to do to have that, I'm in. I'll work all day."

I chuckled softly. "Just sleep in and come over whenever you can."

"It's a deal," he rumbled, and man, did he sound good over the phone. "I'll talk to you tomorrow, but right now I have to write up my deputy for talking to a suspect about a confidential informant. Hopefully three days of unpaid administrative leave will help him retain the lesson."

"This is about me."

"It certainly is."

"You realize the deputy was probably gloating and not ratting me out."

"The three other deputies wanted to kick the shit out of him. They think he should be altogether done. I haven't made up my mind yet, but since he's Pete Waylon, Dean Waylon's little brother, I had thought to get back at Dean for what he did to you, through Pete."

"No, Brody, that's not you."

"Which is why I haven't done it already," he admitted. "Plus, you know, I think Dean already reaped the whirlwind as it were."

"What do you mean?"

He cleared his throat. "Two weeks in at the University of Florida, he got suspended from the football team for drugs and alcohol. They gave him a couple chances to clean up, but he never did and was cut from the team the week before homecoming."

"And he's been here ever since?"

"No. He stayed in Florida. Last I heard from Pete, he was working in Tampa as a security guard, and his third wife was taking him to court for more alimony."

"Yeah, okay. Leave Pete out of my thing with his brother."

"That's what I was thinking. I'll just write his ass up."

I smiled into the phone.

"You're thinking I'm pretty great right now, aren't you?"

"I'm thinking that I really appreciated you being around today even when we argued. Thank you."

"Promise me you'll let me come around."

"I promise."

"Talk to me until you fall asleep."

So I did.

ELEVEN

I'd missed the moment in time that Davis Winter became a crazy person.

"Seven in the morning?" I whined, squinting at him as he stood at the back door. "Davis, I haven't even had coffee yet."

"Which is fine," he assured me, cheerfully, passing me a box of donuts and a huge cup of coffee from Hot Brew, which had been a staple in the town since before I was born. "I brought crullers and bear claws and those cream-filled donuts you used to like."

Used to like meant what I'd loved back in the eighth grade. His reference point for a friendship was almost twenty years old. The important part, though, was that he had made an effort, and so I thanked him, profusely, and had him come in to have donuts with me and Jo.

I hadn't expected that Davis wouldn't only bring the tractor and the bush hog, but a guy to drive it as well. It was Kevin Carlisle, who I had also gone to school with. He was thrilled to see me, made quick work of the weeds, and then his wife, Janey, arrived with the backhoe because, as I suspected, once everything was cut down, the soil needed to be turned. She was lovely, an absolute whirlwind of activity, and when the three boys from the market were there promptly at nine, she gave them all Red Brick Hardware hats and heavy gloves and hoes and showed them how the dirt needed to be smoothed back into rows. She and her husband had worked with Davis she told me, and they had been partners since we graduated from high school.

Angie, Davis's wife, was overwhelmed to see me, hugged me so hard, said how sorry she was for how she'd acted in the ninth grade and that, apparently, from the tenth grade on, much like her husband, she'd tried talking to me, but to no avail. I had missed quite a bit when I was off the soccer field with my head down and earbuds in.

My old coach, Mr. Ochoa, came by with his family, and they brought a huge cooler filled with chicken patties, hot dogs, and hamburgers. He was as thrilled to see me as I was him, and I was even more thrilled to hear that he and his wife, Sydney, who he brought with him, had reconciled. In high school, they had been separated, maybe getting a divorce, maybe not, and his kids had lived with her in Austin. As I'd never met his children before, it was weird to suddenly be presented to a son, who was my age, and a daughter the same age as Maeve.

When the plants started arriving along with rock and gravel I hadn't ordered, I bolted around the first truck as the door opened and the driver jumped down.

"I think there's been a mistake on the order," I informed him.

"No," he said, smiling, shaking his head. "You took care of my sister. Now we're taking care of you." His smile fell away a bit as he leaned in close and his voice lowered. "And please, you don't want to insult my father by saying no to his gift. It's not polite."

I crossed my arms and scowled at him. "You're trying to intimidate me into taking a gift? I told your mother yesterday that—"

His groan of irritation was unexpected. "Please, man, just—it was from this job I overestimated by just a bit."

My mouth fell open as I gestured at the back of the truck. "Are you kidding?"

He winced like his whole life hurt. "My father said, 'Take it to him and see if he wants it. If he wants it, good. If he doesn't, you come back and bag it and make sure it sells.'"

"Are those big pieces flagstone?"

He let his head fall back on his shoulders like he was in agony. "Yep. And the rest is Mexican Beach Pebble and river rocks."

Not in a million years had I even considered such a thing for the garden. I didn't have that kind of money for all I would need.

"Are you sure?"

His head dropped forward, and he stared at me warily. "Yeah. Why? You think maybe you want it?"

"Well, hell yeah, I want it. I just can't afford it if you change your mind."

He clamped his hands on my biceps. "We only invoiced you for the crushed granite gravel, some red brick, and some large calcite pieces my father threw in that I didn't bring."

I didn't need any of that if I had what he brought me. It would be far more beautiful than I anticipated. "Then yes, I'll take it, and please, thank your father for his generosity."

He made a face. "You made his daughter happy, you win. She's the kid that doesn't fuck up, you know?"

"Hang in there, it'll get better, and he'll see you want to help him."

He grunted as he offered me his hand. "I'll let you know when that changes, and I'm Joaquin, by the way."

"A pleasure," I assured him, taking his hand.

Once everything was unloaded, I told the boys—Artie, Mike, and Vance—to go up on the porch and have breakfast with my grandmother and my sister-in-law. Rochelle and Everett had showed up, and Rochelle was making burritos with eggs and peppers and chorizo, and it appeared they were good even if I hadn't gotten one yet. Jo was sitting, pouring orange juice and coffee, thrilled to pieces to have so many people around. She was an extrovert, my grandmother, always had been, and loved to entertain. It was nice to see her in her element, in a beautiful long-sleeved white shirt with the sleeves rolled up, black trousers that came to the ankle, and flat slingbacks. She looked like Audrey Hepburn, lounging on the patio, the messy-pixie style she'd worn since brachytherapy had taken her hair, flattering her features. I loved it the moment I saw it, and now, the style combined with its icy-silver color only added to her beauty.

Walking up on the porch, I checked on Rochelle, who was still cooking for the three boys. The new barbecue converted into a regular grill with the click of a switch, and each of them had already had four burritos apiece—they were small, but still, holy crap, I'd forgotten what bottomless pits boys were at seventeen—and were all looking at her as though she were a goddess.

"I rented some misters and industrial fans from Davis as well," I told her as I came up beside her. "I'll bring you one so you don't overheat out here."

She turned then and kissed me, wiped lipstick off my

cheek, and then smiled like I was the most radiant creature on the planet. "Thank you, Kae."

Moving away from her, I heard my name called and saw more people out in the garden. Everett was waving at me, trying to get my attention.

"Coming," I called out as I bent over Jo. "How are you?"

She smiled at me before she put on the oversized Prada sunglasses I'd bought her in New York when I was there in the fall on a speaking engagement.

"Did you eat?"

"Yes, I did," she reported, grinning as she sipped her morning tea. "Rochelle makes a mean burrito, and your guacamole from last night is still good."

I smiled at her and kissed her forehead. "If you get tired, yell for me. And you don't need to stay out here in the heat."

But as I said it, three girls I didn't know carried a chaise over with a fan and an umbrella that fit into a slot in the deck. They made Jo her own little island.

"Hi," I greeted them.

I understood, after a few minutes, they were the boys' girlfriends, and they came to see what was going on with me, who I was, and decided to stay. The three of them were lovely, but really, Artie's girlfriend, Sandy, was the stunner of the group. Tall and willowy, with luminous ochre skin, she had me pinned in place with her stare until she offered me her hand. When I took it, her handshake was firm and serious, all business, which basically informed the situation for me. She had to be one of Maria De Leon's friends.

"So," she began coolly, sizing me up, scowling as though she already found me lacking. "Maria says that you could give me a list of books to read to prepare for the AP English exam next year. Is that true?"

I winced. "As you know, I'm not on staff there at the high school, and I'd hate to step on anybody's toes by—"

"Mr. Hastings said that I couldn't take the summer course because I wasn't ready," she said, and again I saw it, the laser focus of her dissecting stare. "But I'm in his class in the fall. Already enrolled and everything, so I ask you, what the hell is that about? The boys get the reading list but not me? Not Maria? Not my friend Nidra?"

"Maybe you and your parents and Maria's and Nidra's should all go see your principal."

"Actually," she said, tipping her head at me in a way I knew from my teaching assistant at home, Belinda Galloway. She, too, would tip her head just a bit before she said something horrible. "My father, Hyrum Reed, the Mayor of Braxton, he's going to be by in just a bit to speak to you."

"I'm sorry, what?"

"The mayor," she repeated, slowing down her words, since I was old and couldn't follow along, "is coming by to see you about Mr. Hastings."

"What?" I gasped.

She turned to Jo. "Mrs. Geary, you understood what I said, didn't you?"

"Yes, my darling, and so does he, but he has to go direct those people in the yard, so let him go, and you all read me some *Hamlet*."

I looked to Jo for help.

"Did you know that you can read Shakespeare any way you like, because there are hardly any stage directions in his plays?"

I squinted at her.

"The girls were telling me all about it."

Only then did I notice that all three of them had textbooks. It was summer vacation, and they were going to read *Hamlet* to my grandmother.

"Kaenon!"

I whirled around and saw Everett, arms spread out, and only then noticed that there were at least twenty-five people in the yard, all waiting for me to tell them what to do.

"Sorry," I called over to him, bolting for the stairs.

Rochelle made me grab a burrito on the way, and a bottle of water.

"It's Texas in the summer," Rochelle reminded me. "Hydrate."

I did as I was told.

I REMEMBERED where everything went in the garden, but I purposely pretended not to so Everett could correct me. It was evident he could have placed everything as well, but Jo hadn't trusted him to do so, and that had hurt. He'd put her house back together, after all, and as I stood in Peg's cottage, staring at a new black-and-white chevron tile on the floor in the kitchen—the exact color and design as Jo's kitchen— that gave it a nice symmetry, flat black walls and glossy black and glass door cabinets with silver hardware, I was overwhelmed. Seeing Peg's old mortar and pestle there, as though just waiting for her to use it again, caused a lump in my throat that was hard to speak around.

"Jo didn't tell me you renovated the cottage too."

He was pleased. I could tell from the aw-shucks attitude, the sheepish smile, and the flush of his skin, like he was embarrassed. "I didn't do it all, because I didn't know if you or Peg would have liked that."

The back door of the cottage was a Dutch door, and Peg had always left it open in the summer to let in the breeze from the forest that was a mere ten feet away on the other side of the fence, overgrown and wild. There was a tiny greenhouse there when I was growing up, but it had been gutted by a storm, and Peg had torn it down, saying that all green things wanted to live outside. I wondered what she would have thought of the wisteria that grew there now.

"You planted that?" I asked him as we stood together on what could only be called a stoop, pointing at the gorgeous, healthy plants.

"Yeah," he shrugged. "She liked the smell, remember? That and freesia and the lilac."

I turned to look at him. "Why are we doing this?"

"Doing what?"

"Don't play dumb; it's annoying as hell."

He exhaled sharply. "Really, just—"

"Why are we going through this ruse?" I revealed irritably, tired of him pretending he had no idea where anything went when the opposite was true.

"I don't—what do you mean?"

"Oh for fuck's sake, Everett, you remember this garden just as well as I do! You don't need me out here. You can—"

"But I can't grow anything," he choked out, torn, I could tell, between yelling at me and being afraid to. "You and Peg—Jo's right, you just have this bond to the land that I've never had."

"When did Jo tell you I had a—"

"Years ago," he growled at me. "She said that you and Peg were special, and you both have this thing inside you, this light, and the longer you stayed here, in this town, on the Varlett land, on our homestead or whatever you want to call it, the stronger and brighter the light gets."

"Oh, that's crap!" I insisted, uncomfortable suddenly, feeling caged, the space too small to begin with, now nearly claustrophobic with him taking up half of it even though we were standing outside. "She's been saying that for forever, and we both know—"

"That's how it was for Peg."

"Maybe," I rasped, conceding that and only that. "We both know when she'd come home from being away longer than just the summer—"

"She was gray," he said flatly. "She always looked gray when she came back."

I shrugged.

"It was like she was all wrung out."

"Old," I muttered.

He made a face. "Not just old," he said solemnly. "Drained. She would almost be sapped of her life force, and then two or three days of walking barefoot in the grass and the dirt, she was good as new."

What he was taking as grounding, as her drawing power from the earth, didn't work that way. If that was what had happened, she shouldn't have ever gotten run-down, because there was good old terra firma all over the globe. No, it wasn't the land itself but, instead, being home where she could finally rest. It was as simple as that.

When Peg traveled, she never slept, she drank too much, did too many drugs, and fucked whoever she wanted and was always gone before dawn. She never slowed down because she had to get what she considered her vices out of her system away from Braxton. She wanted to be thought of in a specific way when she was at home. Not proper in the context of how the close-minded people in town would have defined it, but wise. She wanted to be construed as a healer and a witch, but didn't want her carnal appetites discussed, so she never indulged them at home. Until Chief Constable Eustace Coltrane was elected. Him...she just couldn't say no to. I had teased her often that it was because he sounded like Sam Elliot, who she'd always had a thing for. I had hoped he'd move in, but when her doctor found first the lump in her breast and then realized that it had metastasized, the cancer moving to her kidneys with lightning speed, she sent the cowboy with the heart of the lawman away. She wanted him to live. He wasn't about to do it without her.

She lived long enough to see me graduate with my BA, but I could tell, when I picked all three of them up at the airport, how sick she was. She'd squeezed me so hard before she left, and made me promise to fly my grandparents somewhere special when the time came.

"I'll come home," I told her.

"Don't you dare," she ordered, and her voice left no room for argument.

At the end, she was too weak to keep Eustace away, though, and Jo told me that she and my grandfather had waited outside so they could say their goodbyes. Eustace was gone a month later, his great big heart giving out one night as he lay in a hammock on what was then a postage stamp of my grandparents' back porch. It was hard starting grad school in the fall knowing they were both gone, both Peg and Eustace. I was never so thankful for my grandparents after that.

"Listen," I began with a sigh, giving voice to my thoughts. "Before Coltrane, Peg did too many drugs, drank too much alcohol, and broke her heart over too many people. That was what ran down her battery, not being away from the land."

"I don't know," he said sharply. "You have your theory; Jo and I have ours."

"Oh, so what, you and Jo are in solidarity over this?" I asked dramatically.

"Don't do that, don't be all snide. It was probably the hard living, like you said, but there is something to the land giving her strength the same way it does you."

I shook my head before I walked back inside the house. "The land does nothing for me."

"What did you say?" he yelled behind me. "Kaenon? What the fuck did you say?"

"I said," I answered fast, my voice brittle, cold, pivoting to face him as he slammed shut the bottom of the Dutch door behind him but left the top open, "the land does nothing for me!"

"Is that right?"

"Yes, that's fuckin' right!"

"That's bullshit, and you know it."

"No," I corrected him. "What you said was total crap."

His glare was dark.

"You don't believe me?"

"I see you, Kae; you glow." I opened my mouth to retort, but he raised his hand. "It's true. It's nothing to fight about or argue over, it just is. Simple as that."

"I don't even know what you're saying," I stated, frustrated that he was so certain of something that made no sense. Because yes, all my life I'd seen Peg do things that defied logic, but I certainly wasn't her and could never hope to be. Peg had glowed. People, animals, even stupid sunflowers would turn in her direction. Our neighbor complained all the time that his roses uprooted themselves trying to get through the fence, and he finally gave up and told Peg to keep the yellow tabby that was slavishly devoted to her. "You know, Ev, you haven't seen me in years. This is what I fuckin' look like now, all right? It's just me."

"No," he was adamant, his face scrunched up, bristling like an animal in a cage as he began to pace. "You're not listening because it's me and you wanna fight, but just from yesterday to today—you're like some golden lion stalking around here."

I stared at him. He stared back.

When I smiled, slowly, insidiously, arching one eyebrow for him, he flipped me off. "Are you kidding me right now?"

"Fine, fine," he groused, conceding the point, throwing up his hands before gesturing over my shoulder. "What about the plants, Kae? Huh? What about them?"

He was talking in circles. All of us grew things in the garden. He was being ridiculous. "Everett, you—"

"Jo's little orchard went to seed the year you left for college."

"Oh, come on, you know exactly why that happened."

"Yeah, I do know, because I was here," he asserted. "Jo was at the end of her rope. She tried everything to keep those trees alive. She met with horticulturists and tree doctors and all those big firms that promise they can cure anything by spraying."

"The bigger issue was that Jo was just one person, and she didn't have anyone helping her with the—"

"No. Nothing worked because you were gone, and Peg was off traveling. The trees died of a broken heart."

"You have lost your mind."

I remembered how sad Jo had been to lose first the citrus trees—two orange and two lemon. The apple trees went next, the Gala and the Granny Smith; then the avocado, that was the oldest; and finally, the lime before what was, for Jo, the saddest of all, the cherry trees that Peg had brought her as saplings from Japan.

"Nobody who came to save the trees had any idea how to

help. Not really," he continued. I hadn't given the trees much thought at the time as I'd been in New York, attending school and playing soccer. "Everyone said the same thing to Jo, 'Lady, you're lucky they've lived this long, because none of them make any sense in this arid environment.'"

"Well, see? That was probably as long as they were going to live anyway," I said, hearing the guilt in my own voice, wishing I had been able to set foot back in the town before two days ago. The issue was, of course, that when I'd run from Braxton when I was eighteen, I never thought I'd be back. I had arrogantly assumed Peg would outlive all the rest of us, so my presence in town would forever be unnecessary. And it wasn't that I believed what Everett was saying about the magic of me being here, but I had watched Peg care for those trees, and I would have done something, tried anything, to save them. They were Jo's, after all.

"The orchard was good when Peg was home, and then when she was off seein' the world, it still bloomed, it still flowered, and still bore fruit as long as *you* were still around. The second you were both gone—Peg passing, you in another state—the fruit trees were dead."

But that was ridiculous, nature didn't work like that.

"Have you looked at all the cut-off trunks? Have you been back there yet?"

"No, I—"

"It's like a graveyard."

"Thanks for that," I groused at him. "You know, it's not easy to be—"

"Jo told me that in the Varlett line there have always been seers and healers and witches, and whether you like it or not—"

"Nature works or it doesn't, Ev. There's not a lot of mystery to it. The trees died for whatever reason, and I'm not some plant whisperer. Look at the wisteria that you planted outside, I just saw it, and it looks great."

"You don't get it."

"Do you want to go take another look at it, because I promise you, it's growing."

He shook his head. "It's been there, like, three days," he confessed. "I put it in when I knew you were coming, but it won't thrive. It'll either stay that size or just wither away. You should see our landscaping at home. It's stunning, but I don't do it. We have a whole battalion of guys who make it work."

I nodded, studying him—the droop of his shoulders, the resignation that clung to him, and the way he couldn't stand still. I had to focus on something other than what he perceived as a shortcoming. And that, in and of itself, was a huge paradigm shift for me, because really, when was the last time I gave a crap about what my brother thought?

"So," I began, clearing my throat and pointing to the left, into the tiny room beside the back door, "I love that you left her floor-to-ceiling shelves and her locked cabinets in the apothecary. I can tell it was cleaned up in there, but even the barn-wood floors are the same."

"Peg always said that the floors where things were made was where everything that spilled should be left to soak in because—"

"—there are no accidents," I finished for him. "I remember."

He nodded.

"You know, I'm surprised that the shelves are still holding up."

"Why?"

"It's all carved teak."

"Meaning what?"

"Well," I gestured at it. "The termites might not want it, but it's not all that durable."

We both looked at the bookshelves. They looked the same as they always had.

"They look pretty good," Everett said, turning to me. "I wasn't here by then, so I have to ask, did she really have all of this carved in Laos and shipped over here?"

"No. Peg was there and met a beautiful woman who turned out to be an amazing carpenter," I explained to him. "She came over from Laos and stayed here for a year, carving those shelves, and when she was done, she and Peg went to Bali together." I still remembered Vatsana, the carpenter who'd stayed in the cottage with Peg. She was an artist, wholly committed to her craft of carving the shelves from the enormous pieces of imported teak. I got the feeling that being with Peg had been her vacation, and then the time was over. After Bali, Peg came home, and Vatsana returned home to Luang Prabang. Peg had worn the beads Vatsana hand-carved for her for the rest of her life.

"I still can't believe those huge sections are all single pieces."

"Probably worth a lot of money if you uninstalled them," I hedged, waiting.

"I would never," he rasped. "And I know you don't know me anymore, but I promise you the thought never even crossed my mind."

I grinned at him. "I know."

He'd been staring at his feet, but when I spoke, his head snapped up and his eyes focused on me, studying me. "You do?"

"Yeah, I do," I said hoarsely, feeling it in my gut, the change overwhelming in such a short space of time. It was seeing what he'd done, how much he cared about making Jo comfortable, and honoring Peg's memory. I couldn't help but really see him, who he was now, the man standing in front of me, as the memories of the boy who'd betrayed me all those years ago faded into the background just a bit more.

He sucked in a breath and pointed. "Those cabinets in the middle are still locked."

Lifting one of the five necklaces I always wore, three on leather cords, two on silver chains, I showed him the brass key, now patinaed, that hung beside a sterling silver watch key.

Closing the distance between us, he took gentle hold of the key. "Are you kidding me? This key is for that?"

I nodded.

"The hell, Kaenon." He sighed, smiling slowly. "I thought, there's no way that anyone has a key, so I called every locksmith I know in Austin, but they all said that it would have to be drilled out and that, of course, would crack the wood. I couldn't crack the wood."

"So you left it alone," I said, slipping the chain over my head and passing it to him. "Good man. Now you get to open it, and you can have the watch key that's with it when we're done."

He stared at me in absolute shock.

I let out a deep breath and took hold of his shirt, my fingers curling into the fabric as I felt the hot sting of tears before my vision blurred with them.

Holding the watch key, his face pinched, and I saw he was fighting his own tears even as I brushed mine away. "This is the watch key for Papa's watch? For Papa's pocket watch, the one that belonged to *his* father, the one I've had since Papa died but could never wind because it was specially made?"

"Of course it is," I whispered, because my voice was gone.

"He left me that watch," he reiterated, as if I'd forgotten.

"Yes, he did. And he told me to take the key and hold on to it until I forgave you."

It was lucky he'd put new furniture in Peg's cottage. There wasn't much, not much could fit in four hundred square feet, but the loveseat was a nice addition and was apparently sturdy. It took his weight when he dropped down onto it, and at six-two, just like me but heavier, at least two hundred pounds, my brother was not a small man.

He bent, put his face in his hands, still holding my chain with both keys, and sobbed.

I gave him a moment to gather himself and then took a seat beside him and put my hand on his back, gentle but firm enough for him to know that I was there if he needed me. Taking a deep breath, he raised his head and turned to me, eyes puffy and red, tears running down his face, looking like I'd just killed his puppy.

"You kept this."

"Yes."

"But now you're—now you want me to...and it's my watch, so then—Jesus, Kae, what else do you have of Papa's?"

"I have his chess set. I have all his books and his compass. I keep that on my nightstand."

He was trembling as he stared at me.

"Wind the watch and carry it with you. He would like that."

"I can't—I have to—it's too much to just sit here, and so if you're not ready to forgive me, then—"

I leaned into him and grabbed him as tight as I could.

He took a deep, shaky breath and then hugged me back just as hard.

It was short, not like it had been with Maeve. We let go at the same time and stood and scrambled over to the bookcase. He was shaking, so I liberated the watch key from my chain and gave it to him. Forever. I took the other key then, the brass one, and slid the cover aside to reveal the door lock, and slipped the key in place. It turned easily, as though it'd recently been oiled. But craftsmanship was like that, it never disappointed. When something was made with love, it lasted, and worked whenever called upon.

Behind the door, there were drawers. I reached for the first one and opened it, both of us gasping at the same time.

"Take a picture with your phone, or she'll never believe you," I said under my breath.

He got out his phone, but I had to take the photo because my brother was all thumbs at the moment, overwhelmed with me, and, it turned out, his aunt.

Because there, sitting in a drawer all alone, was a red beryl mala with a tiny gold card beside it that read, *For Rochelle, With love, Peg.*

NEITHER OF US was up to going any deeper into Peg's bookcase, so I locked it up and put the key back around my neck. I closed the top half of the back door as Everett waited for me, and then we went out the front together and locked it up behind us. It still took a skeleton key, which Everett passed to me.

"That one goes on your key ring, all right? Not around your neck with—what are all these?" he asked me, touching the necklaces I wore. "I mean—" He gestured at my wrist where the all-original Rolex Blueberry GMT that Peg had gotten me when I graduated from college sat surrounded by beaded bracelets that she had strung herself, and somehow rendered unbreakable. People I knew bought bracelets that broke in a month, and I'd had mine for years. "I know better than to touch the malas, and what's with the cuff bracelet?"

"Peg had that made for me in Tibet when she was there," I explained to him. "It's engraved with the Heart Sutra," I said, lifting my right wrist. "That's what all the writing is."

"Was she a Buddhist? Are you?"

"I'm probably closest to that, but I'm not ready to say I'm anything quite yet, and we both know that Peg was a child of the world. She was baptized Catholic, but she was a fantastic pagan, a devout Wiccan, and every now and then, agnostic. It depended on the day."

He touched my bracelet. "It's beautiful, and she must have loved that sutra."

I nodded.

"It looks heavy."

"Yeah, it is."

"So, the necklaces are what?"

I held up the charm on a piece of leather cord. "Inside this silver cage is a Rudraksha bead that Peg brought me back from New Delhi. She wanted me to remember to always be compassionate."

"It's a what bead?"

"Just—we have shit to do, right?"

"Yeah, no, we do, but go on," he said, crossing his arms, waiting.

He wasn't ready to let me walk away from him. "Fine," I grumbled, lifting the next black cord. "This is a tiny mirror. If a witch casts a spell on you then, in theory, the mirror will bounce it right back."

"You're serious?"

"She never wanted me to be hexed."

"And she worried about this, for real?"

I glared at him.

"Sorry, sorry, go on."

I started to walk away from him. "You know what, I think I'm going to just—"

He grabbed my arm tight and held me until he stepped into my path. "I really am sorry. Please. Keep going."

I showed him the key on the heavy silver chain. "You know what this is."

"I do."

"This one," I began, picking up the bronze charm on a leather cord, "is a vajra, if you're saying it in Sanskrit, or it goes by its Tibetan name, dorje."

"Let me guess, that came home with her from Tibet."

"I can hurt you. I'm big enough now."

"No, I don't mean—I just wondered, what's it symbolize?" he asked, smiling at me.

"It's for protection and symbolizes a great deal, but for Peg, it was about destroying evil and ignorance, and that's what she felt my purpose was."

"All by yourself? Just you?"

"That's it," I declared, striding away from him so fast he had to scramble to catch up.

He was trying to build bridges with me, just to chat, but we were still on shaky ground, so it was best not to push anything. As he caught up, someone called out to me, and I went to check on the depth of the holes that were being dug and that the spiral of the flagstone was being done with enough room for herb planting. And really, it wasn't necessary for him to see the wax seal rendered in sterling silver, of a phoenix rising from the ashes and the Latin underneath that read *luctor et emergo*. That one Jo had made for me when I was in high school. The words, *I struggle and emerge*, had been my motto. I couldn't even count how many times I'd clutched the charm over the years.

"Are you scared?"

I turned and looked at him. "Of?"

"Everything's happening so fast. Me and Rochelle, Maeve and her family, we all sort of bombarded you."

"How else could that have worked?" I asked him. "You and Maeve, you wanted to talk and fix things and…you know, we're all about to lose the one person who means everything in the world to us. That means we *do* fix things right now, because later might be too late. You have to do it as soon as you can."

He grinned at me. "Yeah, yeah, it's true. I wanted to come over the second I knew you were here, but Rochelle said I had to give you a second to breathe since it was the first time you'd been home in years."

"You waited a whole day," I teased him.

"I might've driven by the house a couple times that night."

I shook my head as he bumped me with his shoulder. My brother had wanted a reconciliation with me almost desperately; it spoke well for our future.

HELPING WITH THE PLANTING, down in the dirt, I was peripherally aware of Rochelle screaming my brother's name in happiness. When I looked up and over to the back patio, I saw her leap at him and hook her arms around his neck. He carried her over to Jo, and the two of them crouched down on either side of her. It was nice, seeing them all together, sharing a private moment. I was glad to have been able to give that to them.

My coach's son, Dustin, joined me in the garden, and he passed me the small plants, the clary sage, white sage, garden sage, and then the thyme, rosemary, oregano, and parsley.

"I like this snail shape you got going here," he teased me, hand on my back.

"It's supposed to be a sacred spiral," I said in mock disgust.

He laughed at me before passing over the basil, echinacea, and chives. "You need gloves, baby. Your hands are gonna get wrecked."

Baby? What the hell was that about?

I couldn't have stopped my scowl if I tried. Why was the man trying to flirt with me now? Did he not see that we were all working?

"What?" he asked, giving me a full-wattage smile, the nod accompanied by one lifted brow, letting me know how very smooth he thought he was. It was a bit much for a Saturday of digging in dirt and barbecuing.

"Getting your hands dirty is just part of the process of being in the garden," I stated matter-of-factly, letting my tone convey my disinterest for any suave bullshit. "When I pull all the dead rose branches off the cottage, I'll wear gloves then," I assured him as I planted the catnip and marjoram, the mint, rue, and angelica.

He glanced over at Peg's cottage and then back at me. "You have to pull all the vines off that house?"

I nodded.

"When?"

"Oh, not today," I said, chuckling because there was only so much that even an army of people could accomplish in twelve or so hours.

"Was the cottage covered in roses?"

"Yeah," I said wistfully, looking at the roof now covered in dead branches. "There used to be pale pink New Dawn climbing roses, white Iceberg roses; the Shropshire Lad roses went all the way up to the chimney. They're like a peach color and were my aunt's favorite. Joseph's Coat roses, which are orange and red and pink and yellow all mixed up together, it was really beautiful, and they bloomed all the way into fall."

"How are the dead vines even hanging on?"

"I suspect that they got knotted together," I answered, standing up, towering over him for a moment before I offered him my hand and pulled him to his feet. We were the same height. He didn't have the two inches on me that Brody had, and instantly, I missed the man. "When I get up there on a ladder," I explained, "once I cut where they connect, it'll probably all just fall off, like when you used to cut the net after you guys won a basketball championship. The problem will be gathering it all up and burning it." I thought a moment. "Maybe I'll have a big bonfire."

"A bonfire sounds nice," he said, smiling at me.

"It does, doesn't it?"

"Hey, we've been out here for a bit. Maybe we should get some water," he suggested, taking hold of my shoulder to lead me out of the pile of dirt that was slowly starting to look like something other than just that.

Walking by the boys, they asked me where I wanted the flowers.

"Could you grab me a water?" I asked Dustin.

"Absolutely," he said, and the warmth and invitation in the dark brown eyes was hard to miss. "Anything else?"

"No, that'll do it."

Once he walked away, I explained to Artie where I wanted the carnations and the chrysanthemums, the heather and the honeysuckle. Vance was tasked with putting the hibiscus tree in, and the lilac. Mike got the fun of planting the holly, but I gave him help from some of the men who were there shaking their heads.

"That's mean, Kaenon, to make that poor kid move the holly."

More guys from school, who I'd seen only in passing, were terribly pleased to talk to me now. It was amazing how many people kept showing up, and Rochelle finally came down wearing her mala, and who cared that it was red and she was dressed in khaki and white. The galoshes were a nice touch.

"I had those on yesterday."

"And why wouldn't you? There's going to be water everywhere and lots of mud."

I tipped my head at her. "You like the mala?"

"Uhm, well, yes, Kaenon, I'm frickin' wild about the mala and the fact that she made one just for me, in the exact stone I wanted, I might add, and put it in a locked cabinet so that when you and Everett reconciled, it would be there," she said in a single breath of joy, her voice cracking at the end, fanning her face with her hands. "Ohmygod, please stop talking to me about this. I finally just now quit crying, and I don't wanna start back up."

I held out my arms, and she jumped at me, as my sister had the night before, arms and legs wrapped around me, doing a mean impersonation of a spider monkey.

"You and Maeve are both terrifying," I assured her.

"I love you," she wailed into the side of my neck. "You're being so kind to both me and Everett, and I just—I'm over the moon, Kaenon, and I never want you to leave."

Well, that wasn't going to happen, me staying in Braxton,

but I was glad she and I could be friends. I hadn't anticipated it, and it was a wonderful surprise.

"Kaenon, where do you want the jasmine?"

It was Davis asking, so I put down Rochelle and bolted back out to the garden to show him. I also answered his wife's questions about the marigolds and the aloe. When I was about to leave her, she caught my hand.

"Angie?"

She squeezed tight. "I just wanted to say that I missed talking to you in high school. You sort of closed yourself off after ninth grade, and well...," she said, taking a breath, "I never missed even one of your games except the away ones."

"Ange," I murmured, opening my arms.

She filled them and cried, and evidently, we had been better friends in eighth grade than I remembered, because she'd been sorry a long time.

After that, Davis wanted a hug too, and it was not a problem because he'd been amazing, and I appreciated it so much.

"Hi."

Turning, I found a handsome man, who I was certain I'd never met before in my life. He thrust his hand out at me, and I took it at the same time Rochelle came up behind him.

"Kae, this is my cousin Tyler Galloway. Ty, this is Everett's brother, Kaenon, who I was telling you about," she said sweetly, moving from where she was beside him, to me, and leaning. "See? I told you he didn't look a thing like Ev."

He kept his bright blue gaze locked with mine. "I'd love to help if you just tell me what you need."

"Can you cook?"

His eyebrows lifted. "Not as well as you, at least from what I've heard, but I can certainly grill burgers and hot dogs and chicken patties."

"You're hired," I said with a laugh. "I need to feed these people before they all bail at the same time."

"Well, then, absolutely," he agreed, dropping my hand only to take gentle hold of my bicep. "But you will take a break and sit with me, won't you?"

"You realize there's a crapton of people here and that," I said, pointing at the cooler beside the grill, "is full of meat."

Yes, very attractive man, handsome in that all-American way, in a "Captain America after he lost his shield" way, Chris Evans with the beard and mustache. I was betting that both men and women followed him wherever he went. Much like Brody, he was out of my league, and it was fun to watch him jolt when he realized what he'd signed on for.

"Don't worry," Dustin said, walking up beside me and passing me a bottle of water. "I'll help if he needs it."

"I'll be fine," Tyler assured him. "I'm good under pressure. Day traders have to be."

"So do attorneys," Dustin said snidely.

"What kind of attorney? Personal injury?" Tyler scoffed, and I wasn't crazy about his tone. Why he was trying to belittle Dustin, I didn't get.

"I specialize in commercial, constitutional, and tax law," Dustin told Tyler. "I can give you my card."

I wasn't sure what was going on as Dustin gave me a wink, the smoothness he was working so hard at was *not* something he'd picked up from his father, at all. I'd seen Coach Ochoa get flirted with once at the state soccer finals, and when the woman hit on him, the man had nearly passed out. I understood now, he was still in love with his wife at the time—and was presently as well—and wasn't about to do anything to jeopardize their eventual reconciliation. But the look of horror on the man's face before he bolted had been quite amusing. It was one of the few times the rest of the team had laughed *with* me and not *at* me. Dustin had moves his father did not possess.

"Excuse me."

Another man I didn't know offered me his hand, this one tall, with sun-streaked chestnut-brown hair and vivid emerald-green eyes. He was tanned dark, I was betting from making a living outside. When I took his hand, the calluses were hard, his grip strong.

"I'm Conner Hill. My grandmother is Lois Hill, out on Calumet Way. She has the jasmine hedge that you and your aunt planted after my grandfather died."

"Oh, yeah, I remember your grandmother. How is she?"

He made a soft sound. "She's in a nursing home in Wimberley now, but she always said that if I, or anyone else, ever saw any work being done to bring this garden back to life that I was to offer you one of the many plants that you helped her grow."

It was so kind, so thoughtful, and I took hold of his forearm, squeezing gently. "Thank you so much. I would love to have some of that jasmine."

His smile was gorgeous, and he took a step closer to me and inhaled deeply. "I figured you'd say yes. Who in their right mind turns down jasmine? So where would you like them? You direct me, and I'll put 'em in the ground."

"Right by the front gate, please," I told him as I turned him toward the back deck. "Will you come say hello to Jo?"

"I would love to," he said. "Lead the way."

"I'd like to say hi to her as well," Tyler suggested.

"Yeah, come on."

"I didn't say hello to her earlier," Dustin pointed out, his hands on my hips as he walked up behind me and spoke close to my ear, bumping his nose on the side of my face.

"I'm coming as well. Besides, I need to show Tyler everything that's in the cooler."

"I think I can figure it out."

"Yes, but I brought it."

The three of us crossed the dirt and went up the stairs, greeted the people there, lots of Rochelle's friends, and I realized that there were others coming in and out of the house, carrying trays of veggies, fruit salad, and wedges of watermelon and cantaloupe.

Jo was drinking a tall glass of lemonade and sharing pieces of cubed cheese and apples with the girls, who were now reading *Rosencrantz & Guildenstern Are Dead* to her.

"Oh, well, now," she said, sitting up from her lounging position and giving everyone her most regal smile. "Look at all the gorgeous men flocking to my side."

They were all charmed, no way not to be. This was Joanna Geary, after all.

She was thrilled to see them, but there were others bustling around and lots of people called out greetings. I took the moment before she started holding court, when the three men were distracted, to crouch down beside her, close.

"I'm having a weird day," I whispered in her ear.

"That's because you're drawing men like bees to honey," she replied under her breath, the two of us sounding like spies in a bad B movie. "And I know you're not used to so much attention. I mean, let's be frank, you're usually going through a dry spell."

"I'm sorry?"

"Oh, don't sound so affronted. We both know it's true."

It was, there was no use denying it. I didn't normally get so much attention. I wasn't the guy who stopped traffic, I was the other one. The whole experience of guys flocking, seemingly interested in just me, was more than a little strange.

"Your milkshake brings all the gay and bi boys to—"

"No." I cut her off before my brain exploded.

"That song was on all the time, don't you remember?"

"I do but you shouldn't, and I certainly don't have a milkshake," I said sounding, I realized, both horrified and completely insane.

Her eyebrows lifted. "Technically couldn't—"

"No," I said again, louder, more adamant, standing up so I could glare down at her and bully her into quiet submission, which would never, in a million years, work. This was my irrepressible grandmother I was trying to intimidate, even playfully. "Do not gross me out."

"When did you become such a prude?"

"I—"

"Oh," she said suddenly, smiling up at me, looking quite pleased with herself. "How about *It's Raining Men* instead?"

"I'm leaving," I announced and would have, but she grabbed hold of my hand.

"It's the combination of you and the land, love," she said authoritatively. "Just like it was with Peg. She was absolutely magnetic, don't you remember?"

"You're cute, but you're deluded."

"And yet...they're coming out of the woodwork."

I was going to argue.

"Here he is, Dad," Sandy said behind me.

Pivoting, there was yet another man I didn't know. He was older, polished, professional, and he was wearing a polo tucked into slacks, like he just got off the golf course. Handsome man, and after a moment, I recognized where Sandy Reed got her penetrating stare. It was from this man, her father.

I tried to wipe my hand off on my cargo shorts. "Sir, allow me to run inside and—"

"That's not necessary," he said with a smile, offering me his hand.

Taking it quickly, we shook, and I watched him put his arm around his daughter, draw her into his side, kiss the top of her head, and then gesture a woman over. His wife, Denise—stunning, elegant, with deep golden-brown skin and obsidian-colored eyes. She was carrying what appeared to be a grape salad. It looked amazing.

"I hope you brought that for me."

Her chuckle was warm. "Well, for Jo, so you can have some."

Of course, the mayor's wife knew my grandmother. That just stood to reason. She passed me the dish before she walked over, stepped between the men towering over the matriarch of our family, and took a seat beside her on the chaise. Sandy joined them, and Jo reached up and took hold of her hand, I was sure, regaling her mother with how much fun they'd been having.

"So, Mr. Geary," the mayor began, drawing my attention back to him. "Could you tell me a little about what's going on with Mr. Hastings up at the high school?"

"Please, call me Kaenon, Mr. Mayor, and I don't know that I'm qualified to say what—"

"But there seems to be a problem, wouldn't you say?"

I had to be honest. "There seems to be a pattern, but I could be reading too much into it."

He squinted at me. "Well, I've asked Mr.—Oh, here he is now."

And now another man, this one in an actual suit, no tie thankfully, but to show up in dress shoes to a backyard swarming with people shoveling dirt was not the best idea ever.

"Kevin," the mayor called over to him, and the man took the stairs two at a time, hand out as he closed in on us.

They shook and then the man turned to me. He was probably a few years older than me, handsome in that bookish way where you could imagine him strolling the halls of academia in tweed sport coats with suede elbow patches. The silver wire-rim glasses accented his pale gray eyes, and his thick blond hair was cut short on the sides and in back but long on top, falling over his forehead. The smile that he gave me lit his face and added to his appeal.

"You must be the amazing Mr. Geary I've been hearing so much about," he greeted me, offering his hand. "I'm Kevin Rossiter, the high school principal."

I took it quickly and was surprised when he didn't let me pull free, tightening his grip on me instead. "I doubt you've heard about me from anyone but Maria De—"

"Oh no," he said, taking a step closer. "I've heard from several parents of Maria's friends, from the mayor yesterday, from your colleague as well as the dean of your college, Eleanor Chavez."

What the hell...?

"She said that I would be foolish to not have you on staff for the summer in whatever capacity I could get you."

"No, wait," I said easing my hand from his so I could cross my arms. "I'm here to take care of my grand—"

"Summer classes are just half days, Mr. Geary."

"Kaenon," I corrected him.

"Kaenon," he repeated, my name sounding guttural and low when it came out of him.

"I can't work at the high school. I have to—"

"Oh, we're not asking you to teach," he said, and he

included the mayor, who gave me a smile as he too crossed his arms. It felt odd, us there, facing off, sizing each other up like we were two mob bosses discussing how we were divvying up the turf of someone we just whacked. "We're asking you to advise whomever we get in there to teach now that Mr. Hastings has been placed on administrative leave."

"Over two kids?" I prodded, concerned that they were moving a bit fast on Mr. Hastings.

"There's a pattern," he explained. "And it goes back quite a way, always with the same issues—race and gender."

"Why allow it to go on?"

"I just took over at the end of last year," he explained.

"Got it."

"So, can the mayor and I count on you then to advise the teacher we're bringing in?"

"Of course," I assured him, glancing at the mayor, who smiled and gave me a little nod. "Just let me know."

"Could you come by the high school, say around nine?"

"Sure," I agreed, noticing Artie, Vance, and Mike clomping up the stairs toward the coolers where the bottled water was. They detoured when they saw the principal, however, and walked over to say hello.

He was surprised to see them, even more so to see them cluster beside me, Vance putting his hand on my shoulder. They greeted the mayor as well, Artie being the only one who seemed nervous. Since he was the one dating the man's daughter, I understood his hesitancy.

"Hey," Mike said to me after a moment. "There's a lady who needs to talk to you."

"I'm sorry?"

"There's a lady at the front gate, and she's got two guys with her, and she asked us to come tell you that she needs to talk to you."

"Excuse me," I said to the mayor and Mr. Rossiter, leaving them with the boys as I walked over to the end of the deck and leaned over. There, at the front gate, was Carrie Wedge, who was my mother's age, her husband, Enoch, and her son, Hollis. When Peg had died, Jo told me that she had given them her bees.

Taking the stairs fast, I jogged out to the gate.

"Carrie," I said in greeting as I closed in on her.

Her glare was not friendly. "We refuse to give you back all the hives, Kaenon. We just can't, but we'll certainly—"

"Back up," I said, reaching the gate and putting my hands on it as I stared at the three people there. "What about the bees?"

Enoch moved around his wife. "Jo's stipulation when she gave us the bees was that if and when you returned to Braxton, the bees would revert back to you. That was in the original transfer. It goes on to state that you, and only you, could amend the number."

"O-kay," I said on an exhale. "I don't want any bees, Enoch. You've been taking care of those hives for years. They're yours. I have no interest in them."

All three of them looked utterly gobsmacked.

I grinned at them. "You all should see your faces."

"Move back," Carrie demanded, and when I did, she opened the gate and lunged at me, hugging me tight as the fear that she'd been eaten up with came out with her tears.

I returned the hug, and then Enoch was there, his hands on my face, giving me a pat as he had when I was younger, and finally his son, Hollis, who didn't touch me but did smile.

"We brought honey over for you," he said, and I saw his eyes take me in, look me up and down, and then settle on my face. "I'll go fetch it."

"Thank you."

It was strange to see him, Hollis Wedge, who was the same age as Everett but who had gone to the local trade school instead of Braxton High. I had seen him in passing, growing up, and we'd never spoken, but I never felt the same dread with him as I had with others. He'd come into the store once years ago, when it was raining, just stood near the front window, watching the deluge of water but said nothing to me. I could still recall his face in profile, the shadows of the raindrops running down his cheeks.

"Kaenon."

I stopped staring after her son and returned my attention to Carrie.

"May I ask, are you going to supply Rochelle's new boutique with smudge sticks and loose smudge, dressed candles, rose water, Florida Water, incense, oils—"

"Wait, what are you talking about?"

"Well, I know Peg showed you how to make those amazing bath salts of hers, and how to mix those oils, like the fertility one and the soul mate one that smelled so amazing people would drive all the way from other states to—"

"Oh, Carrie, no," I assured her. "I'm not a—I would never presume to do what Peg did."

"But she trained you to be a rootworker just like she was."

"No," I corrected her. "She trained me in the shop, and I can make smudge just like everyone else—hell, you can learn to do it by watching a video on YouTube—but card reading, runes, bones, candle work, and petitions, that was all her. I had neither the interest nor the aptitude to do any rootwork."

She searched my face, and I wasn't sure what she was looking for, probably checking to see if I was lying.

"You and I both know that I'm not her. I'm not Peg," I said, my voice rusty because so much thinking about Peg in one day was making my heart hurt. I had forgotten how much I missed her. "I've gotten pretty good at mixing up sugar and tea, but that's about it."

"Tea?" she said, sounding interested, her eyebrows lifting. "Could I taste some?"

"I'll put some in a bag for you," I assured her. "Maybe you all would like to stay and have some lunch."

She nodded quickly. "I'd love to help with the garden too, Kae, if you'd like. And I have some mature slippery elm and ginger and senna plants I'd love to give you."

"That would be wonderful."

She was beaming at me now. "I have yarrow and wintergreen as well."

"Anything you'd like to bring me, I would love."

Her sigh was deep as she leaned into her husband.

"You see there," Enoch said to his wife, putting a hand on her back and rubbing gently. "I told you. He ain't puttin' you out of business."

"What are you talking about?"

Enoch turned back to me. "Ever since she heard you was back in town, she's been frettin' on how long before you put us out of business. We got us a shop front downtown on the corner of Main and Rose, where the place was that sold all those high-priced cupcakes."

"Oh, uh, what was it, Sweet Sugar or something like that?"

"Sweet Sugar Buns," he said and rolled his eyes. "They didn't even make no kind of buns in there, just them cupcakes that was more frosting than cake."

I snickered.

"Anyway, so we been there about ten years now, and there's a few other places that popped up around town, the Silver Witch Crystal Boutique, and Sun & Moon, which sells bath oils and essential oils and is more organic-based beauty products, but we're the only place that does what Peg used to."

"Got it."

"We sell honey and Carrie makes candles and incense and smudge. She makes spell kits as well as witch balls and wreaths, corn dollies and the like."

"The only thing Peg sold in her store were her oils and her malas," I reminded Carrie. "She made and dressed candles but never to sell, and for Beltane she'd make those vine hearts with the little besoms on them," I said, thinking of the one that hung in my kitchen at home that never failed to receive a compliment from people who visited. "And the wreaths for Yule, remember? But she never sold them; they were gifts for specific people."

"Yes, but what you have to remember, Kae, is that anything Peg made was just so charged with her intention. I'm still learning, but I have a witch ball she made me years ago that's still more powerful than anything I've made, ever."

"Here we go," Enoch announced, and I realized that Hollis was back.

In his arms were four jars of honey, three the same golden amber color and the fourth, lighter and clouded. I took them and he tapped the lid of the last one.

"That one has lavender in it, so you have to put it in the fridge."

"This is great, thank you," I said, smiling into his warm brown eyes. "Y'all want to come up to the porch and visit a spell with Jo?" Man, my accent was coming back fast. I needed to make a conscious choice to curtail it.

"Oh, I would love to see her," Carrie said, "but I'm not certain she'll want to see us now that we're not retuning the bees."

"I can assure you that she won't give a damn."

Both she and Enoch looked unsure, but they walked ahead of me toward the patio, waving at people they knew on the way.

"Kaenon."

I looked sideways at Hollis, who was walking beside me.

"You liked boys in high school. Is that still the case?"

I exhaled slowly, because of course he would have a problem with me. "Yeah, Hollis, that's still the case."

He nodded. "Well, that's just fine, because you have to be about the prettiest man I've ever seen, and you smell like sunshine and roses and dirt, and it's about all I can do not to jump you right here."

I stopped walking and stared at him.

His grin was wicked when he stepped in front of me. "How 'bout you meet me out by the pond tonight, the one behind the Dawson place, and you and me can have us a talk."

Talking was not on his agenda, and I would have told him that Brody Scott was the only man I was meeting at a pond, but Dustin jogged up before I had the chance and offered to carry the honey.

"I can help him," Hollis groused at the man.

"No, I've got it," Dustin assured him, taking two of the jars from me as Conner joined us.

"Kae, Jo would like a word with you."

"'Course," I said, smiling at the three men before continuing on to the porch.

As soon as I reached the stairs, Tyler yelled over to me so I could see he had every inch of the grill covered in cooking meat. Principal Rossiter gestured for me from where he was standing with the mayor and several teens, including Sandy and Artie, and Dustin told me I should take a seat in the shade for a moment.

"You haven't slowed down all day, Kaenon."

"Excuse me." The words, almost growled out, rippled through me, and when I turned toward the sound, Brody was there, scowling at me.

"When did you get—"

"Here," Brody directed, taking the jars of honey out of my hands and passing them to Conner. "Go show those to Jo," he ordered the man before taking my hand in his and leading me into the house.

There were several people in the kitchen, mostly women, and I could hear the blender going and see things being chopped and mixed, a whole assembly line of food preparation. I would have thanked them, would have stopped to talk, but Brody walked on, tugging me behind him, through the living room and down the short hall to my bedroom.

Inside, he yanked me through the door, rounded fast, slammed the door shut, and then knocked me back into it, his hands on my hips as he stood and stared into my eyes.

"Do me a favor and stay here," I directed, smiling up into his face before I eased free of his hold and darted to my bathroom to wash my hands. Since I was hoping to touch him, I didn't want to do it with dirt and whatever else I'd managed to pick up today on my hands. Although, the thought of leaving my fingerprints all over his perfect skin was giving me ideas, something I'd have to explore later.

When I walked back into the room, he was pacing. "What's wrong with you?"

"Are you kidding?"

It was adorable how annoyed he was, and looking at him—at the powerful lines of the man, his long legs, narrow hips, and wide shoulders—gave me heart palpitations. The way he nervously carded his fingers through his hair, leaving it tousled and sticking up, made me sigh just looking at him.

"Don't smile at me," he warned gruffly, his frustration only adding to his allure. The man was a grouchy, growly mess, and since I suspected that I was the cause, I wanted to kiss him and make it all better.

"No smiling," I teased him, closing the distance between us down to nothing. "Got it."

"This is not funny," he snarled at me.

"No," I agreed, trying to make my face as serious as his.

"What the fuck, Kaenon?"

The sound of him, even mad or scared, I couldn't tell yet which, was a decadent silky rumble that was all sex and heat and possessiveness, and the throb of want that tore through me made me tremble in response to him. For the life of me, I couldn't recall wanting anyone more than I wanted Brody Scott. And yes, there were several handsome, even beautiful, men outside, but the one in front of me now was the only one I wanted. Only Brody made my breath catch and my pulse race and my cock thicken in my shorts. The blood pounding in my ears was enough to cause a whimper to slide out of my throat.

"Brody," I managed to grind out with difficulty.

"Jo's right," he said roughly as he leaned in and kissed me.

I opened for him, arms lifting, wrapping around his

neck as he clutched me against him, one hand sliding low, over my ass, the other on the small of my back, keeping me still as he ravaged my mouth. I was all hands, wanting to touch him, taste him, suck him off again, and get him into my bed. He did wild things to my libido, drowning my brain in absolute devouring lust.

Shoving him off me, panting, I asked him what Jo was right about.

"What?" he rasped, pupils blown.

The russet-brown of his eyes was really something. It reminded me of deep, rich carnelian or petrified wood or polished mahogany. I was a big fan. "You said that Jo was right." I reached out to trace the veins in his bicep, and when he shivered from the contact, I couldn't control my smile. He loved it when I touched him, and that was a huge turn-on.

"When I got here, she said that there were guys sniffing around after you, and if I wanted you, I had better stake my claim," he said, his voice coarse and husky. "I thought she was screwing with me, but then I saw them all."

I shook my head and gestured him to stop. "None of those guys are important. I was never going to go to the pond with Hollis Wedge."

"I'm sorry, what?"

I started laughing because no, I hadn't meant to make him jealous, and I wasn't a game player, so he didn't have to worry, but seeing him all pissed off and irritated was pretty hot.

"Kaenon!"

I lunged at him, arms around his neck before I kissed him, laughing into his mouth, sucking on his bottom lip to get his mouth open before I rubbed my tongue over his.

He kissed me back, hard and deep, taking, not gentle,

voracious and demanding until I went boneless with submission.

"You smell so good," he said thickly into the side of my neck, licking over my skin, sucking before I felt his teeth, "Like oranges and mint and dirt, of all things."

He smelled clean, and his hair was still slightly damp, and I wanted him under me in bed more than I wanted to breathe. "You took a shower before you came over here," I said as I kissed him, walking him backward, my hands on the button of his well-fitting beige shorts, loving the long-sleeved white linen button-down with the rolled-up sleeves and open collar that he had tucked into them. "And you thought, 'I bet Kaenon would love to take this shirt off me.'"

"I—what?"

He was lost, and I loved it. I especially loved how easy he was to move when his entire brain had shut down from what I was doing to him.

When the back of his knees hit the bed, I pushed him just hard enough to topple him down onto the comforter.

"Kaenon," he said like he was going to protest, so I came down on top of him, pinning him under me as I ravaged his mouth and got the shorts open, zipper down, and my hand under the waistband of his briefs. When I took hold of his length, he groaned like he was in pain and bowed up off the bed.

Scrambling fast, I got up, rolled him over and shucked down his shorts and briefs in one rough movement, baring his ass.

"Kaenon, we have to—"

"You're the idiot who was worried," I said, rushing to my nightstand to retrieve the lube and a condom as he started to get his hands under him to push up off the bed.

I fell down behind him, and when I licked the top of his crease, he froze. "The fuck are you doing?"

Quickly, deftly, because I'd been undressing men for years, I yanked off his shoes, and the shorts followed.

"Kaenon, we have to get back out to—"

Stepping between his legs, I urged him up onto the edge of the bed, and he did as I directed, moving to his hands and knees for me.

"People are going to come looking for—Kaenon!"

The yell happened because I shoved my tongue in his ass.

"Fuck," he moaned hoarsely, going facedown into the comforter, his arms giving out, his ass still in the air as I spread his cheeks and spit. I wasn't only going to use saliva, but that's where I was going to start, and I knew what it felt like rolling down the crack of my ass, so I suspected Brody was going to like that just as much. Part anticipation, part actual stimulus, I knew I was right when he moaned my name.

I spit a second time and a third, using my fingers to spread it around before I began licking and pushing inside, sucking and laving, opening him up, pushing in deeper, one of my hands moving to his cock to stroke him from balls to head over and over.

As he began riding my tongue, pushing back into my face, I flipped open the lid on the lube and coated two fingers. Lifting my head, I kissed up his crease as I slowly, gently, slid first one inside and then the other.

"Kaenon!" he yelled as he pushed back fast, taking both fingers to the knuckle.

"I'm trying to be gentle," I said with a low chuckle, watching as he leaned forward and then shoved back again. "But you should see your ass open for me."

"Oh, Kaenon, please."

Putting the condom between my teeth, well-versed with this maneuver, I had the foil packet open and the condom on, all with one hand as I screwed three fingers into his ass, hitting his prostate again and again until my name was on an endless loop of pleading.

When I finally eased my fingers from his hole, he hissed out a warning before I pressed the head of my cock to his entrance.

His hands scrabbled on the comforter as I pushed in slowly, stretching him open, curling over him, my hand working over his still-hard, leaking cock as his body swallowed my dick.

"Jesus, Brody, you feel so good," I said, plastering my chest to his back as I buried myself to the balls and then eased back, languidly, letting him feel every inch of me, no pounding, no rutting, instead a joining, a smooth rolling urgency that built with every slide to his core.

When his hand closed over mine, I let go of his shaft, whispering that he needed to show me how he liked it as I filled his ass.

"I want to—I need to see you. Your eyes."

"You can look at my face the next time," I assured him, thrusting harder, to see what he liked, and was rewarded with his muscles tightening around me.

"Fuck yeah," I rumbled as he let go of his cock.

"I'm gonna come, I'm too close, just your breath on the back of my neck is gonna send me—please," he begged as I dug my fingers into the hard curve of his ass, loving the feel of him, the power in his frame, his sleek, smooth skin.

He normally topped, he told me he did, so the fact that he was trusting me with his submission was a heady thing.

As I began a deep, sensual thrusting, I relished the feel

of him, of his satin heat sucking me in, milking my length as I buried myself to the hilt. "Next time I want your legs over my shoulders, and I'll fuck you so hard that you scream my name."

"I'd scream myself hoarse now, if your house wasn't full of people," he promised, and shuddered as he came, spilling onto the bed, my name a ragged cry on his lips.

I followed right behind him, my orgasm rolling through me as his body clenched around me, and I was left weightless and reeling for long moments until I came back to myself in a jolt.

"Sorry, I—let me move so we can clean you up and—"

"In a second," he said, his voice raspy, dark. "I love the feel of you breathing on me, and your skin is hot on mine, and…next time…no condom. I want to feel all of it."

"Turn your head and kiss me."

I liked how fast he followed orders.

TWELVE

He went out first, and I stayed behind and washed my face and hands before walking back through the kitchen on my way outside. Once I reached the deck, I saw that Brody had taken over the task of grilling. I was halfway toward him when Tyler stepped in front of me.

"Kae, now that Brody's doing the cooking, I'd love to talk to you for a second."

"Absolutely," I assured him, "I just need to have a quick word with the Chief Constable and then check on Jo."

"Of course," he said, stepping sideways.

Walking over to Brody, I put my hand on the small of his back, and he turned to look at me, smiling languorously, the look primal, lustful and also possessive. He was looking at me like I belonged to him, and as I stood there and soaked that up, all of it, every drop of his attention feeling captivating and powerful, it hit me what I was going to be missing when I went home at the end of the summer.

No one else was ever going to look at me like that. Not

for the rest of my life. There were secrets in the depths of his eyes, in the curl of his lip, and in the way his hand felt when it slipped around my hip and drew me close.

"How come you always smell like that?" he murmured, nuzzling his face against my temple, into my hair.

"Like what?"

"Hell if I—like summer."

"I've been outside all day," I answered, my eyes closing because of him, because of his nearness, with the memory of sex and how much I wanted to be back inside of him. How was I supposed to let someone else learn all there was to know about him? How was I supposed to leave him for someone else to claim?

"Not just today," he whispered, inhaling. "You smell like that all the time. It was there when I first saw you at the outdoor market. It's like this woodsy smell, like a forest if it was full of mint and black tea and sandalwood. I just wanna breathe you in."

"Awfully poetic of you, Constable," I teased him.

"I can't help it. You smell so good."

It was from being in Braxton, in the garden. People would always say that Peg smelled like white sage and mandarin oranges, like cedar and ginger, peppermint and bergamot. I knew I did too, because people remarked on it when I first got to college and then again, whenever I'd get a care package from Peg. She'd send me a chunky scarf that smelled like vetiver and geranium and lavender, and it would infuse everything, down to my skin, for weeks before it faded.

At a house party once, I was coming out of the bathroom when my roommate's brother, who had treated us both to dinner the night before, shoved me back inside and pressed his face to my neck. I had no idea what to do; he was older, out of college, a lawyer, and he had his hands all over me.

"God, Kaenon, you smell so good, all earthy and sweet, like freshly turned dirt and oranges and sun on clothes that have been outside on the line all day."

"Is that good?" I asked him.

"Yes," he husked before he kissed me.

That night I learned that scent had power and that it could be just as alluring as physical beauty, a kind spirit, or a clever mind. When I got care packages from Jo or Peg, they made me smell like me. But what made no sense now was that there was nothing in the garden, nothing to cling to me, but somehow I was covered in scent from memory. How was that even possible?

"Kaenon?"

Turning, I found Dustin, and he smiled as he took hold of my arm. "Jo would like to talk to you right now."

"Oh, okay," I said, giving Brody one last look before I followed Dustin over to my grandmother. She was sitting with two of her daughters, my aunt Rose, the oldest of her children, and my aunt Linda. What was funny was that both of them were dressed in capris and knit tops and summer scarves like it was their uniform. My grandmother, much older than both of them, was dressed far more fashionably.

"There you are," my aunt Linda said almost sadly, getting up, appearing haggard, hands fisted at her sides. "I don't know what you're trying to pull, but Mama can't—"

"No," Rose said softly, standing as well, taking a step toward me, reaching out like she was going to take my hand but stopping at the last moment and drawing it back. "We're not here to accuse you, Kaenon, but Mama has no idea who we are or what's going on or—"

"What?" I asked her, looking at Jo, worried that something had happened while I was gone. I took a seat on the chaise beside her.

Jo was looking sideways, not out at the garden where everyone was, but toward the back of the property that ended at the fence and beyond it, the overgrown trees and shrubs that lined the canyon before the steep slopes.

"Hey," I said to get her attention.

She turned to look at me, and all I saw was black because she was still wearing her oversized sunglasses.

"Take those off, please."

She lifted them, putting them on top of her head, and I saw the same clear blue eyes I'd been seeing all my life.

"Well?" she asked me pointedly.

I scowled at her.

She tipped her head toward Brody.

I huffed out a breath. "Could you stop screwing around, please, because you're freaking out your daughters, and they're going to try to have you committed or something."

Both Linda and Rose were staring at Jo, openmouthed like she was speaking in tongues.

"Are you hungry?"

"Yes, but not for a hot dog or whatever else is on the grill," she told me, reaching for my hair, tucking a piece behind my ear.

"Oh, I know. How about a BLT and some grape salad?"

"You'll make it the crisscross way your grandfather always did?"

"Of course."

"And you don't mind frying the bacon?"

"Do stars twinkle?" I asked her, using one of my grandfather's favorite expressions.

Stand In Place

"Such a good boy, give me a kiss."

I leaned over and kissed her and then got up to go make her sandwich. Since the kitchen was filled with people, and the mayor's wife was directing everyone, I asked her if she could please have someone fry me up six slices of bacon.

"Coming right up," she assured me with a smile. Me, assisting with the class this summer, to help out her daughter, had earned me some brownie points.

I was making Jo's sandwich when Rose joined me, along with her daughter, my cousin Selene, who had come with her. I just hadn't noticed her earlier. Rose had three other children, but for the life of me, I couldn't think of their names at the moment. Selene I always remembered, because the goddess was Peg's favorite.

"Kaenon, what's going on?" Rose asked levelly, doing her best, it sounded like, to keep her calm as she spoke to me.

I continued making the sandwich. "I don't know what you mean?"

"Look at me."

Doing what she asked, I noted that Selene, too, was dressed older than my grandmother.

"I promise you that when Linda and I sat down, Mama was not there. She had no idea who we were or who Selene was."

"Okay."

"But after you sat down, she's suddenly fine?"

"She asked me if my daughter was going to stay in Memphis now that she's graduated from college," Selene chimed in.

"Is she?"

"Well, yes, but that's not the point."

"What is the point?" I asked, thanking the kind older

gentleman who put a plate with still-sizzling bacon down beside me.

"We've got a long table coming over from the community center to put out on the back deck so we can get everyone fed," he informed me.

"Oh, thank you so much," I told him, squeezing his shoulder.

"Anything for Jo; she's one of the pillars of our community."

I gave him a smile and then realized that Selene was waiting for me. "Sorry, go on."

"Kaenon, do you realize that a month ago Jo had no idea who my kids were," she informed me. "But suddenly you're here, and she remembers that my oldest daughter just graduated from Rhodes College in Memphis? What the hell?"

"Selene," Rose scolded her and then suddenly caught her breath.

"What?" I asked, worried that something had startled or scared her.

"You're—you make the basket weave with the bacon like my father used to."

"Well, yeah," I said with a shrug. "Papa always said that it was the only way to get bacon in every bite."

She nodded quickly. "Yes, yes…I'd forgotten."

I took a breath and turned, facing my aunt and my cousin. "Listen, I don't want to fight, and I'd love it if you all want to visit every day this summer, but if you're just going to come over here to check and see if Jo is okay, I can promise you she will be. As long as I'm here taking care of her, she'll be great."

"And what about at the end of the summer when you have to go home, Kaenon?"

I exhaled sharply. "Well, then I have to make a decision about where she's going to be."

"What do you mean *you* have to decide?"

"I have power of attorney over Jo," I told her. "All her property is in my name. I'm the cosigner on her bank account. And the house, the land, all Peg's property that transferred to Jo when she died, that's under my purview as well."

"And how did you manage that?"

It wasn't a surprise that she didn't know. Jo had never been one to share what she construed to be boring information with anyone. "I'm the executor of the estate and—"

"You son of a bitch," Rose shrieked at me, slapping me across the face, hard.

It was a surprise. I hadn't been hit in years, but I recovered and stepped back so she couldn't do it again as Denise Reed, the mayor's wife, stepped up beside me and ordered Rose and Selene out of the house.

"I'm Jo's daughter," Rose yelled at her. "You can't—"

"You just hit him," Denise said icily, enunciating each word. "I suggest you leave before I have the Chief Constable remove you for battery."

"I—"

"Now," she commanded, and I heard the sharp order of a powerful woman who was not used to being second-guessed. I was betting that when people appeared before Judge Denise Reed in Civil Court that they weren't given many chances to annoy her.

Rose and Selene went out the back door, and I was going to follow them to make sure they didn't bother Jo, but Denise stopped me.

"I need to make sure—"

"My daughter is still out there," she informed me,

holding her left hand up and behind her as though waiting for someone to pass her something while touching my cheek tenderly with her right. "And so is my husband. No one is going to bother Jo."

A moment later, a Ziploc bag full of ice wrapped in a dish towel was placed in her hand by another woman, and she gently pressed it to my cheek. "I heard a bit of that exchange," she said, her voice soothing and calm. "And it's amazing to me how money, or the promise of it, can tear families apart at the seams."

"My brother and sister didn't have the same reaction to the news at all," I said, taking the ice from her and taking over the pressure.

"That's because they're your siblings and they're thinking that your money will eventually be their money."

I wasn't sure that was a fair assessment, but I didn't correct her either. I was still coming to terms with whatever boundaries I was going to draw around my renewed relationship with Maeve and Everett, so I let it pass.

"Sorry," she continued as if she'd heard my thoughts, "that wasn't particularly kind of me to assume. But listen to me, Kae, it's understandable that Jo's children might be mad as hell that they get nothing when she passes, so I want you to know that if, when the time comes, you need legal services, it's been said I'm well connected," she said with a wink, and I couldn't help but smile at the judge who, of course, would know all the right people. "Wills and estates and money can get ugly, so I'm going to assume that you have all the pertinent documents in order, but if you do need advice, you know where to find me."

"Thank you, that means a lot to me." I offered her my hand, and she took it. "She wants everything just the way it is now."

"Including the garden returned to its former glory."

I smiled at her. "She showed you pictures."

"Oh my, yes, so many pictures. It was quite the lovely space. I can see why the Braxton Nature Conservancy had all their luncheons here."

"And don't forget the Women's Auxiliary and the Braxton Historical Society."

She chuckled. "Well, once you have the arbor covered in roses again and the air smells of honeysuckle blossoms, lavender, and sage, I might ask you to give us the space for the garden club charity fundraiser to benefit the Women's Health Center here in Braxton."

"Oh, I don't know if a black-tie affair is—"

"If you restore it to its former glory, I think it will be perfect."

I smiled at her. "Well, if I can make it happen before the end of the summer, you're welcome to my Aunt Peg's garden."

The expression on her face was both warm and understanding at the same time. "Darling, I suspect that you have roots here, in this place, that you're not even fully aware of."

"No."

"Don't you find that when you stand in place, sometimes even for a moment, you feel as though you're home?"

I scowled at her.

Her laugh was good, like Jo's, deep and throaty, filled with life. "Finish the sandwich; I'm sure Jo's starving by now."

It took me a few more minutes, but I made Jo a beautiful plate and poured her a glass of sweet tea and walked it out to her. I found her sitting at the table, under the umbrella, in the same spot she'd been the night before, chatting with

Rochelle and several other women, but I didn't see Rose or Selene anywhere.

Taking a seat beside her, I put the sandwich and glass down in front of her.

"Oh, this looks marvelous, my darling," she praised me, then picked it up and took a bite, pleased, I could tell from her deep sigh of contentment.

Rochelle's eyes got big as she noticed my face, but I shook my head slightly so she wouldn't say a word to Jo.

"I'm sorry about Rose and Selene, my love," she said, turning to look at me, her hand lifting to my face, her fingers gentle on my chin, tipping my head sideways so she could see where her daughter had hit me. "Sandy was inside; she told me what happened."

"She's a little narc," I groused, glancing over at the teenager, who waved at me, not knowing that I was calling her a name.

"We knew it was going to be like this," she said flatly. "That's why we did it. They keep hoping I go senile and sign away the land to them and give them access to my bank account."

"Which is hysterical, because I have more money than you," I told her. "This is Braxton, for crap's sake, not San Francisco. The house, the little plot of land it sits on, and a bit of land in the canyon, it's not worth nearly as much as I suspect they think it is."

"It's worth something combined with the rest," she told me. "Just like Everett said about him and his cousins working on a deal to—"

"Oh no, Jo," Rochelle said in defense of her husband. "He's not—he would never do anything to jeopardize his new relationship with Kaenon. I promise you, he's not the man that either of you think he is."

"No, I'm sure he's not," Jo said kindly, smiling at Rochelle. "But he was working on something with them, with the others, was he not?"

"Yes, but really, not anymore."

Jo nodded. "That's fine. The important thing is I made certain that I was pronounced utterly sane and in complete control of all my faculties when I signed over everything to Kaenon. In fact, I saw a shrink at the hospital who said that not wanting any more chemo, as it would kill me before the cancer does, was the sanest option available to me, no matter what my son and daughter-in-law believe. It's all documented."

Rochelle nodded. It had to be weird for her since she and Everett both worked for my father. The whole divided loyalty thing was a real consideration.

"Mom, may I talk to you?"

I had forgotten about Linda, but she was there, and when Jo patted the chair beside her, Linda hustled around the table, taking the seat.

"I just wanted to tell you that I'm thrilled to see you looking so good. I'm going to come back tomorrow and bring Tate and the kids, all right?"

Linda, I remembered, had two kids, Tate and Charlotte, I thought, and it sounded like Tate had kids too.

"I can't wait for you to meet them, Kaenon," she told me. "They're the same age as Maeve's kids. I'd love for you to tell them all about Peg, and they'd love to see her rock collections or anything else that you might have. Tate was telling me this morning that Maeve and her kids had a wonderful time with you."

I glanced at Jo, who just narrowed her eyes and nodded like I should just shut up and make polite conversation. And it was smart; Linda was being nice to Jo, after all, so I smiled obediently. "That's great, I'm looking forward to it."

"So you'll be back tomorrow," Jo said brightly, and I saw the wince at the same time, like *please, God, no*. My grandmother was an extrovert, it was true, but she also liked the quiet. She always said that my grandfather was the only man who could be silent for an entire day while never once letting her feel lonely. And me. I could be that same kind of calm, which was why we fit together like the pieces of a puzzle. She loved all her grandchildren, and great-grandchildren, but the noise was constant with them, and that could be tiring.

"Yes, as I said, I'll bring Tate and his kids. I understand that Maeve will be here with hers as well."

"I believe so," Jo agreed, watching as a long table was carried up the stairs to the middle of the patio. A late lunch was about to be served.

"May I ask," Linda began with a wince, "will Robert and Tessa be by?"

"No, I don't think so," Jo responded. "I don't think they'll be in Braxton until the Fourth of July weekend."

"That's my understanding as well," Rochelle said, glancing at me.

"And, Kaenon," Linda continued. "Will you be with us for the Fourth of July?"

"I doubt it," I told her.

"Well, that might be for the best."

Jo was about to say something, but I took hold of her hand. When our eyes met, I gave her a tiny headshake and then heard her quick exhale.

"I agree," I said, leaning close to Jo so she could touch my hair and kiss my cheek. Always she'd been demonstrative with me, and that had never changed. "Thank you for your input, Aunt Linda."

She seemed pleased, if her smile was any indication.

Food started coming out of the house then, a stream of people setting up two rows of side dishes, from cornmeal-fried okra, potato salad, pinto beans, and onion rings to corn on the cob, sweet potato casserole, and french fries. There was tossed salad and fruit salad as well, and Brody set huge platters of hamburgers, chicken patties, and hot dogs at the front of the line for everyone to take.

When I got up to thank everyone for coming and told them to dig in, there was a round of applause before people started getting in line. Shelly Tate had apparently been in the kitchen, helping, and when she walked over to give me a hug, she brought her husband with her for me to meet. Her boys were somewhere in the yard, still digging holes and watering plants.

Dustin got me a paper plate, but I told him I wasn't quite ready to eat yet. Tyler assured me that I should, as hard as I'd been working. Conner said I needed to as well, and Hollis explained to me that he'd eat when he returned, but he had to run back to the family nursery to get the plants his mother promised me. I could go with him if I wanted. The accompanying smile was almost lurid. Principal Rossiter offered to sit with me to discuss more in depth my role of advisor to the teacher he had coming in for the summer.

I took a deep breath and then closed my eyes, tipping my face up into the sun as Brody came up behind me, wrapped his arms around my neck, and pressed his face into my hair. I put both hands on his forearm resting under my chin and held on.

"Well, okay then," someone said.

The pure masculine grunt that came out of Brody Scott,

the sound a sexy rumble in my ear, made me smile over the show of raw possessiveness.

"You're ridiculous," I assured him, giving him more of my weight.

"Until you go," he said, his voice rough, thick with emotion, "you're mine."

And I had not one problem with that.

THIRTEEN

People stayed until the sun sank below the horizon, putting in a hard day's work. Small towns could be like that, neighbors pitching in and helping neighbors, enjoying a meal together and some good conversation in the process. Jo helped fill disposable plasticware with leftovers and enjoyed sending folks off with food and a hug. Dustin and Conner left together, which I found interesting and sort of hopeful. I had always liked to see new things beginning in unexpected ways. Hollis left and came back, bringing the plants his mother promised me, and then said that if anything changed with Brody to let him know. He wasn't about to get anywhere near me while I was entangled with Chief Constable Scott.

"He's the law in Braxton, you know," he said as though I wasn't aware.

Principal Rossiter told me, as I walked him to his car, that he hoped he hadn't given me the wrong idea about him. He wasn't hitting on me; that wouldn't be appropriate. I worked for him now.

"I will say, however, that I did have an alternative agenda

for wanting to get to know you," he said, giving me a kind smile.

"Oh? What is that?"

"I'm looking for an assistant soccer coach for the coming year."

What part of leaving after the summer was he missing? "That's very flattering," I said to be nice.

"You led the Braxton Bulldogs to the state championship in both your junior and senior years of high school," he said, as though this was news to me also. And what was the deal with people telling me things I already knew?

When I was walking back after saying goodbye to the principal, I saw Brody and Tyler speaking next to his car. Brody had his arms crossed, and Tyler was talking with big animated gestures, hands flying in punctuation of whatever it was he was saying.

"I wonder what that's about?" I said to Everett as I moved the hose, beginning the watering that was going to take the rest of the night. Davis had brought me several sprinklers and two more hoses, which was extremely helpful. He said he'd add it to my bill.

"God, it's going to be epic," I'd groaned at him.

"We have payment plans," Davis had assured me with a waggle of his eyebrows.

"I know what that's about," Everett said a few minutes later when I followed him into Peg's cottage so we could get it locked up for the night. "Brody and Ty were shackin' up for a month or so when Brody first moved back."

"Really," I said, trying to sound nonchalant, wondering why neither of them had mentioned that to me.

"Yeah, but it didn't take."

I coughed softly. "Do you know why?"

"Well, yeah, of course," he said with a shrug, walking

into the apothecary, looking at the shelves full of the clear-glass hermetically sealed jars that Peg was so fond of. "Brody's a dog, and Ty's a serious guy. That's why Rochelle introduced you to him. She wants you to stay, of course, and if you and Tyler got to be a thing, that would help."

I was quiet.

"I would...like that too."

Looking over at him, I found him staring. "Ev?"

He took a breath. "Yeah, ya see? Already with the Ev, and it's only been a day, and I missed that for so long, and I would kind of like you to hang around and keep saying it."

I studied him.

"Awww man, what?"

"No, nothing, never mind," I said, because really, it wasn't my place.

"Please, Kae, speak your mind about everything until this thing—us—moves like it's supposed to, with well-oiled gears."

I knew what he meant. We were trying, both of us, but it was new and spooky, and we were like two cats closing in on something unknown, jolting and jumping over every little sound or movement.

"It's really none of my business."

"Oh, for fuck's sake, Kae, just spit it out."

I was fiddling with some of Peg's jars, the older ones, the ones with the wire bale lids, not the newer ones with the metal hinged clamps. The ancient ones had belonged to her and Jo's mother, Willa, and they predated the marriage of my grandparents.

"Don't open anything," he warned me. "You don't know what'll come out."

He wasn't wrong.

"Kae."

I took a breath. "I just think that you're wasting your time doing whatever it is you do at the car dealership when you have an obvious gift for interior design."

I didn't look at him; instead, I looked at Peg's jars and thought about all the things she had meant to make. Now, looking at all her herbs, I couldn't imagine how I, or anyone else, would ever figure out what was there. Nothing was labeled; that wasn't her way. She knew by touch and scent, could tell the difference between dried agrimony, dried St. John's Wort, or dried horehound, just by looking at it. I couldn't, but neither did I want to. I was a teacher, and I enjoyed it, healing and nurturing, moving kids to their next step in life. Peg had enjoyed that too, in different ways.

"Yeah," he said into the silence. "You're right."

I turned to look at him as he opened two drawers and took a bag out of each.

"Explain to me the difference between a spell bag and mojo bag?"

"You're changing the subject."

"I want to know the answer to this before I forget to ask. I always meant to but never got around to it."

"This question is consuming your mind?"

"Yeah."

No, it wasn't, but that was fine. We were talking around something else. "A spell bag you use what's in the bag, the ingredients, to do something specific like, I don't know, cast a spell."

"Hence the name."

"Exactly. Peg would make them and stock them on the shelves in the store. If someone wanted a luck spell or a money spell or love, they'd just grab it and take it home."

"That's this," he said, holding up a gauzy yellow bag tied with a bee charm.

"Yeah."

"And so this is a mojo bag," he said, holding up another pouch with a drawstring closure, the second one silk, not organza like the first.

"No, that one's a spell bag too. There won't be any mojo bags in here."

"Why not?"

"Mojo bags are made for a specific person. They're alive. They have to be taken care of like a pet. That's why, when you get one, you get oil with it, or incense, so you can feed it."

"You're serious."

"It was your question."

"I still don't understand why one of these can't be a mojo bag."

"Because you get a mojo bag and then keep it with you for, like, a week or so at first, in a pocket or a bra; you get the idea. And then after that, you hide it, because no one else can ever see it but you. If someone else sees it, it's done, and you have to start all over again."

He looked at me, smiling.

I shrugged. "Believe or don't."

"But you clearly do."

"I—Peg taught me to believe, she drilled it into me, but to her, a mojo bag was something that worked for you, with you, and no one else could see it, ever, so that's why there wouldn't be any in here just lying around."

"And you think what?"

"I think a mojo bag is about your intention and attracting the energy you want and need in your life."

"But that's not magic."

"Who's to say," I said, grinning at him. "After people saw Peg, they felt better, and maybe that was magic, and maybe that was just her, but again, could be they're one and the same."

"You're not talking about Peg anymore."

"No."

"You think I enjoy fixing up houses, and because it makes me happy, that positive energy, or whatever you want to call it, is radiating off me."

"Yes."

He let out a deep breath.

"You think so too," I reasoned, certain I was right.

"Yeah, and so does Rochelle," he said with a resigned sigh. "I've got to quit, and Dad is gonna tell me how stupid it is for me to flip houses for a living when nothing about the real estate market is secure. And he's going to tell Rochelle that most clothing boutiques go bankrupt in less than six months, and me failing, and her failing, are both very real possibilities."

I kept quiet, letting him reason it all out in his head.

"If we fail, that will be bad enough, but to live—I mean, just to be able to eat—we'll have to go back to him, defeated, with our tails between our legs, and just thinking about that makes both of us want to play it safe because…shit. The alternative to success is failure plus a big steamy plate of humiliation."

I went back to looking at Peg's large canisters and jars, shaking a couple and having the *aha* moment of knowing what I was looking at.

"Don't you have anything to say?"

I shrugged. "I'm not any better. The idea of failure at anything has always filled me with absolute dread, because if I failed, I had to come back here, and I couldn't do that, so there was always that pressure plus knowing that, someday,

I would need to take care of Jo and Papa and Peg. I was sure they would all be living with me."

"They have other family."

"Yeah, but they basically put everyone else on the back burner to raise me the rest of the way."

"I can see that."

"So, it was up to me to pay them back and, of course, my privilege to do so."

"Then you understand."

"Yeah, I understand."

His eyes met mine. "Then what?"

"Oh, come on, you know what," I said, chuckling. "You jump, for crissakes. This is your life, Ev, not anybody else's. You don't plan; you never plan. You just go."

"Not everyone can do that."

"It's like what Peg used to always say about the box."

He was scowling at me. "What're you talking about?"

"Don't you remember? She used to say that just because you build a box, or find a box, or buy one—whatever way you got it —it didn't mean that you had to find something to put in it right away. You didn't have to go home and look around for something to put in the box. Sometimes it stayed empty a long time, but eventually, what was supposed to go in there would appear, and you'd think, man, that's lucky. I have the perfect thing."

He smiled slowly as he stared at me.

"Don't be in a rush to fill the box."

"Don't be in a rush to give up on your dream."

"Nope. Because maybe the perfect thing is just waiting for you," I told him.

"You know," he said as we walked back across the yard from the cottage. "I think you might be magic after all."

"Don't tell anybody."

"Absolutely not," he said and draped his arm over my shoulder like he hadn't done since I was fourteen. It turned out I'd missed it just a bit.

After trudging up the back stairs, I dropped down into a chair beside Jo.

"Well?" she said after a moment, turning her head to look at me.

"I told Everett he should be an interior designer. He already had the idea, and he wants to quit working for Dad and flip houses."

"I think that's a marvelous idea."

"I reminded him about the boxes."

She grunted.

"What?"

"She didn't come up with that gem, you know. That was my mother's."

"Really?"

Another grunt.

"She took all the credit."

"She took the credit for a lot of things."

"It sounded better coming from her. Sage-like and shit."

She rolled her eyes.

"You know she had a way."

"Did she? I can't seem to recall."

I laughed at her, because there was nothing about Peg that Jo didn't remember. They were the kind of sisters that were into movies and old books, the devoted kind who were best friends. They used to talk for hours and at other times they'd sit, for the same amount of time, and not say a word, both of them reading or watching the rain as they drank tea.

"It sounds like we're going to have another full house tomorrow," I informed her.

"Joy," she said, her voice dripping with sarcasm.

"I thought you liked Maeve and her kids."

"Everett and Maeve never visit me because neither of them can sit still like you can. Maeve cleans," she said, giving me an evil grin, "and she dusts the top shelves better than me. Everett fixes faucets and oils door hinges. Rochelle busies herself on her laptop, and the kids and I play games on their PlayStation."

I suspected that she watched them play, and napped as well, but that could be fun too.

"It's going to be different now. Everyone wants to see you."

"Because they all think I'm going to die like, I dunno, Tuesday."

"Well, you're not."

"Most likely no, but in the event I do, make sure you get rid of all my porn and all my fancy undergarments. And I still have the belly dancer outfit your grandfather liked too."

I let my head fall back as I tried to will the images out of my head. It was hard. I could still remember when she took belly dancing lessons to turn on my grandfather. She even learned to balance a scimitar on her head.

"I wonder if I still have the zills somewhere."

"What are you talking about?"

"The...you know, the little finger cymbals."

I stared at her.

"Love?"

"You can remember the word *zill*, but you can't remember your grandchildren?"

"Some of my grandchildren are pills who just want my money."

I couldn't argue with that.

"I'm sorry Rose hit you," she apologized again, reaching for my face. "But it doesn't look like it's going to bruise."

I scoffed at her. "She'd have to have hit me a hell of a lot harder than she did."

"Well, I called her and told her that until she was ready to apologize to you, I don't want to see her."

"Oh no, Jo, that's not—"

"You're my golden boy," she said, taking my hand in hers. "No one hurts you while I'm here to protect you."

I leaned sideways and gave her a kiss, and the smile I got, so pleased, made it impossible not to hug her.

"So," she said after we were quiet for a few minutes, the two of us enjoying the warm summer breeze. "Did you top or did Brody?"

She was lucky I hadn't taken a sip of my water.

I SMELLED the rain and got Jo inside, and the umbrellas closed and leaning up against the side of the house, and the two tables covered in tarps right before the cloudburst. In the kitchen, I was finishing up the last of the cleaning as Carrie Wedge helped me, her husband, Enoch, sitting with Jo, having tea. Brody was doing some Tetris stacking in the refrigerator, but it wasn't looking good.

"Kaenon, your tea is amazing," Carrie said, taking another sip of the Red Rooibos she had wanted to try. "Is there bergamot in this?"

"And mint and cinnamon and vanilla bean," Jo said with a yawn. "He's good at knowing what goes together."

"Yes, he certainly is," Carrie praised me. "Do you think you might want to make it in bulk for the shop?"

"I don't think so," I told her, as Brody came up behind me and gently squeezed the back of my neck.

"Give Carrie some of the others," he directed me. "Jo's given me the lemon balm, peppermint, and rose one as well as the chamomile with dandelion and dried orange."

I turned to look at him. "You two sit together in her parlor quite a bit."

He shrugged, leaned over and kissed her cheek. "She's easy to talk to."

Jo elbowed me gently, and when I bent close, she whispered in my ear, "He wants me. I told you he was bi."

"Oh God, it's time for you to go to bed."

"I need a shower first; I was outside all day, you know."

"Go already," I ordered her.

"I'm going," she told me, and then turned and gave Carrie a hug that shocked the woman to silence, and then went into the living room and did the same with Enoch before heading toward her bedroom.

"Oh my God," Carrie said shakily, looking at me, her hand over her heart. "Jo has never hugged me in over forty years."

"Well, she's getting old," I teased her. "She's getting a bit sentimental."

She nodded quickly, too choked up to say anything more.

After packing her a plastic sandwich baggie full of tea, I said goodnight to Carrie and Enoch on the front porch. We all stood for a moment, watching the sheets of rain fall.

"I thought I heard Hollis say that you and he were going to take a walk down by the pond tonight," Carrie said, chuckling. "I'm thinkin' that's gonna have to wait."

"It's off the table indefinitely," Brody quipped before opening the screen door and going back into the house.

Carrie squinted at me as Enoch gave me a pat before darting out to their Dodge pickup truck, needing to move it closer to try and keep his wife as dry as possible. "That Brody Scott is a fine lawman, and I voted for him, but he's a hound of a man, Kaenon. Hollis would be much better suited to you and would understand your gifts."

I suspected that her son was just as much of a "hound" as Brody was. "Thank you for your concern, Carrie," I replied, kissing her cheek. "I'll keep it in mind."

"See that you do," she said, and then we both ran out into the rain.

I opened the door for her as she climbed in and closed it, then returned to the porch as fast as I could. Even in those few seconds, I was drenched, and was shaking my head when Brody walked back out onto the porch with a dish towel.

"That isn't going to do it," I said, laughing as he started drying my hair and being none too gentle about it.

"I know," he agreed, leaning in to drop a quick kiss on my mouth before continuing his ministrations. "I just need you to make it to the shower without dripping all over the hardwood."

"You're saying I need a shower too?"

"Yes, you need a shower. I'll wait for Jo while you take a quick one, and then it'll be my turn in there."

I nodded, slipping my hand around the side of his neck, my fingers threading into his thick hair. "You want us both clean for some reason?"

"My plan is to be naked in your bed this time, and I'm not leaving after."

The surge of molten heat that rushed up my spine made me shiver there on the porch. "You're going to stay and sleep with me?"

"If that'd be all right?" he asked softly, and the warm, sensual smile I got made it hard to breathe.

I answered him with a kiss.

When I got out of the shower and walked out to the living room, Brody was walking around, turning off lights and checking that the front door was locked.

"Where's Jo?"

"She came out for a glass of water and then said she was going to bed. I got a kiss, but she said you had to go in there for yours."

"Shower," I stated, pointing back over my shoulder.

"Yes, sir," he said with a snort, slapping my ass as he walked by.

I could get used to the easiness of this thing we had going on.

Jo was in bed, holding her leather-bound and worn copy of *Pride & Prejudice*, but close to her, facedown and open, was a hardback edition of *Anna Karenina*.

"Why?" I asked her.

She rolled her eyes. "Well, I promised your grandfather I'd read that horrible book before I died, so I figured I'd better get to it in case I go in the night and he meets me at the pearly gates and wants to discuss it."

I smiled at her. "And so, what's with Elizabeth and Mr. Darcy?"

"Honestly, I can't possibly be expected to read it right through, so I take breaks and read my favorite."

"I see."

"But I'm tired so I'm going to bed, but I forgot to turn the night-light on in the bathroom."

"I'll get it."

"Kiss me first."

So I did. When I was at the door, leaving it open a crack, she called over to me.

"Tell Brody I'm a heavy sleeper so he can scream all he likes."

"He'll never get a hard-on again if I tell him that."

She was cackling when I left.

At the door of my room I stopped, because Brody was on the phone.

"No, I think it's great that you were the guy sleeping with whatever moved, but somehow I got stuck with the reputation for being a player because I screwed Hollis."

I opened the door, and he was standing there with a bath towel wrapped around his waist and nothing else. It clung to his perfectly round ass, and the rest of him, the six-pack abs and muscular chest, those impossibly broad shoulders and tree-trunk arms were there for me to admire along with his long, powerful legs, and that gorgeous tawny-tan skin. I heard my breath catch. He was a beautiful man.

"Bye," he snapped and tossed the phone onto the bed. "So, I need to tell you something."

I closed the door behind me, and as I walked over to him, I pulled the t-shirt I'd put on up and over my head and dropped it on the floor.

His eyes narrowed as he watched me. "I've slept with two of your admirers from today, both Hollis Wedge and Tyler Galloway."

"Have you," I mumbled, shucking down my sleep shorts and stopping for a moment to let them fall to the floor, pooling at my feet before stepping out of them.

Naked, I closed in on him, not stopping until I reached him, putting my hands on his hips before slipping them around to the front of the towel where he had it secured.

"Christ, look at you," he croaked out, his hands on my shoulders before sliding them up my neck to cup my face. "Every part of you is gold."

I lifted for the kiss.

"Kaenon, I don't—I'm not—If I'm in a relationship, I don't sleep around. I would never betray a trust or—"

"I know that," I assured him, taking his mouth slowly, gently, sucking on his bottom lip until he opened for me. When I slid my hands up his chest and pushed, he took a step backward and sat down on the edge of my bed.

Tugging on the towel, I pulled it free as I kissed him thoroughly, feeling the submission I was after even as I straightened up. His eyes remained closed for a moment, and when they finally drifted open, I saw again the blown pupils from earlier in the day. His response to me was so honest, so transparent, that I said a quick thank-you to the universe for giving him to me.

"What?" he asked, staring up at me.

"Nothing. Get up on the bed."

He did as directed, dragging himself over the comforter to the headboard, leaning back and slipping his hands behind his head to grab on.

Following, I crawled over the bed to him, to his hard body, and bent over his already erect cock and licked a long, slow line from base to tip.

"On my phone," he rasped, "I have the...I have my results from my last...Kaenon." He moaned loudly as I licked over the glistening head, wet with precum.

"You're trying to tell me that you don't want any more condoms," I said, before I leaned sideways and got into my nightstand, needing the lube there.

"Yes," he said, taking it from me. "That's what I'm saying."

Since I was up for whatever he wanted, when he rose up off the bed and pushed me down, I waited, watching as he straddled my hips, pinning me under him to the bed, surprised when he reached for my shaft with his lubed palm.

"Brody," I just managed to get out, because looking at him, all that beautiful carved muscle under his smooth, sun-kissed skin, was making it impossible to think. "I have a thing too, results that tell you it's safe with me. I'm safe."

"I know," he said, lifting over me, my cock still in his hand, the anticipation building, coiled in my balls, at the base of my spine, sending pulses of electricity over already stimulated nerves.

I wanted to be inside of him. I wanted to dig my hands into his hips and wrench him down on top of me, stuff him full in one long, hard thrust. At the same time, the thought of him working my length inside of him, slow, controlled, taking me in a little at a time, the long, languorous agonizing slide of feeling him open in tight, convulsing intervals, was just as hot.

When he sank down over me, taking the head of my cock, and then more, into his body, the punch of emotion I felt that accompanied his action nearly made my heart stop. He stared down into my eyes until he was impaled. His ass muscles clenching around me and the heat of his body were almost more than I could bear.

"Oh, Brody, please, baby, you have to move," I pleaded, trying not to buck under him.

"Yeah?" he asked, lifting up, rolling his hips, curling forward to anchor his hands on my chest before clenching his ass tight.

I almost swallowed my tongue with my need for him, and I knew I was changing right there, in that moment. I loved sex, always had, but it had always been something I did, that I participated in, that I made good for others. But this, with Brody, I could feel the joining, the connection, the notching into place. It was terrifying.

My lizard brain sensed danger, that remaining there, in bed with the gorgeous man who was grinding down onto me in sinuous motion, harder and faster, milking my cock as his fingers dug into my pectorals and his eyes closed as he abandoned himself to anything but his own pleasure, was a trap. I would become addicted to being with him, of feeling like this, and extricating myself would become impossible.

"Roll over," I begged him, my voice not my own, guttural and low.

He lifted up off the end of my cock and fell down beside me, putting his hands under the headboard of the bed, holding tight.

Grabbing the pillow, I shoved it under his ass before curling forward, lifting his legs, one after the other, over my shoulders. With my hands on his thighs, I drove forward in one long, smooth slide.

"Kaenon," he husked, and I lifted my eyes to his, and for the first time in my life, it was as important to kiss as it was to fuck.

I ground my mouth down over his, chasing his tongue, wanting it, my body taking over, pumping into him even as I kissed him breathless. When he twisted his head away to gulp for air, I straightened up, his legs falling to my waist, ankles crossed behind my back as I pounded inside of him, the pistoning relentless as I continued to hold on to his thighs, certain I'd leave bruises.

He arched up against me, trying to press tighter, and against the solid brace of him, of his body, I lost myself, using him hard, my thrusts wild, savage, the only thing that mattered being as deep as I could get so I'd be stamped, forever, on his body and mind.

Nothing else, no one else, could ever be this for me. I had searched and of course found the one man I needed right where I'd started. The idea that we'd both returned to the same place was unfathomable and perfect at the same time.

"Don't stop," he implored me, and when I saw the tears, I changed my angle and took hold of his leaking cock at the same time.

He howled my name as he came, spilling hot and thick over my fingers, my hand, and wrist, the satin heat of his muscles clamping down around me as I drove to his core, hearing the continuous slap of skin as I pounded into him. And then the rush of coming so hard blurred everything together for a moment, sight, sound, smell, all of it as I lost time. Between us, our skin was hot and wet and slick, and I kept coming, pumping all I had into him, making him wholly mine.

It took long minutes for me to come back to myself, to notice the quiet and then become aware of the man under me. The two of us were a sticky mess of sweat and semen, and I could not have been happier, or more content.

"Get off me," he ordered, voice cracked, broken, his body trembling, and I was suddenly terrified that I'd hurt him.

"Brody?" I tried to retrace what I'd done, looking for anything I'd missed. There had been pleading for more but no word of stop, of that I was certain.

"I need—" He was panting, working to calm his breathing, waiting, not speaking until he was ready. "I need to get up."

Why? What was driving him? Why did he need to leave me? I was just as naked and vulnerable as he was. I was still inside of him, and this close, this connected, this fused, neither of us could hide. But he was on his back, on display for me, and for some reason he wasn't comfortable with me seeing whatever it was he was trying to hide.

"You need to hold on a second," I soothed him, not asking questions, waiting, watching to see if I could figure it out. "My muscles aren't working yet." It was the truth, and his, those muscles in his hot, perfect ass, were still spasming around my cock. It almost hurt because I was oversensitized, but it was still the good kind of pain that was pleasure as well, that edge that went both ways from moment to moment.

He threw his arm over his eyes, trying to hide, and I understood the need. He was just as flayed open as I was. We were both naked in more than just the physical sense.

"Look at me."

But he didn't move, instead swallowing over and over, and I knew he was gulping down tears that he wasn't about to let me see.

It hit me then, the why of his desire to run, and I felt stupid for it taking me minutes and not seconds. But it was his fault; sex with him was mind melting.

"You have complicated my life," I whispered, lying down on top of him, kissing his throat, then the line of his jaw, each press of my lips softer than the last, delicate, careful, until he took a deep breath and moved his arm, turning to look at me from red-rimmed eyes. "And yeah, this is going to be a gigantic pain in the ass, because you flying up to see me, and me flying down here to see you, is going to be rough."

He sniffled and rubbed his eyes before he cupped my face in his hand.

"But cheating isn't going to be our problem. I don't want

to do this with anyone but you. I don't think it's going to feel like it just did with anybody else, so if it can't be as good, why would I want it?"

Quick nod from him as his eyes tightened up to keep any more tears from falling.

"Brody," I husked, not sure what I wanted to say as I eased my spent cock from his body even as I was caught, fixated, as my cum leaked from his still-spasming hole. It occurred to me then that I couldn't have that, that I needed to leave something of myself behind to mark him. And that feeling of possessiveness, of want and need and gut-clenching, raw yearning as I brushed my fingers over his warm skin, massaging and soothing him as my breath caught on his sigh, made everything crystal clear. "I'm ready to do anything to make this work with us. Anything at all."

He rolled over on top of me, wrestling me under him, his lips sealing over mine as he took possession and claimed what was so very much his.

Me.

I was his. Without question.

FOURTEEN

It was early in the morning, and I woke up hard and aching. As my eyes opened, I was treated to heavy-lidded, mahogany eyes glinting in the near-dark. His hand was lazily stroking over my rock-hard erection.

"I wasn't gentle with you last night," I whispered, nuzzling my face into the side of his neck. "I don't want to hurt you or—"

"You didn't hurt me," he promised, his voice a silky purr in my ear as he passed me the lube from under his pillow at the same time he rolled to his side.

Slicking myself fast, I pressed myself to his back and slid my cock between his cheeks, parting them as I first notched against his entrance and then pressed inside.

"This is a lot," I murmured in his ear, my left arm under him and across his chest, my hand gripping his right pectoral, the other wrapped around his throat, holding him still. "I want you to be able to walk."

"I can walk just fine," he moaned, grabbing hold of the edge of the mattress.

I pushed forward, my groin flush with the curve of his

ass, fully seated, before I withdrew a fraction only to thrust back inside.

He leaned his head back, his staccato breathing letting me know how turned on he was, and the hand that had been at his throat slid over his shoulder, down his rib cage, around his hip to his cock.

"If you miss topping you can have me any—"

"No," he said, his voice brittle and dry, full of gravel as he pushed back and I shoved forward. "I'll tell you if I change what I want."

I stroked and milked him, the pearly precum leaking from the thick head making the slide through my fingers easy. He felt so good, so tight, so hot, and I made each snap of my hips harder, faster, wanting nothing more than to be buried in him as deep as I could get.

When he reached back, snaking his hand under my arm, not wanting my hand off his dick, and grabbed hold of my ass, pushing me forward, keeping me close, tight, I understood that he wanted me there, plastered against him, my breath on the back of his neck as I rolled my hips forward until he slid free and scrambled to his knees, needing more than I could do on my side. The pounding I delivered, once I had leverage, made him bite his lip so hard he drew blood.

He came, and I followed, the orgasm charging up from the base of my spine, sparking over my skin like a live wire. When he collapsed down onto the bed, I followed, crushing him under me, which was apparently funny, because the throaty, seductive chuckle came instantly.

"Let me get off you," I murmured, licking up the side of his neck, the taste of him nearly as good as his smell, all musky and warm.

"Just wait," he rumbled, arching his back, which lifted his ass against my groin, driving my cock inside of him a fraction deeper. "I like how full I am and that I can feel your —feel you. It's hot sliding between my thighs."

The man did not have a problem with me coming in his ass. It turned him on just as much as it did me.

"Kiss me."

He was laughing as he complied, and I hungrily devoured his mouth.

"I hope you have no plans to go home tonight."

"I have a crappy little apartment close to the station house," he said between kisses. "You can keep me here as long as you want."

"Don't make idle promises."

"I wouldn't. I'm all yours."

I was going to hold him to that.

THE SMELL of coffee woke me. When I opened my eyes, Jo was there, looming over me, with a "cat that ate the canary" smile on her face.

I glowered at her.

"Oh, come on," she whispered sharply, indicating Brody with the cup in her hand.

There was stubble burn on his throat and collarbone, his lips were red and puffy, and there was a bit of bruising on the side of his neck, and when he rolled over to his left, a distinctive bite mark on his right shoulder.

"Maybe don't try and eat him when you two are in bed tonight."

"Give me that cup and get out."

She shook her head. "You need to get up and shower," she informed me. "It's after nine; people are going to start showing up."

"It's after nine?" I whined.

She waggled her eyebrows at me. "If you have sex all night, you're not going to get all the shut-eye you need."

I grunted.

"I suspect you don't care."

Pulling the pillow out from under my head, I covered my face with it. I felt the bed dip beside me ever so slightly as she sat down.

"What's it going to be, love?"

I groaned.

"That bad?"

Moving the pillow, I looked up at her.

She snorted out a laugh. "You look so miserable."

"Monthly flights," I whimpered. "All the time."

Valiantly she tried to kill her smile, pressing her lips together tight.

"It's not funny."

"No."

"This wasn't supposed to happen."

"Yes, well, as the poet said, dear, the best-laid plans of mice and men and all that," she said, paraphrasing good old Robert Burns.

"I blame you," I assured her.

"Me?" She pretended to be affronted.

"Not once did you say that Brody Scott was back in town."

"Oh, that again? I'm certain I did," she said innocently.

"You lied the other day, and you're lying now."

She gasped and clutched at her heart. "You cut me to the quick."

"Get out so I can shower."

"I want strawberry crepes today," she announced haughtily.

"Yes, ma'am."

She stood up then. "And put new sheets on this bed, and open the windows until it gets hot out. This room needs airing out. It reeks of sweat and spunk."

"Oh, could you not," I groused at her as she left the room, cackling.

I was going to give Brody hell, but his snore told me he was still sleeping, though how, I had no idea. The fact that when I curled around him, he nestled back against me, made me smile like a simpleton. I so very much more than liked him, and God, what a mess.

After I took a quick shower, I closed the door behind me and went out to the kitchen to start on Jo's crepes. Fifteen minutes later, Everett and Rochelle showed up.

"We brought trees," Rochelle imparted, walking up beside me and kissing my cheek. "And men."

"Awww," I said to her, "guys for me? You shouldn't have."

She laughed and I could tell she was tickled. "No, dingus, to dig up the old stumps in the orchard and plant new trees."

"Everett," Jo spoke in awe. "You brought me new trees?"

"And surprise," he revealed, walking over to her and taking her small, soft hands in his. "I got a sapling from Mom's garden, from that same cherry tree that Jo brought you back from Japan. I called her yesterday and asked if I could have one of the younger trees, and she said yes."

I was quiet because I didn't want anything from my mother, ever, but it would make Jo happy, and that was all that mattered.

"Kaenon," she said knowingly, and when I lifted my eyes from the strawberries I was slicing, her eyes were like lasers on me. "Is that all right?"

"Of course," I replied fast, hoping to sound nonchalant.

"Are you certain?" she pressed me.

I took a breath. "Yes, Jo, I'm certain."

She turned her attention back to Everett then. "Thank you, my darling."

And I watched my brother melt to the floor, right then and there, under my grandmother's pleased smile, adoring gaze, and words of thanks.

A half an hour later, when Maeve and her family showed up, there were crepes and eggs and bacon and turkey sausage for them. The kids both wanted banana and chocolate crepes, Maeve wanted blueberry and whipped cream, and Will wanted strawberry and mascarpone, if it wouldn't be too much trouble. I appreciated Rochelle taking care of the eggs and bacon for me, though she drew the line at turkey-anything other than the kind you had at Thanksgiving. She also made breakfast burritos, as she'd done the day before, for the guys who were digging up the stumps in the orchard and planting the new trees.

"You know, I hired all three of those nice boys you had over here yesterday for my shop," she told me.

Nice boys? "Oh, you mean Artie and Mike and Vance?"

"I thought it was Hoyt?"

"It is, but he goes by Vance."

She grunted. "I guess I would too, if my name was Hoyt."

"That's exactly what I said."

"Yes, well, I hired Artie to be in the shop with me. He's quite charming and polite and just as cute as a button, so he'll be my sales associate, and Mike is going to be my delivery driver, picking up inventory and dropping off consignment items, and Vance will be in charge of the stockroom. Both Artie and Mike said he's quite organized."

"What about when school starts?"

"I'll cross that bridge when I come to it."

"That's really nice of you."

"Well, they worked so hard for you yesterday, and you can tell a lot about young men from how they treat their significant others, and they were wonderful and kind and polite to their girlfriends."

I had to agree.

"It sounds like your Saturday was filled with just a crazy amount of people," Maeve chimed in, getting up from the kitchen table and walking over to me, her hand on my back, rubbing gently.

"It was amazing," I told her. "So many people came to see Jo."

She scoffed.

I glanced over at her.

"To see you, Kaenon, not me."

"Both of you," Everett said, playing peacemaker. "Equally."

"Your aunt Rose hit Kaenon," Jo told Maeve.

"I'm sorry?" she said abruptly, bristling, her tone like ice.

It was nice to see her get instantly defensive, and I could almost hear "the hell you say" in the undercurrent of her voice.

"Because everything is in his name," she explained.

"So what?" Maeve snapped. "What is anyone going to do with the house or the land or anything else, anyway? Sell it?"

"That was Everett's plan," Jo said honestly, shrugging.

"A piece," Everett stressed to her. "Only the parcel that drifts down into the canyon, nothing else, for crap's sake. I would never part with the house or the garden or Peg's cottage," he railed at her. "The hell kind of monster do you think I am?"

It was quiet, even the kids didn't say a word, and into that silence walked Brody, one eye open, one closed, not all the way awake, in a pair of basketball shorts and a t-shirt that had seen better days, given how faded it was.

"Oh, well," Maeve said brightly, leaning on the counter, arms crossed, head tipped, looking like an evil pixie. "Good morning to you, Constable."

He scowled at her, and Everett snickered, and Will, who was standing close to him, said that maybe he should shower.

"Why are you people here?" he groused at them all.

"Come here, sweetie, let's have some coffee," Jo said indulgently, waving him over. "Kaenon, get the poor man some coffee."

When he sank into the seat beside Jo and buried his face down in his folded arms, and her eyes opened wide, all of us but the kids dissolved into laughter.

"I hate you all," he muttered into the table.

Jo just stroked his hair.

EVERETT AND BRODY and Will and I all had to help dig up the stumps with the five men that my brother had paid extra to work on a Sunday. It was fortunate that Davis had left the minitractor one more day, or we would have never been successful. As it was, Jo was standing at the edge of what had been her orchard and eyeballing where the trees were supposed to go. After the third hole that I dug—and she thought the lines were still off, had been, she said, when the original trees were planted—Everett went to his truck and got twine and his tape measure. Math would triumph over "a little more to the left," he promised.

Brody smelled better after his shower but was soon as sweaty as he'd been the night before—without the added aroma of semen. I missed it. The idea of my cum drying on him gave me a perverse pleasure that I wasn't about to confess to anyone.

Before lunch, others started showing up.

"Kaenon!"

I was filling the trench around the avocado tree with water when I looked to Maeve and she was gesticulating wildly. Handing the hose off to Everett, I joined her and was surprised when she reached for my dirty hand, grasped it, and faced a man with me.

"Kae, this is Tate, Aunt Linda's oldest son. I don't know if you remember him."

Tate looked like most of the Gearys, the dark chestnut-brown hair and blue-black eyes. He was handsome. He looked a bit like my grandfather, and a bit like Everett, and not a thing like me at all.

"Hi," I said, not offering my hand because for one, Maeve was holding it in both of hers now, and for two, I was dirty. "Nice of you to come by and see Jo."

"Of course," he said kindly, smiling at me. "But it's you, Kaenon. I'd love for my kids to spend some time out here in the garden with you, if you don't mind."

"I'd love it," I said, hoping my sincerity was obvious.

I had his son and daughter after that, ten-year-old Liam and eight-year-old Callie, along with Bebe and Kurt, who had nearly climbed all over me when I'd answered the door that morning. They were thrilled to be back and had brought me rocks and pieces of shells, and Bebe even had some fossils that she'd gotten from Will's sister who worked at the Field Museum in Chicago.

"I want to know what plants I can eat," Liam said excitedly.

"Maybe let's not start with the plant eating," Tate said, grinning at me.

I had the kids watering and shaking plant food in the garden when my aunt Debbie arrived with her son, Justin, and his two kids, teenagers both, Naomi and Paul. They did not want to be there, both of them on their phones at the picnic table on the porch. I saw Jo pull Brody aside, and he went into the house moments later.

"I'm going to go sit with Jo for a bit," Maeve told me after she brought Tate and me both bottles of water.

She ran back up to the porch just in time to sit down beside Jo before Debbie joined them. Everett put a hand on my shoulder as Tate made a noise in the back of his throat.

"I'm missing something," I said to my brother and my cousin.

"Debbie's getting on her mother about thinking that Justin's gonna steal something," Tate explained to me. "Last month, one of Rochelle's rings?" Tate asked Everett.

He nodded.

"Yeah, one of Rochelle's rings went missing after Justin visited, and he's already pawned all the silver that Jo gave Debbie, plus all his mother's jewelry, except for what she's wearing on her fingers."

"Oh, you're kidding," I said sadly. "Why?"

"Justin hurt his back in a construction accident, like, ten years ago now, and he got really addicted to oxy when he was hurt."

I nodded.

"And so after that, it was heroin, and once he got out of rehab, then back to pills and alcohol, and it was a mess. That's why he and Ciara got divorced."

I saw Debbie lean forward at the table to point her finger and say something to Jo that Jo only shook her head at. When she raised her voice, I took a step forward, but Everett stopped me at the same time I saw my sister put up her hand and shake her head at my aunt as Jo turned away, cringing over whatever was being said.

At that moment I realized again how inflated my ego had been. Everett loved Jo and so did Maeve, so dearly, so much. Maeve was not about to let her aunt give her grandmother even a second of whatever she was trying to dish out. Jo had sent Brody inside to lock doors, making certain my things, hers, and even his, were all safe from my sticky-fingered cousin. She still loved her grandson, he was in her home, after all, but Jo didn't want him walking through her home without supervision.

"We should start working on getting out some leftovers and firing up the grill again," Everett told me, and I agreed.

When Brody came out of the house, Justin, who I hadn't even seen go in, followed him out. Both men walked to the table where Jo and Debbie were seated, and they both sat down, Brody beside my grandmother and Justin next to his mother. It was interesting to watch Debbie almost deflate before Brody leaned forward and took her hand.

"He's been trying to get Justin into a program in Wimberley, at a horse ranch, for the last three months, and maybe he just now agreed."

Anything was possible.

"You know, it looks like it might just rain again today," Everett said, glancing up at the sky, and I checked too, noting the gathering storm clouds. "At least it's not as hot as it…was…yes…ter…holy shit."

I turned to look at him. "What?"

"Jesus, Kaenon," he rasped.

I followed his line of sight to Peg's cottage. What had been dead vines the day before were now dotted with rosebuds.

"Oh, that's great," I said, grinning at him. "They weren't

dead, after all. They just needed some water. We'll have to find all the roots today and get some more water in there and fertilizer and use the rest of those bags of mulch Davis left to cover them."

He was staring at me and shaking his head.

"What?"

"You're so stupid," he growled before he called for Jo.

She looked over at him, and he pointed at Peg's cottage.

I watched as she stood up, walked to the edge of the stairs as though in a trance, and then took hold of the railing to take the steps slowly to the ground below. Bolting over to her, I gave her my arm, which she grabbed with both hands.

"What are you wanting to do?" I asked her, waiting.

"I want to see the roses," she told me.

Walking her out into the garden, she looked cute in her cropped white denim jeans, black and a pale blue collarless linen shirt with puffed sleeves. Her leather wrap belt, which Rochelle had brought her from her boutique, looked great with her wedge sandals. She was easily the most stylish woman there, besides Rochelle, with everyone, including my sister, dressing older than the eighty-seven-year-old.

"You're going to get your shoes dirty," I warned her.

"Oh, Kaenon," she breathed out in a whisper. "Oh, honey, look what you did."

"Joanna Geary," I admonished her, stopping so she had to as well. "You and I both know that roses don't just pop up overnight. They're there because—"

"Of you," she cried, and I heard the sob in her voice before I turned and saw her eyes fill as she took my face in her hands. "Oh, love, you did it; you put down roots. You're grounded like Peg never was, like she never could be, even with Eustace, even though she loved him so much, more than anyone, she still wasn't settled, the road still called to her."

I shook my head even as she held me.

"You've been fighting it so hard, even in these few days back, but really, you've been fighting since you left, because you knew you were never supposed to."

"No, I...Jo, I never belonged—"

"You always did, even when it was hard, even when people were so very stupid, you still were only ever supposed to be right here in this place, in this town, on your land, Kaenon. You and this ground, this dirt, my home, your home, your cottage, your trees, your flowers, your—my God, Kaenon, don't you see? Everything is trying to climb right out of the earth to touch you."

I grabbed her arms, harder than I meant to, or should have, but she only smiled through her tears, her face so bright, luminous as she beamed up at me. "Do you know how crazy you sound right now? Do you have any idea?"

She tilted her face up to the sun. "I thought it would take all summer," she murmured to the breeze. "I thought, please, God, let me live to see Kaenon find his way home again. Because it's not just the family you have, like me and Everett and Maeve, but also your friends who love you just as much as we do. We've all been waiting to see you brave enough and strong enough to forgive so you could love again with your whole heart."

I let her go and took a step back, angry and hurt at the same time. "You've been thinking what all these years? That I haven't been able to love myself?"

"Yes, I do."

"Why? Because I'm broken inside?" I almost snarled at her, and it felt ugly and wrong to be mad at Jo, but she wasn't talking sense, and that was so converse to who she was and what she stood for in my life that the anger boiled out of me.

"You're not broken," she soothed me. "You've been so angry, so betrayed, so hurt, and there's been no place to vent that."

I shook my head. All my simmering rage had been directed at many people over the years.

"You never got to confront anyone."

"No, that's not—"

"Think about it," she cautioned me. "Your parents went away, your brother, your sister, all of them disappeared from your life, and you never had any closure."

I began pacing. This part I knew. My closest friends, they had all said the same thing to me at one point or another, that I buried the hurt my family inflicted down deep inside and left it there to rot.

"Not everybody needs the magic epiphany of closure," I told her. "The whole 'what doesn't kill you' bit, and all."

"But that's not you. As you well know, before that day, before school started, when you were fourteen, you were one person. Afterward, you were another. That moment changed every part of who you are."

"I—"

"You've insulated yourself behind this protective wall, and you never let anyone see the real you again because that person, that boy, was enraged."

I crossed my arms as I paced, resisting the urge to hug myself and withdraw.

"You couldn't ever be mad at me. I saved you," she said implacably. "The same is true for your grandfather and for Peg."

I bit my lip so I wouldn't say a word, afraid what would come out.

"Peg could be horrible, and your memory is so kind, but she baited you and railed at you, and I've heard you tell people that Peg made you believe in all the things she herself did, but that's not true. You've always sifted through what made sense and what was logical, and learned that and jettisoned the rest. She thought you were just like her because you never said a word in argument, never set her straight."

I choked out a laugh. "You wanted me to fight with Peg?"

"I wanted you to tell her what was in your heart."

"I loved her. That's what was in my heart."

"Of course, I know that, she knew that, but you couldn't, wouldn't allow yourself to, fight with her, or me, or your grandfather, because you sainted us the second we stepped between you and the fire."

"Sainted is not a verb, it's an adjective. You can't use it to--"

"Kaenon Geary, do not nitpick my language!"

I groaned.

"Listen to me."

"I don't understand what you're trying to—"

"You've never been able to unload how you felt in that kitchen all those years ago, or how you were treated by the community."

I swallowed down how badly I wanted to yell at her, and just stood there.

"You never got to vent at your family," she explained, stepping back close to me and taking hold of my hand. "At anyone who was horrible to you at school, or anyone who tried to hurt you. When you were small, you did your best to avoid them, and when you got bigger, you ignored them. But you never showed anyone your true face. First, because you were small and afraid. But then you grew into the man you are today, and you refused to give them the satisfaction."

"I—"

"Your grandfather saw it, so did I," she said with a sigh, sounding wistful, almost sad. "So many of your classmates were sorry. Deep down in their bones, they realized, too late, that you being gay didn't matter a whit, only missing your friendship did."

Davis had illuminated that piece for me, how thoroughly I'd shut people out of my life, no second chances, no do-overs.

"But all of it, every scrap of it, has been festering inside of you until you saw Brody Scott at the farmer's market."

I scoffed at her. "So now you're saying what, Brody saved my life?"

"No, dear," she said, giving me back all the sarcasm I'd just dished out. "What I'm saying is that because you could forgive him, forgive Brody, that opened the door for you to deal with all the rest of it."

"No."

"Ohhhh, yes," she said, drawing out the words.

"Brody's not—"

"Forgiving Brody, talking to Brody, that allowed you to do the same with Maeve and then with Everett," she declared, utterly certain of herself. "And in so doing, you finally got to realize something I've suspected for years."

"And what is that?"

Her smile, as she gazed at me, was full of so much love I had to glance away. "That somewhere during all that time, the anger and betrayal and hatred and eventual apathy, it all became sympathy for what they'd lost."

My head snapped back to her as my gaze locked with hers. "What they lost? What the hell did they lose, Jo?"

Her face was serene with the confidence of her conviction, her eyes so full of love for me. "You."

And that word, that single word coming from her, almost broke me. "I don't think so. I don't think the two of them not having me in their lives was some great loss for them. It's not like that."

"But you knew how much you loved them," she corrected me, her voice so strong and powerful, giving no quarter as she stood toe to toe with me and argued. "And you knew that the two of them missing out on that love was, in fact, a horrible, dreadful loss."

"Jo—"

"Because it would have been for you, were the roles reversed," she said, hammering home her point. "If the shoe had been on the other foot and you had abandoned them, had hurt them and then had no way to mend that bond, it would have killed you."

And it would have. No question.

"So you forgave them just in case they ever had the balls to come to you."

The words took a moment to sink in, and when they did, I laughed with relief. "The balls?"

She beamed, the wicked grin back, making her eyes glint.

Deep breath, I exhaled and then breathed in the truth of her words. "You're saying I've been lost a long time, carrying around all this crap inside me that I've never let out."

"Yes."

"And I never allowed myself to dump it on anyone, because I knew it wasn't fair."

"You said it wasn't like you to think too much of yourself, and that's true. But it's also very you to be careful of what you say and do in every situation. You analyze and dissect and forget to feel and just *be*, and because of that, because you're so in your head all the time, your heart gets left completely out of things."

I grunted.

"And that results in people like Aidan Powell in your life, who you can walk away from and never look back, because you never gave a damn in the first place."

"Fuck."

"Well said," she pronounced, taking a deep breath of air.

We stood in silence, watching each other.

"You think you know everything about me."

"Because I do," she said soberly, the tenderness there in her eyes even as her smile faded. "You've been sailing through your life, Kaenon, not because it's been easy, but it has been blessed in so many ways."

"With you, with Papa, and Peg," I offered.

"And with your friends and people who look at you and see your worth in seconds, recognizing someone who's ready to help."

"That's a nice thing to say," I said mischievously, baiting her.

"Yes, well, it's true. But it's also true that you have not once, since you left here, put down an anchor. You stay in places, sort of drifting on the surface, but it's easy to hoist the sail, to go wherever the wind takes you."

"I am digging this metaphor."

"And me without a shovel to hit you with."

I snickered, and she reached up to cup my cheek.

"But now you're here, and you forgave Brody because you've never stopped wanting him, but the second you did forgive him, your head finally took a back seat to your heart and look around you now. The land itself knows its boy is truly, finally, home."

I pointed at the roses on the roof of the cottage. "You got all that from a bunch of flowers that we mistakenly thought were dead?"

"Did we?" She scrunched up her face like she wasn't so sure. "Think they were dead? Or did we *know*, beyond a shadow of a doubt, since they haven't bloomed since Peg died, that they were dead as a doornail."

"Clearly they were not," I countered, crossing my arms as she did the same.

"Or they were and now aren't."

I shook my head. "Let's agree to disagree."

"And Brody?"

"Oh God, what about him?"

Both eyebrows lifted knowingly.

"Leave it alone, crazy person."

"Isn't it interesting, when you see all the pieces fall together, that without him coming home, you wouldn't have either?"

I chuckled and kissed her. "I am not staying here," I told her stridently, adamantly, but felt the words ring false for the first time. There was a twinge in my chest, an ache in my throat, a tightening of my skin, and a sinking in my stomach that signaled that which had been separate from me for so long—dread.

Other lovers that I'd been impressed with and thought of as more cultured than me, articulate or worldly, when I walked away, there was no regret. I dissected the why of it, of course, what had prompted my initial choice, but as Jo had pointed out, the process was a purely cerebral one, not grounded in any tender emotion, merely lust and attraction changed to a laundry list of logical reasons to remain coupled. Brody was...different.

Just the thought of being separated from the man made

it hard to breathe, like the air was being sucked from my lungs in agonizing slowness. My heart hurt, thinking about driving away with him standing behind me, waving goodbye in the rearview mirror. It seemed the absolute opposite of what I *should* do, a mistake to be avoided at all cost.

"Oh no? You're not going to stay?"

I glanced over at the back deck as Brody came down the stairs and began toward us as we stood near Peg's cottage.

"Don't talk out of your ass anymore," she warned me playfully. "You can't just throw out words and think they don't mean anything."

I groaned as Brody sped up, jogging to reach me faster.

"The roots are all around you," Jo whispered, "you just need to open your eyes and see them for what they are."

When he reached us, he glanced at Jo before slipping around in front of me and putting his hands on my hips as he gazed into my eyes.

"Are you okay," he asked softly. "It looks a little serious out here."

Ruggedly handsome man, staring at me with more tenderness than any other lover I'd ever had.

"What is this?" I snapped at him, taking out all my uncertainty and fear and frustration and flight response on him. Running would be the best, and worst, thing possible.

His slow, sexy smile told me he would not be baited into a fight. "We're gonna be an us," he announced. "We're gonna be together, and already I'm excited about the foundation."

I whimpered, and his smile went into dangerous megawatt territory.

"Oh come on, it's gonna be great."

"I hate this town."

"Uh-huh," he placated me, drawing me forward to lick over my lips for entrance.

I opened for him, and I heard his breath catch before he laid a kiss on me that nearly melted me right into the dirt.

"Oh," Jo murmured with a sigh.

"Aww, baby, you made the roses grow," he whispered before he kissed me again, and I wrapped my arms around his neck so he couldn't get away.

"Isn't it romantic?" I heard Maeve say somewhere close.

And my aunt Debbie said yes, yes, it certainly was.

FIFTEEN

I was surprised on Monday morning when Jo and I got to Braxton High to see how much it had changed. Gone was the sort of penal-code vibe it used to have, from the ten-foot-high chain-link fence that used to encircle the school to the prison-gray buildings. Now, there was glass everywhere, enormous walls of glass and redbrick, natural lighting and a rainwater harvesting system. The glittering display cases filled with trophies and ribbons, plaques and framed photos of past champions was stunning. I enjoyed seeing myself, as captain of the soccer team when we were all-state champions in both my junior and senior years, hoisting the silver cup high in the air. Jo rolled her eyes at me when I pointed out the picture.

"Why am I here?" she groused at me.

"Because I didn't come to spend my summer away from you," I reminded her.

"It's half a day," she grumbled. "We have to spend some time apart. You're suffocating me."

When I scowled at her, she threw up her hands in defeat.

In the front office, we were waiting for Kevin—Principal Rossiter—when the door of his office opened, and a man I knew stepped out into the hall.

I groaned in disgust before standing. "Come on, Jo, we're out of here."

"Don't you dare move," the man said sharply, and Jo's smile was full of mirth.

"Oh, whatever this is, is about to get good," she said excitedly.

Standing my ground, I waited, arms crossed, battle ready.

The man, Dr. Tolliver Knighton, took a few steps but decided to abandon all propriety and bolted over to me.

"No," I said distinctly.

"Kaenon," Principal Rossiter said sharply, "Dr. Knighton is the chair of the English department at the University of Texas-Austin and—"

"He knows who I am," he confirmed, taking hold of my arms, squeezing tight, staring at me, smiling, and then letting out a quick exhale. "You look great."

"You look old," I said, tipping my head since he was holding my arms, indicating the graying temples and streaks of silver in his dirty-blond hair.

"It was one book," he reminded me. "How long are you going to hold it against me?"

"Let me think," I grumbled, trying to take a step back, but to no avail.

"You would be in charge of the dual credit courses as well as freshmen advisor. You could bring your symposium on Shakespeare, Drama, and the Effects on Literary History to UT, and the book you're working on with Sylvia Whitley at Oxford about feminist writers and witchcraft and what's missing from the canon—I can send you to England."

Stand In Place

"All your professors are PhDs, Stormy," I said snidely.

His jaw clenched over the old nickname. "You have an MFA, and you'll get your PhD one of these days, I have no doubt."

"I garden now," I told him. "And besides, I'm only here for the summer."

Jo scoffed.

"Lasa called me and told me you were here, and I called Principal Rossiter and he explained that you were going to oversee the new AP teacher here."

I was quiet.

"I'd rather have you in the English department at UT, still overseeing the program here but teaching at the college, holding classes there, and then in the fall—"

"You don't need another person doing research at your school. You're full up with—"

"I only have one other professor who writes pieces for popular presses and not just academic journals. I need the diversity."

"No."

"I have a lot of people doing research, but you have three published books that people I know and respect are teaching from, and again, essays in magazines that those outside academia actually know of."

"No."

"Your podcast, *Logos Garage*, that you do with Maytal and Ramon, is so clever. I love that you talk about everything from gender studies to world myths to religion and witchcraft. I think it's great how many amazing guest stars you've had, and that there's going to be a book that complements the series."

"Don't suck up," I warned him, trying to make him explode with the power of my mind.

"It was ten years ago," Tolliver declared irritably. "Maybe it's time to let this go."

"I hold a mean grudge, ask my grandmother."

Jo nodded. "He does, I'm sorry."

"I'm sorry you're related to him."

"Stop talking to my grandmother," I demanded.

"Kaenon, love, you're being a bit argumentative and—"

"I'd say extremely argumentative," he chimed in belligerently, at which I smacked him in the abdomen hard enough that he gasped and bent forward.

"Kaenon!" Principal Rossiter half-yelled, looking appalled.

"—combative," Jo finished, taking hold of my arm. "Kaenon Lee Geary, what on earth has gotten into you?"

"Dr. Knighton, I'm so sorry that—"

"No," Tolliver interrupted Principal Rossiter, surprising him, if Kevin's mouth dropping open was any indication of how adamant Tolliver was. "Professor Geary and I go way back to grad school. He can take a swing at me if he wants."

"I'm going to do more than that if you don't—"

"Just stop," he muttered, sounding frustrated even as he took hold of my right arm. "You and Niall Collins did not need my collaboration on that article in the *Rose and Thorn*. You both covered the romantic ideal of courtly love as expressed in poetry and gardening in a way that has yet to be surpassed."

I rolled my shoulder to get him off me, and took gentle hold of Jo's hand to lead her back to the car.

"Wait, wait—crap," he grumbled to himself, catching up to me fast and then barring my path. "I'm sorry."

"We both know you're not," I retorted, my voice dangerously low, growly.

"Kaenon!" he yelled at me. "You can take a sabbatical

from Pollard and work for me. We both know you get asked to speak and lead classes all over the country, which is why you need to teach a reduced class load. I'll give you that."

"I already have that," I told him.

"But it's been a strain on the department at Pollard since it's so small," he stated logically, which only annoyed me more. "If they get rid of you, they can hire a new person who can take on more, which you can't do because you're in such high demand."

I let go of Jo's hand and crossed my arms again, hating that I was listening to him.

"Constance Aguilar joined the faculty at UT. Did she tell you?" he asked me just as one of the many doors that led into the school opened and we all heard the click of high heels on concrete somewhere behind us.

"Have you lost your mind?" I asked him seriously.

"I'll give you until July first to decide."

"I'm not going to work for you."

"Just think it over," he insisted. "I really want you there with me."

I shook my head. "Why?"

"Because you're great with students and faculty, and wherever you go, people follow like bees to honey, and I can use the help."

I was going to argue with him, but we were interrupted.

"Am I late? I had no idea where I was going, and Stor—shit, I mean Tolliver, am I late or is he not—oh! Kaenon! Ohmygod, you're really here. I thought he was messing with me!"

"Why would you want two people who hate you there working with you?" I muttered to him before I turned to face Connie, another one of my oldest friends from grad school.

She flew into my arms, wrapping hers around my neck, a

vision in pale pink and Christian Louboutin Mary Jane pumps. After squeezing me tight, she eased back just enough to look into my face. "Hello, you gorgeous thing, I missed you."

"I missed you back," I grumbled, and she leaned in and kissed my cheek, reaching out to wipe off the lipstick she'd left behind.

"Can you imagine having two of us there who hate him?" she said under her breath, eyes wide, concerned about the man's sanity. "I mean, really, do you think he's doing drugs again?"

Tolliver's groan was loud in the cavernous, echoing hall.

"And who knew that Stormy Nightmare was going to be a department chair at a place that either one of us would ever want to work?" she continued, laughing softly. "That is just crazy, am I right?"

She most certainly was.

AFTER LUNCH WITH ROSSITER, Tolliver, and Constance, Jo and I were walking arm in arm down Main Street, looking at the shops there that I'd never seen and that she had wanted to check out but had just not gotten around to doing.

"Your friend Constance is really lovely," Jo said softly, yawning after another moment.

"She acted like me starting at UT was a done deal," I replied irritably. "They both did, and I have commitments at home that—"

"Kaenon, sweetheart," Jo began with a chuckle, "how many different signs do you think one man needs to show him the way?"

"What?"

"You know, all the men in our family are blessed with being handsome, and I've always thought how lucky that is."

"Since we're all dumb as rocks, right?"

"Now let's not undermine rocks, that's just rude."

I growled at her, and she laughed as we passed an ice cream shop. Jo wanted a waffle cone, a small one, so in we went.

Outside, sitting on the bench, without fanfare or the Wicked Witch of the West music from *The Wizard of Oz*, we both saw my mother, Tessa Geary, walk out of the law office of Richard Travers, the man who had been my parents' lawyer for many years. Or, he was until they gave me up to my grandparents. When I was officially adopted, he brought the legal papers to the house that had been signed, notarized, and filed in family court. I was surprised when he hugged me on his way out, telling me that I was better off. Jo told me that he stopped doing business with my parents after that, so it was surprising to see her coming out of his office, and also amazing to lay eyes on her. On my mother.

Everything about her, from the wavy tousled hair pulled into a low chignon, to the crisp white collared button-down shirt, gray pencil skirt, and heels, was immaculate. She looked just like she had the last time I'd seen her, as elegant and graceful as ever.

"I wonder what my mother is doing at Travers's office," I said off-handedly to Jo between licks of my cone.

"Signing the divorce papers, I suspect," Jo replied nonchalantly. "Because even though they live in Austin, the lawyer's here, right?"

I did a slow pan to her.

"Oh," she said, making a face, "did I not mention that?"

"They're getting a divorce?"

"Mmmm."

I felt the sting of being left out. "Why didn't Everett tell me?"

"He doesn't know. Neither does Maeve," she assured me, patting my knee. "No one knows but me, and your father and mother, and now Richard Travers or some other lawyer in that office of his."

It took me a second to find the appropriate words. "Holy shit!"

"Indeed."

"What the hell, Jo?"

"Why are you mad at me?"

"I'm not mad. I-I'm-I'm stunned. I'm—a divorce? Them?"

"Well, they've been separated for over nine months already."

"How did they keep that from Everett and Rochelle?"

"Everett and Rochelle live here, darling, and they see your father quite a bit at work, but not your mother."

Huh. "And when did you find this out?"

"Yesterday, when your father called to tell me," she explained gently.

"Why didn't you tell me?"

"Well, you've been very busy with the garden and reconnecting with your family, and of course there's Brody."

"Jo, you—"

"And besides, your father asked me not to tell anyone until he talked to you and Everett and Maeve personally."

"You mean Ev and Maeve, not me."

"No," she corrected, her tone brusque, setting me straight. "He meant all three of you."

"Yes, but he has nothing to do with me."

"Which, as I've suspected for many years, he'd much like to remedy."

"I see," I said, which was pretty good, considering that

my heart was in my throat. I continued to eat my cone and turned back to watch my mother walk down the sidewalk until she reached a coffee shop where she stopped and pulled her phone out of her purse.

"Well?"

"Well, what?"

"Any twinge when you look at her?"

And what was interesting was that there wasn't one. My mother's side of the family had been adamant about separating themselves from me, cutting me out of their lives as though I had never been there. From what I understood from Everett and Maeve, though, no one on that side was particularly close, people scattered all over the country, with the annual Christmas card exchange being their only communication. I wasn't missing out on anything. Even though, thanks to my mother, I resembled the Cabots more than the Gearys. It was so strange.

"Are you all right?" Jo asked, turning to look at me just as I did the same and looked at her. "Are you going to fall apart, seeing her?"

"No, I don't think so," I said, and I meant it.

"You look like you might need a Xanax."

"Do you have a Xanax?" This was also a surprise.

"No, but I'm sure Rochelle does. We could call her."

I nodded in agreement as we both turned back and watched my mother as she texted on her phone.

"So, how do you feel?" Jo leaned her head on my shoulder as we sat there, both of us eating in the shade on the bench, watching my mother.

"I don't know," I said, crunching the waffle cone. "But this is really good ice cream."

"It is," she agreed.

"I thought maybe I'd cry," I told Jo.

"When you saw her, you mean?"

"Yes."

"But no? You don't feel like it?"

"Uh-uh. I wonder why."

"I have a thought," she said, sounding sad and resigned at the same time. "Perhaps that day in the kitchen, at that exact moment, you knew that you and she were done."

"Maybe."

"Or," she continued, "it could be that having Everett and Maeve back in your life, and their spouses, and in Maeve's case, a niece and nephew, has given you a new perspective on what family really is."

"And what is it?"

"I think it's people, related to you or not, who will stand still in one place with you and be counted in your life as someone who matters and who you know you matter to back."

I nodded.

"And also, I think this goes back to Brody."

"How do you mean?"

"I mean that loving Brody, and being loved in return, sort of insulates you from her, or your feelings from her. You know you're loved, because he does. Love you, that is. It's written all over his face when he looks at you. His whole heart is in that smile of his, just as yours is with him."

"That happened too fast, maybe."

"What's that?"

"Me and Brody."

"Who's to say?"

"Jo––"

"No, really. Who's to say? You were ready to see him. He was ready to be seen. Peg took one look at Eustace, and that was that. Everyone has their own timeline, darling."

It was hard, for a second, to breathe.

"You can't doubt he loves you."

I couldn't, no. Because when he looked at me, every single time, it was like he was looking at his home. "You loved me first," I said, taking her left hand and squeezing it gently.

"No," she said with a sigh. "Your father did when they laid you in his arms."

I would choke if I tried to speak in that moment.

"And your mother did, once upon a time. The thing is, in her heart of hearts, she can't see beyond the gay, and it's a pity, but it's a fact."

Quick nod from me, because yes, I knew that. She had two children, not three. I didn't exist anymore. She couldn't be who she was if I was part of her life, so she'd cut me out with surgical precision and never looked back. And while I'd lied to Maeve and said I never thought of her, because of course I did, it was different with my mother. Usually people assumed she was dead as I never, ever, spoke of her.

"I'm sorry she is how she is, but these are old wounds, aren't they?"

"Yes," I croaked out. "They are."

"I can't worry that you're still in pain over—"

"I'm not," I promised her, needing her to hear the truth in my words. "I'm not that scared kid anymore, I swear to you."

"Good, that's good," she said, exhaling her worry. "Because I need you all in one piece for Brody, and for the life that you're about to have with him here."

"Jo, I am not moving back to—"

"Darling," she rushed out, twisting on the bench to face me. "This is what I was saying earlier. How many signs do you need from the universe before you heed them?"

"What signs?"

She smacked me on the arm. "Don't be obtuse."

I was going to defend myself, but there was the screech of tires and a horn blowing, which moved my attention from Jo. There, stopped in the middle of the street, with another car behind him, was my father in a Mercedes SUV.

All his attention was on me, and when I checked, my mother's was as well. Both of them had their eyes riveted on my face.

"Park the car, Robert," Jo called over to my father. "You're holding up traffic."

His mouth hung open as he stared.

The guy in the Ford pickup behind him leaned out to yell, but noticed Jo and me and waved instead of swearing at my father. It was one of the guys Davis had brought with him on Saturday, who had helped put the garden back together. I waved in return, and Jo did as well, on general principle.

"Who is that?" Jo asked me as she smiled.

"Adam something?"

"Who?"

"He helped with the garden," I explained.

"Yes, but, darling, didn't everyone?"

"Not everyone," I said pointedly as Adam whipped around my father and drove away.

"Well, yes," she agreed with a sigh as my father finally moved, parking the car in the crappiest parallel parking job I'd ever seen.

"I bet Brody writes him a ticket for that," Jo muttered as he got out of the car, didn't lock it, didn't look both ways as he charged across the street. He was lucky he didn't get run over.

Dumping the remainder of the waffle cone in the trash, I stood up and braced myself.

"Kaenon," my father gasped, striding toward me, staring.

It was surreal to see him, because my brother looked like him, as I had thought when I first saw Everett, and now I realized how much more my father resembled my grandfather. So as I waited for him to reach me, swamped with memories, missing Harvey Geary, who'd been gone now for over eight years, it must have shown on my face. My father walked right up to me, without pausing, and took my face in his hands.

It was wholly unexpected as was my smile at him.

"Kaenon," he whispered harshly, and the tears that filled his eyes nearly undid me as he let go and grabbed me at the same time, yanking me into his arms and hugging me tighter than he ever had. "I'm so sorry, Kaenon. I couldn't be any sorrier, son. Please, please, please give me a chance to make it up to you. Please, I beg you. Forgive me my ignorance."

And I could. I knew I could. Give him a chance, because I wanted, needed, to know what had brought about this change of heart in the man.

Forgiveness, however, would take time. The words "you threw me away" were still there on the tip of my tongue, though they'd begun to taste stale over the course of the past few days, as if they'd exceeded their shelf life and I could let them go.

Still, he was my father, the man who was supposed to love me no matter what. I wasn't sure if I could ever demand an explanation for what he'd done. Truly, there was no justification he could offer that would ever take away the dulling sting of his abandonment.

But time, and a chance, I could give him.

"Oh," Jo whimpered, and when I looked at her, she had pulled tissues out of her purse to wipe her tears away.

I didn't look for my mother, and she didn't join us, but finally, that was, all the way deep down in my soul, all right. We all had limits, and I understood that, probably better than a lot of people. Some of us had endless reservoirs of strength and forgiveness, others did not. I was more than blessed with the people I had in my life. And now, suddenly, like a gift, I had my father back. There was really something to that prodigal business.

EVERETT AND MAEVE both showed up at the house after five. Jo was walking my father, her son, around the garden that had seemingly started sprouting overnight. They were arm in arm, and he was smiling and nodding as she talked in an endless stream. He stood there, frozen, as though he'd seen a ghost, staring at Peg's cottage now covered in full-blooming climbing roses, the colors vibrant and the blooms healthy.

After standing there for several minutes, he turned to look at me. "How did you do this?"

I smiled at him and said a word I hadn't used in more than half my life. "Dad, it's the sun, lots of water, phosphorous in the fertilizer, mulch with organic compost, and all the pruning that Peg had me do year after year when I was in high school."

"Yes, but it's been *years*," he said, stressing the word, "since you were here. This shouldn't be able to happen."

It was stunning, the bloom of color everywhere. "I don't know what to tell you."

He reached for me, hand on the back of my neck, hauling me close, his arm around my shoulders, unable, it seemed, not to touch me. His hand found my hair a hundred times, and when he sat me and Everett and Maeve all down together and explained that he and our mother were done being married, Maeve grabbed his hand, and Everett and I sat there and assured him that everything would be all right. He shocked the hell out of us when he explained that in their separation, both our parents had found new people to spend time with. Our father's new friend was named Yael, and she was originally from Israel but lived in Austin now, and was one of the top real estate agents in the area. She wanted to talk to Everett about an idea she had.

"Doing what?" Everett asked my father.

"She's considering starting to buy and sell houses herself, and since you're so good at seeing the potential in old and run-down property, and you have such a wonderful eye for interior design and remodeling, we both thought that talking to you would be a great idea."

I glanced at Everett, who looked back at me like a deer in the headlights.

"But," my father said, clearing his throat, "neither of us wanted to push you or make you feel as though you were being disloyal to your mother."

"Yeah, no, totally," Everett agreed, glancing at Rochelle, who appeared stunned.

"But your mother has met Yael, and I've met your mother's beau, Eric, and really, there's not a problem," he stressed to Everett. "I was going to bring her with me on the Fourth of July, unless you'd all like to meet her before that."

"I would love to meet her this weekend," Maeve chimed in.

"So would I," Jo told him, taking hold of his hand, so pleased with him that she was glowing with pride.

Later, as Jo was giving my father a tour of the house and all the amazing things Everett had done, which made him so happy he couldn't stop smiling, Maeve got a text on her cell and went out onto the back deck while Will played games with his kids on the PlayStation.

"Hey," I said, announcing my presence as I joined her, passing her a cup of tea.

She wiped her eyes and smiled at me, sniffling a second before taking a sip. "Oh, that's yummy," she told me, taking a deep inhale from the cup. "You can really smell the rose and the bergamot in this."

"What's wrong?" I prodded.

She shook her head.

"Mavis," I said, using an old name that she'd always hated.

"Kaenon, I...."

"Please."

She groaned. "Okay, so Mom texted me and Everett and asked us to meet her for dinner tomorrow night to talk about the divorce. She also wants to introduce us to her new guy."

I nodded. "Good. Thank you for telling me."

She took hold of my arm. "I won't go. I don't want—"

"No," I said, covering her hand with mine. "I won't take you away from her the way she took you away from me. We're not going to do that, not again. Never again."

"But I love you," she stated quietly. "And I need her to know that."

I grinned at her. "Doesn't stop you from telling her, does it?"

"No, it doesn't," she agreed, smiling at me and then taking a breath. "She told me once that you're the spitting image of her grandfather. I don't get how she can turn her back on the only one of her kids that looks anything like her."

"You got her great cheekbones," I reminded her.

"So did you," she said with a sigh, "and her gold coloring. Your eyes are your own, though. Where on earth did hazel come from?"

"Peg told me I was a changeling," I said, waggling my eyebrows at her.

"That would explain the roses," she remarked, gesturing at Peg's cottage.

"I really need to explain to you people how mulch works."

"Yes, dear," she soothed, leaning into me. "I'd love to hear the whole thing."

SIXTEEN

The new woman in my father's life, Yael Huber, showed up the next evening with him, and we all agreed, after having her there for only a couple of hours, that she suited him well, with her laughter, gracious candor, and innate kindness. She enjoyed spending time with all of us and was really excited to sit with Everett out on the deck and chat about flipping houses, until she noticed the blue clematis on the other side of the fence.

"That's lovely," she said pointing. "What is that?"

Everyone turned to me, and the stunning woman with honey-gold hair and dark brown eyes and deep dimples, smiled warmly. "Well, Kaenon, would you walk me around the garden when you have a moment?"

"Of course," I agreed, grinning at her.

After taking the tour, admiring the lavender and roses, the lilac and gardenia, and the hydrangeas and bridal spirea, she asked if I would be interested in doing landscape work for the homes that she and Everett were going to flip together.

"It won't work," Everett explained to her.

"I'm sorry?"

"It's dry here for hydrangeas, right?"

"A bit," she agreed, "yes. Though once it rains more, the humidity will help."

"It doesn't matter if it rains or not to everything in here," he said, including the whole garden, which was already coming up. "It'll grow for Kaenon."

"It's true," my father agreed, hand on my cheek. "He's always had a green thumb."

Jo grunted.

"You disagree?" her son asked her.

"No, no, not at all. I just think it's a bit more than that."

Later, Yael was thrilled to meet Brody, as was my father, both of them excited to hear that he and I were beginning something.

"Why does she care if I'm serious about you or not?" I asked him as I cut the peach pie that Jo had made earlier.

He flicked me on the side of the head.

"Owww," I complained, threatening him with the knife I was cutting with. "The hell was that for?"

"Why do you *think* she gives a crap?" he groused at me. "Did you consider that maybe she wants you to stick around?"

"Why?"

"Because your father's happier when you're around, just like your brother and sister and your grandmother and everybody else in the whole damn town."

"I think you're overdoing it a bit."

He shook his head. "The shit you don't see is a lot."

I leaned in for a kiss, and he met me halfway. "I see you," I said when our lips parted.

"Which is really lucky for me," he said with a sigh and a smile.

. . .

A WEEK LATER, I was watering the magnolia tree, which I didn't know we had until it was suddenly there, behind the cottage, when I found myself looking at the wild, overgrown foliage on the other side of the back gate.

"What are you doing?" Brody asked.

When I turned to the sound of his voice, I noticed the long, blue shadows and the sea of fireflies surrounding him in the too-long grass I needed to mow.

"Jesus," he groaned, stopping where he was, five feet or so away from me.

"What?"

"You out here in the yard, barefoot, in old jeans and a t-shirt that's seen better days, lookin' finer than any other man I've ever laid eyes on."

"You're too easy to please," I assured him, tipping my head at him. "Come here."

Joining me, he kissed me deeply, hands roaming, one up under my t-shirt, on the small of my back, the other on my ass.

I dropped the hose so I could attack him when he pulled back suddenly, panting. "What are you doing, come back here."

"I need to tell you before I forget that I need another couple bottles of the smokeless smudge spray you made me so I can clear out three of the patrol cars. There were some guys harassing tourists out by Blue Hole, there on the Cypress Creek, and afterward they ran off before the law in Wimberley could make any arrests."

"But you guys picked them up."

"We certainly did," he said, forcing a smile.

"And they did not smell good."

"No, sir, they did not," he confirmed, standing there, not moving.

"What's wrong with you?" I asked, realizing that he was trembling just a bit, like he didn't have full control over himself and had perhaps used the story about the men he'd arrested and the need for sage to try and calm down.

"I'm…fine."

"You're not fine," I argued, taking a step toward him. "And why don't you want to kiss me? What did I do?"

He shook his head. "You don't get it. I want to do more than kiss you."

That sounded promising. "Oh yeah? Like what?"

"I'm not—I can't be—"

"Careful?" I offered.

"I just fuckin' want you," he said gruffly, his voice full of teeth and claws.

"I'm yours," I told him. "Have me."

He lunged at me, closing the distance between us predator fast, kissing me soundly, both hands on my ass, kneading, groping while he mauled my mouth.

I couldn't think, couldn't form words, even if I'd wanted to, so when he walked me backward, pressing me against the cottage, holding me there, hands on the button of my jeans, working it open, then the zipper, snaking a hand under the waistband of my briefs, I was whimpering with need.

"I want to…I need…." He turned me around and lifted my hands to the wall, indicating with a squeeze that I should leave them right the hell there while he shucked my jeans and briefs to my ankles. "I saw Hollis Wedge in town today and he asked after you," he told me.

"Oh yeah?" I managed to get out, which was impressive

considering that every brain cell I had was consumed with what he was planning to do to me.

"Yessir," Brody drawled, his voice low, dangerous. "He got me alone and explained that he thought about coming over here quite a bit but wanted to know my intentions."

"And what'd you say?"

"I told him that I'd serve him his balls for a snack if I saw him anywhere near you."

"Brody, you shouldn't have--"

"Oh yes, I fuckin' should have," he half-shouted. "And the only way he ever sees you is if I'm standing right there beside you."

"That's very protective and possessive of you," I tried to tease him but found myself loving the idea of Brody standing between me and the world. It was pretty damn romantic.

"You have no idea how precious you are to me."

I would have responded but jolted instead as he slipped two lubed fingers into my ass, and I saw the empty foil packet fall near my feet. The man was prepared for me, but I had no time to think about that before he took firm hold of my throat and tipped my head back at the same time the wide head of his cock notched against my entrance.

"Tell me no and we'll switch places right now," he husked against my skin, his teeth closing on my earlobe as he pressed my body up against the cottage wall.

"What do you need?" I managed to find my voice, even writhing in his grip.

"You," he ground out, his voice a gritty rumble in my ear. "I need you to know that you're mine, that you belong to me."

I knew that, though. Felt it, felt the weight of it, the truth of it in my heart every day. "Fuck me so I'll know," I whispered back.

Letting go of my throat, he ran a hand over my ass and took brutal hold of my hip before he pushed inside of me, not stopping, opening me up, and stretching me wide around his thick pole of a cock until he was buried to the balls in my ass.

It hurt and I wanted to scream at him, tell him to pull out, but then one hand was back on my throat while the other found my softening dick and started to stroke. I turned my head until his lips were hovering over mine.

"I should have gone slower, but everything hurts, Kae, every part of me."

"Tell me," I demanded roughly.

"It's just…I want you so bad, and I lie there in bed at night, holding you, and my heart hurts when I think about you leaving. There's this hard ball in the pit of my stomach when I see someone else wantin' you, and a constant knot in my throat 'cause I can't say what needs to be said. That I need you here, in this town, at home, in bed, waitin' on me every night."

And there it was, the ultimatum that I'd known was coming even though we'd already agreed to a totally modern, grown-up, utterly logical alternative to cohabitation.

My skin washed hot and cold, knowing that one way or another, already, that this, us, the two of us together, was an all-or-nothing thing. He didn't want to have a geography discussion with me, because he didn't want us to be apart. It wasn't an option for him, and really, I'd been kidding myself that it was an option for me, either. I wanted him, plain and simple, and I would turn myself inside out to keep him, but until this moment, I hadn't realized that me living happily in

Stand In Place

Braxton was even a remote possibility. But suddenly it was, and I knew why. Somehow, some way, the idea of home, or what I identified as *home*, had shifted back to Braxton. It was both scary and a relief.

"Kaenon, baby," he murmured, his fingers sliding over my thickening shaft as he eased back only to thrust up against me, sliding deep, pegging my gland, making me squirm on the end of his dick. "You feel so good."

It was him. He felt like heaven. The way he shoved inside of me, filling me up, I couldn't stop the shudder that tore through me in response to the manhandling and domination. I had no idea I would ever want anyone to hold me down, but neither had I ever had a lover who could.

"Brody," I moaned his name as he pounded into me, pressing my face to the cool wood of the wall, holding me there, immovable, while he had me and took what he wanted.

I nearly came right there.

He slammed into me hard and fast, letting me feel the power in his body as I coated his fingers in precum, thrusting my ass back to meet each grinding roll of his hips.

"I want you to fuckin' stay with me," he snarled in my hair, using me, and the submission, the giving over of my power, of not having to be strong on my own, being able to lean on another person, sharing all my fears, my hopes, dreams, all of the corny things mixed with all of the real things—like how broken I would be when Jo finally died, and how I knew he'd be there, always, if I just let him. "I want to be the one, Kae. I want you to marry me and hyphenate your name and live in this tiny town in Texas with me forever."

It was ridiculous. I'd run so far away only to be right back where I started. Who did that?

"Kae," he murmured, rucking up my shirt and pulling it up over my head and off to kiss a line up my spine, the warm summer breeze on my bare skin feeling as decadent and primal as the now languorous rhythm that Brody had set, taking his time to make me come apart.

It worked too well, the brief pain replaced by aching, drugging arousal slithering up my spine, drowning everything but my yearning for him, my absolute savage hunger.

"Don't go slow," I begged him. "Please."

He unleashed himself on me, all desire and desperation and the ravenous need to penetrate me to the core.

My knees nearly buckled, but I braced myself on my hands and took the pounding I craved more than I thought possible, lost in the cooling shadows of twilight and the furnace-like heat of the man at my back as he stroked inside of me.

I came hard, with a muted shout, eyes closed, trembling in his hold as he, too, found his climax, pouring himself into me, hot, searing, and I felt an irrevocable change in myself, from *I* to *we*.

It could never again be, what would I do, what would I choose, where would I go again? It wasn't just my life anymore, my choices. It was ours.

"What did you do," I murmured into his temple, my head thrown back, resting on his shoulder, his bent forward, his cheek rubbing against mine, my rough stubble sliding over his smooth jaw. He had to shave every morning, and I did not. One of those little details that couples learn about each other along the way.

"What did I do?" he asked brightly, still buried inside of me, clutching me tight, savoring the feel of my skin under his hands. I could tell it from the endless stroking and the gravelly purr of contentment.

"You made it impossible for me to go home."

"You already are home," he insisted. "Your home is with me. Wherever I am, that's it. You know it's true. Now, say it is."

"I'm a lot of trouble, you know."

"No, you're not," he said, chuckling and I could feel the joyous sound down deep. "You're easy, like summer, and I love everything about you and everything you are."

"I'm easy?"

"I knew you were gonna fixate on that," he said softly, nuzzling the side of my neck, kissing everywhere he could reach.

"I hate you," I muttered. "You messed up all my plans."

He snorted, easing from my body and turning me around to face him, lifting my chin so he could look in my eyes, which made hiding impossible. "You love me. You can't keep your hands or your mouth off me, you talk about me all the time, and when you smile, I see nothing but love."

"You're deluded."

His smile was wicked, and my heart fluttered in my chest.

"I don't even like you," I lied into the russet-colored eyes that I wanted looking at me for the rest of my life.

"Except that you want me wrapped around you, around your life from now on, so just say that you'll stay here and live with me and your grandmother, because I could move in tomorrow and we could get married next week."

I squinted at him.

He growled.

"Perhaps——"

"Okay, fine," he said with a sigh, like he was giving in after some long-involved back-and-forth had occurred.

"How about me just moving in and we'll work on the marrying?"

"You know, not everyone in town is going to be crazy about their constable being with me."

"As opposed to what?" he asked as he used my t-shirt to clean first me and then him.

"I need to put that back on," I groused at him.

"Oh no," he ordered, grinning at me, and I realized for the first time that he was in his uniform and the only thing he didn't have on was the duty belt. His badge, however, was glinting in the moonlight. "The only place this is going is the trash."

"You didn't even take off your uniform?" I found this somehow almost sacrilegious, to be screwing me behind my aunt's cottage in his uniform.

"I'll bet you Coltrane and Peg got busy a lot while he was still in his uniform." He leered at me when he said it.

"That's disgusting," I grumbled, yanking up my underwear and jeans, zipping up but not buttoning. I needed a shower. But I noticed that he looked great, all put together, ready to go back out on patrol. "How are you so clean? Did you even pull your pants down or did you just unzip?"

He was laughing at my outrage as I tried to stalk by him. "Oh no, you don't, you haven't answered," he said, grinning crazily, grabbing my bicep and yanking me back to face him. "And how come you didn't notice I was in my uniform?"

I looked at the ground and answered him.

"I'm sorry, what was that?"

Growling, I lifted my head. "I said that the only thing I saw were your beautiful eyes."

Slow nod from him. "My beautiful eyes, huh? Do you think you maybe want me looking at you for the rest of your life?"

"Yes," I said, confessing what was in my heart, that I had thought, almost verbatim, minutes earlier. "I love you so much, and I want to be here, with you, from now on."

The smile I got was breathtaking. "You see? Was that so hard? Why ya gotta be so difficult?"

"You said I was easy!"

He gestured at me. "Well, yeah, to get into bed, but getting the I love you outta you—that took for-fuckin'-ever."

I rolled my eyes at *his* idea of for-fuckin'-ever, and gasped as he tackled me onto the soft grass, laughing as he did. After that, his uniform wasn't clean either.

When we were walking back toward the house, his arm around my shoulders, his hand threaded in my hair, he suddenly stopped and kissed me.

"Tell me again."

"I love you, Chief Constable, and this is fast for me, so you better take good care of my heart," I whispered, a bit overcome with emotion.

"I love you too, Kae, and I always take excellent care of what's mine."

Meaning my heart, of course.

"You should call your old school tomorrow and tell them you're quittin', and then ring up that nice man who offered you a job out at UT, and accept."

"Already you're telling me what to do?"

"Just makin' sure you got a list is all."

Jo was sitting on the back porch, sipping a glass of iced tea. When we came up the stairs, one of her eyebrows lifted.

"Just don't say anything," I grumbled as Brody chuckled, bent, and kissed her cheek, and then went on into the house, leaving me to drop down into the chair beside her.

"You know," she said, smiling at me. "If you give away the milk for free—"

"Oh shut it. He wants to marry me."

There was a silence.

"Well, now," she said, reaching for my chin and turning my head so I was looking at her instead of out at the garden. I noticed earlier that the stream orchid, or chatterbox, that grew wild near streams and lakes and in the sandy soil of marshes in the southwest, was somehow thriving this far inland, in our garden. Peg had planted it some years ago, but we all figured it had died until I noticed it the other morning. "He wants to marry you and make an honest man out of you?"

I rolled my eyes at her.

"And where will you and the Chief Constable live?"

"In the room next to yours, of course."

She stroked my cheek. "Well, that sounds lovely," she said, and I could hear the catch in her voice, which told me how happy she was. "And will you be having nookie in the garden every night, or just on Wednesdays?"

"God," I groaned, sinking down in the chair.

"Don't make fun of the pretty, half-naked man," Brody warned Jo as he walked out the back door, balancing one plate with a couple of steaks on it and another with two enormous Portobello mushrooms. "He's sensitive because he's worried he's easy."

"Well, he's only easy for you because he loves you so much."

"There, you see?" he told me, gesturing at Jo. "Is that so hard?"

I looked over at her.

"The orchids came up," she sighed, offering me her glass of tea. "Did you see?"

"Yes, I saw them, but they're not supposed to be there, you know."

"Anything can grow anywhere, my darling, it just needs what we all do: some good dirt, a little bit of sun, a lot of water, and someone to lend a nurturing hand through the rough spots."

"Is that right? That's it?"

She nodded and tapped her cheek. "Yes, my darling, that's it."

I gave her a kiss and stopped to give Brody one as well on the way in to take a quick shower before dinner.

"Make it fast. I want us all sitting down together," he ordered, because he was naturally bossy.

"Yes, dear," I agreed, and made sure to hurry.

A NOTE FROM THE AUTHOR

~

Thank you so much for reading Stand In Place. I hope you enjoyed Kaenon and Brody and especially Jo's story, and if you did, please consider leaving a review on Amazon for my people. It would help so much with the book's visibility. There are more books yet to come, including Croy's book, *In A Fix*, the second book in my Torus Intercession series that started with Brann's story.

Want to stay up-to-date on my release? Join the mob!

Thank you so much for joining me for my homecoming story, I hope to see you soon!

ALSO BY MARY CALMES

∾

By Mary Calmes

Published by DREAMSPINNER PRESS

www.dreamspinnerpress.com

Acrobat

Again

Any Closer

Floodgates

Frog

The Guardian

Heart of the Race

His Consort

Ice Around the Edges

Judgment

Just Desserts

Kairos

Lay It Down

Mine

Romanus * Chevalier

The Servant

Steamroller

Still

Three Fates

What Can Be

Where You Lead

You Never Know

CHANGE OF HEART

Change of Heart

Trusted Bond

Honored Vow

Crucible of Fate

Forging the Future

L'ANGE

Old Loyalty, New Love

Fighting Instinct

Chosen Pride

THE VAULT

A Day Makes

Late In The Day

MANGROVE STORIES

Blue Days

Quiet Nights

Sultry Sunset

Easy Evenings

Sleeping 'til Sunrise

MARSHALS

All Kinds of Tied Down

Fit To Be Tied

Tied Up In Knots

Twisted and Tied

A MATTER OF TIME

A Matter of Time Vol. 1

A Matter of Time Vol. 2

Bulletproof

But For You

Parting Shot

Piece of Cake

TIMING

Timing

After the Sunset

When the Dust Settles

WARDERS

His Hearth

Tooth & Nail

Heart In Hand

Sinnerman

Nexus

Cherish Your Name

ABOUT THE AUTHOR

Mary Calmes believes in romance, happily ever afters, and the faith it takes for her characters to get there. She bleeds coffee, thinks chocolate should be its own food group, and currently lives in Kentucky with a five-pound furry ninja that protects her from baby birds, spiders and the neighbor's dogs. To stay up to date on her ponderings and pandemonium (as well as the adventures of the ninja) follow her on Twitter, Facebook, Instagram and subscribe to her newsletter.

Printed in Great Britain
by Amazon